Also available from Therese Beharrie and Carina Press

Also available from Therese Beharrie and Harlequin

This book deals with the following issues: grief, dementia, deceased parents, adoption, terminal illness and pregnancy scares. If any of these are triggers for you, please put your mental health first.

ONE LAST CHANCE

THERESE BEHARRIE

carina
press

**carina
press**®

Recycling programs
for this product may
not exist in your area.

ISBN-13: 978-1-335-91832-1

One Last Chance

First published in 2020. This edition published in 2021.

Copyright © 2020 by Therese Beharrie

This edition published by arrangement with Harlequin Books S.A.

For questions and comments about the quality of this book,
please contact us at CustomerService@Harlequin.com.

Carina Press
22 Adelaide St. West, 40th Floor
Toronto, Ontario M5H 4E3, Canada
www.CarinaPress.com

Printed in U.S.A.

For my husband, who loves who I was, who I am, and who gives me the best reasons to grow. For my loved ones, who celebrate my growth with me. And for the readers who are trying. That's enough. You are enough.

My intention with *One Last Chance* was to write a lighthearted romance about two best friends falling in love, getting married and ending things, then rediscovering their love for one another. I succeeded in everything except the tone. Turns out, it's hard to write an entirely lighthearted romance when two people are completely broken and need mending—at least for me.

But there are lighthearted moments in this book. There's laughter and banter and hope. Most important, there's love. I hope all of it will resonate with you.

ONE LAST CHANCE

Part One

'Let's get married.'

Chapter One

One Day, Six Years Ago

'You don't have to do this,' Sawyer Wilson said for the third time. After two years of pretending to be in a relationship with his best friend, those words were part of their routine. Still, he cast a worried look at her. As usual, she looked ready to steal someone's heart. As usual, he layered his defences to make sure it wouldn't be his.

Zoey Roux looked over. Smiled. Reminded him that those defences were pointless. She'd already stolen his heart.

'I keep my word, Wilson.' Her insistence was also part of the routine. 'Seven years of friendship should mean you know that. Two years of pretending to be your girlfriend, too.' She fluttered her lashes at him.

'I know.' He waited. Wondered if he should say it. Did anyway. 'But things are different now.'

Zoey rolled her eyes. 'I'm not going to stop living my life because my... Because of what happened.'

Emotion, sharp and angry and sad, damn it, flushed her cheeks. He shouldn't have brought her to his cousin's graduation party. But what was he supposed to do? She had known about it. If he told her not to come, that he found someone else to be his date, she would have been pissed. Not because of jealousy, unfortunately, but because she would have known it was an excuse. A convenient one, designed for her not to have to attend this hellish party.

'Personally,' he said conversationally, guiding the car into a space in front of the large hall, 'I would have jumped at the chance not to come to this.'

She released a little puff of air. When he looked over, her cheeks were back to their normal colour. There was a teasing light in her eyes. She was never down for long, his Zoey.

His Zoey. What a joke. She wasn't his. Would never be.

'If I hadn't come, your grandmother would have set you up with Kyra from church in an instant.'

'Was that her name?'

'Tammy? Mia?' She scrunched her nose. 'I don't think the name matters. Grandma Carla just wants her grandson to be happy.'

'She has countless other grandchildren to worry about,' Sawyer said darkly.

'But you're her connection to the child she lost so tragically years ago. The only thing she has left of her daughter and son-in-law.' Zoey gave him a sweet smile as she echoed Grandma Carla's words. 'The only one who needs constant reassurance he's loved.'

That last part was Zoey, not his grandmother.

He rolled his eyes. 'Does matchmaking mean I'm loved?'

'Hey, if you accept the brownies she bakes you every

time you visit, you have to accept this. It's the good and the bad with family.'

'Sure,' he muttered, getting out the car and walking around to her side to open her door. 'That's why you're pretending to be my girlfriend. Because you think I should accept her matchmaking ways.'

'I'm here because you told me, and I quote, "I don't want to bring a new woman along every time. And if I don't bring anyone, my grandmother will marry me off."'

'To which you replied, and I quote, "She can't marry you off until you're done with university." Which we both know is a lie. She managed to promise several women, from when I was sixteen, that I'd be a good husband someday.'

Zoey chuckled, putting her clutch under her arm and reaching up to straighten his tie. His breath hitched before he could stop it. He hadn't prepared himself for her touch, though he should have known better. Their years of friendship had taught him that Zoey would touch him whenever she wanted to. She was free with affection. Since he was her best friend, that affection was aimed at him, too. Which would have been totally fine had he not been harbouring feelings for her.

'What?' she asked, frowning. Apparently, righting a tie required concentration.

'What, what?' he replied dumbly.

'Why did you gasp?'

'I didn't gasp.'

'Of course you did. I heard you.'

'You must have heard wrong.'

Her hands brushed against his skin. He gritted his teeth.

'What's going on with you?' Zoey asked, her gaze flickering between his face and his tie. 'Do you want to go in there with a skew tie?'

'Okay.'

'Sawyer,' she said, stilling in front of him. Rich, dark brown eyes that had gone from amused to concerned peered up at him.

'It's fine, Zo,' he replied, gently taking her hands and lowering them to her sides. 'I'll fix it in the bathroom.'

'Or I can fix it—'

'No,' he said too sharply. He cleared his throat. 'It's fine. No one will think less of us because my tie's skew.'

She studied him. He worried she'd see right to what he wanted to hide from her. Instead, concern was replaced by light and seconds later, she pushed him back against the car. It wasn't the strength she did it with that had his breath leaving his lungs. It was the surprise.

'What…the…hell?' he gasped.

'Let me fix your tie, damn it.'

Her hands were on his tie before he could stop her, which accounted for his instinctual reaction. He blocked her. Slid an arm between himself and her body and blocked her.

'What are you doing?' she asked, still struggling to get to his tie.

'I'm protecting myself against this vicious attack.'

'It's only vicious because *you won't let me fix your tie!*'

Her efforts intensified. For a few minutes, they struggled.

'When did you get so strong?' Sawyer asked when she took one of his arms and pinned it to the car.

'Why…are you…holding…back?' Her words were interspersed by little huffs of breath.

'You'd get hurt if I didn't,' he retorted, then let out a startled laugh when one of her hands clutched at his side. 'No,' he gasped now, realising her plan. 'Don't. This is underhanded—'

He broke off when she began tickling him in earnest, and his attempts to defend himself became clumsier. He twisted, but that gave her access to the side of his body she knew was the most ticklish. She showed him no mercy.

'Stop…it.'

'Not until you tell me why you won't let me fix your tie.'

'Fine, if it's that important, you can fix it.'

She lifted her hands in pseudo surrender. 'Are you going to tell me why you didn't want me to fix it in the first place?'

He eyed her hands warily, but didn't answer. What would he say?

When you touch me it's hard to remember we're only supposed to be friends.

That wouldn't work. If he were ever inclined to reveal his feelings for her, he wouldn't choose now. They were in an empty parking lot. There was a fast-food restaurant across the road; next to it, the post office. Some homeless people slept under the shelter of the post office building. A couple of drunk people staggered down the road from the bar he knew was nearby.

It didn't exactly scream romance. Besides, he was about to attend a family function. Everyone, save for his aunt and uncle, who raised him and his cousins, thought Zoey was his girlfriend. And so it would remain until he finally got a serious girlfriend. Or until Zoey got a serious boyfriend.

'You were taking long,' he said, grasping at the first excuse he could think of and ignoring the way his heart complained at the prospect of Zoey being with someone else.

'I don't believe you.'

He smiled. 'Okay.'

She narrowed her eyes. 'Something's going on.'

He widened his smile, hoping it would hide the faint alarm sounding in his head. It was unlikely that after seven years of friendship—and seven years of unrequited love—she finally saw it. He clung to that thought like his little cousin Carly clung to a beloved snack when she got home from school.

'You'll never be safe from a tickle attack,' she said now, sniffing. 'I know you're lying to me, and I *will* get answers.'

'By means of torture?'

'If necessary.'

He thought about it. 'Well, then, you give me no choice.'

In quick movements, he dipped until his shoulder was at her waist and tipped her over.

'Sawyer!' she squealed.

He ignored it. Made sure he had a secure hold and that her dress was still protecting her modesty. He also tried to ignore that her butt was next to his face. If he didn't, he might have to fight the temptation to do something ridiculous like kiss it.

Kiss ass, his cousin, Phil, had once called him. Sawyer had taken Zoey's side in a debate. Sawyer vowed Phil would never discover how tempted he had been to make that accusation literal.

'You gave me no choice.'

'I'll give you one now.' She sounded a little winded. 'You either put me down, or you'll live to regret it.'

'Yeah?' he asked, unconcerned. 'How so?'

'Hi, Grandma Carla!'

Sawyer instantly put Zoey down, and turned to face his grandmother. She wasn't where he thought she might be based on Zoey's voice. He looked around, stopping only when he got a light punch in the shoulder.

'Hey!'

'That was for picking me up.'

He rubbed his shoulder. 'No need for abuse. Especially with Grandma Carla around.'

Zoey quirked a brow. He realised there was no Grandma Carla. She grinned, somehow managing to make it menacing and cute.

'You deserved to think she was.'

She stepped closer, her eyes narrowing. It took him all of three seconds to figure out her intention. He stood perfectly still, bracing for her touch. She fixed his tie, then patted him on the chest.

'You should know by now that I always get what I want.'

She winked. It made him want to kiss her.

He wished he had the power to get what he wanted, too.

Chapter Two

One Day, Now

'Zo, would you mind helping?' Sophia asked, irritably. Not far from her usual tone of voice, though Zoey knew this wasn't a usual day. She moved to help her sister without a word.

'That's it?' Sophia asked as they packed picnic baskets onto a table. 'You're not going to complain?'

'What would be the point of complaining?' Zoey deliberately kept her voice light. 'You'd get me to do it eventually, and we'd have to go through a whole thing about how I offered to help and "you shouldn't say you're going to do something if you're not going to do it."'

'Was that you trying to imitate me?' Sophia's brows rose. 'Since when do I sound like James Earl Jones?'

'Oh, you're right.' Zoey cleared her throat. 'It's actually "way up here, isn't it?"' She laughed at the glare Sophia threw her. '*You* asked for a more accurate rendition.'

'I regret it.'

'You shouldn't ask for something if you don't want it,' she told her sister solemnly, and laughed again when this time, Sophia pulled a face. 'I'm beginning to think this event is stressing you out.'

Sophia unpacked the last of the baskets in her box, set her hands on her hips and looked around. 'It just seems very important, you know.'

Zoey followed Sophia's eyes, taking in the concert stage that had been set up metres away and the banner that hung above it.

Summer Charity Concert for Dementia Research.

She softened, and reached over to take her sister's hand. Sophia wasn't generally the kind of person who inspired affection. Or someone who wanted or needed comfort. But Zoey had recently learnt those kinds of perceptions didn't do her sister any favours. In fact, it had put distance between her and Sophia. So she'd offer Sophia reassurance because that's what her gut told her to do.

'I know,' Zoey said, squeezing Sophia's hand. 'But you and Parker have done a hell of a lot to get this event ready. It'll be great.' She frowned. 'Except for the part where you're making me run a thousand kilometres in an hour. No, wait, the fact that you had me here since five in the morning *and* you expect me to run a thousand kilometres.'

'Do you think I wanted to be here at five in the morning?' Sophia asked, letting Zoey's hand go, although she gave it her own squeeze first. 'Kirstenbosch's management told me someone needed to be around while the guys set up for the concert. And the delivery of the picnic baskets was coming in early, so here we are.'

Sophia started unpacking another box. She eyed Zoey, who was still on her first. Zoey stuck out her tongue, and unpacked her box before moving on to her second.

'And it's not a thousand kilometres.' Sophia scowled minutes later. 'It's a run, for like, ten kilometres max. And you could totally walk it.'

Zoey waited for more. When it didn't come, she shook her head.

'What?' Sophia asked.

'I'm thinking about how you took ten minutes to come up with that reply.' She shook her head again. 'You really are stressed about this.'

'Shut up,' Sophia said, but there was no bite in her words. Which told Zoey that her sister *was* stressed. She made a mental note to stop teasing her about it, and kept working until all the boxes were empty.

As she worked, she gave a fleeting thought to Angie, their oldest sister, who'd got out of helping by using her baby as an excuse. Zoey had always been jealous of people who could use their kids to get out of stuff. Kids could also make tea and peanut butter sandwiches when they were old enough. That did a lot in favour of having kids, in her opinion.

Her heart twinged. She expected it, so it didn't make her too sad. Still, the fact that it was there bothered her.

'What are you doing here?'

Zoey looked up in time to see her sister's boyfriend, Parker, walking toward them.

'Hello to you, too, darling,' Parker said mildly, pressing a kiss to Sophia's lips.

Their eyes met, held, and Zoey could feel the love and affection from where she was standing. The twinge in her heart turned into an ache. It was a familiar pain that followed her around as a ghost haunting the house it died in would. Which made sense. Something had died inside her to cause that pain. She'd lost her best friend, and she had no one else to blame but herself. She deserved to be haunted.

Pushing it aside, she said, 'It's too early in the morning for this kind of disgustingness.'

Parker looked over. 'Wonderful. I have two of the Roux sisters to contend with. One as delightful in the morning as the next.' But he winked at her.

'What are you doing here, Parker?' Sophia asked again, though she cuddled into his side.

'Evie's mom's plans for this weekend fell through, so Evie ended up having a babysitter for her kids this morning, after all. She's with Mom now so I could be here.'

'That was nice of her,' Sophia said.

'Yeah.'

'She was planning on attending today though anyway, wasn't she?' Zoey asked, gathering all the empty boxes now that they'd unpacked the baskets.

'Yes, but only later, because of the babysitter situation,' Parker told her. 'Besides, it was always to help my mom out. It's work.'

Parker's mom had been diagnosed with dementia a year and a half ago. Evie was her companion. The charity event had been Parker's brainchild after he'd found out about his mother's diagnosis. It had taken a year to plan, but the day was finally here.

It was clear to Zoey that Sophia's stress had less to do with the planning of the event, and more to do with the personal investment she had in its success. The early morning run, the picnic that afternoon, the concert following it... Planning them had become cop-

ing mechanisms for Parker. Sophia had shared that
over drinks the previous week. She was worried that
if things didn't go well, Parker's mental health would
decline.

Zoey didn't think it was a fair concern, honestly.
If Parker's mental health did take a dip, it would be
understandable. Having a sick parent was hell on the
brain. On the body. On decision-making abilities. Or
was that one just her? Either way, Parker had a right
to take a moment to recover, and Sophia should know
that. Except Sophia was very much in love with Parker,
hence the excessive amount of worrying.

'You know, the least you could have done was bring
coffee,' Zoey said when she was done stacking boxes.
'That way, your appearance would have been welcome
for all of us, not just Soph.'

'You're right,' Parker said. Zoey was immediately
suspicious. Her sister had found a boyfriend with more
or less the same personality as her. Which meant jabs
like the one Zoey had given him weren't met with
agreement. 'We should go get some.'

'We?' Zoey asked slowly. 'As in you and me?'

Parker's expression tightened. 'Yes, you and me.'

That was more like it.

'But why—'

'Are you going to be okay here?' he asked Sophia,
cutting Zoey off. It was very strange. Zoey decided to
keep quiet to see how it played out.

'I guess so.'

Sophia's face was strained, as if she were keeping
herself from saying something. It was unlike her sister, and it added another layer to the tension in the air
between them. Though Zoey wasn't entirely sure what

was happening, she followed Parker down the steep decline of the botanical garden.

Kirstenbosch was a popular destination during the summer in Cape Town, particularly for picnics and concerts like the one for the event. It was gorgeous. Greenery everywhere. Pops and bursts of colour from flowers. Table Mountain close by. But damn if it wasn't the most *inconvenient* place to walk. The garden inclined and declined since it was nestled at the foot of Table Mountain. Even the walk to the bathrooms was exercise.

For the first time, Zoey considered whether it was the best venue for the older generation attending the day. Almost immediately, her father's voice sounded in her head, telling her off for discriminating against the elderly. She smiled, then shook her head when she remembered Parker was acting weird.

'Hey,' she said, running after him since he was walking ahead of her. 'Aren't we supposed to be doing this together? Or are you going to run ahead and make me feel like I'm chasing after you when you obviously wanted me and not Soph to come with you?'

She nearly bumped into him when he stopped.

'It was obvious?'

'That you didn't want Sophia to come with?' She stared at him. 'Pretty obvious, dude. In fact, I think she thinks you're having a mental breakdown.'

His expression changed. She couldn't quite tell what it was. Satisfaction? Concern? Smugness? All of the above?

'Good,' he said, and started walking again.

'Good?' she repeated. 'What the hell's going on,

Parker? I swear, if you're trying to rope me into some weird—'

'Zoey,' he said, stopping again. This time, she did bump into him, and staggered back from the impact.

'You better have a good reason for acting—'

'I want to propose. To Soph. Today.'

Zoey stared at him for a long time, then slowly nodded. 'I guess you do have a good reason then. Cool.'

'Not that I mind accompanying you to this, but remind me again why Byron couldn't?'

Sawyer jogged on the spot before kicking out his legs, sending blood into the stiff ligaments. It was six in the morning, and he was about to do a run. Generally, he didn't mind the morning. It was an occupational hazard for someone who worked in Cape Town. He was a logistics manager for a transport company. His portfolio included a range of international clients who required him to be awake at late or early hours. But waking up on the weekend to run wasn't work. He wasn't sure what it classified as.

Torture.

How, after all this time, he could still hear his ex-best friend's voice in his head, he didn't know.

Didn't care to know.

'He got in late last night after the game ended,' his sister said. Lisa's husband played rugby for a provincial rugby team. 'I didn't want to wake him up this early to do something he does for a living.'

'But you gladly woke me up,' he said darkly.

'And me,' his nephew, Ryder, added.

'Thanks for that.' Lisa gave Sawyer a look. 'You remember I gave you a choice, right? I asked you if you wanted to do this with me. You said yes.'

'That was before I knew I'd be sacrificing sleep for it. Besides,' he continued before Lisa could protest, 'I couldn't leave Ry at your mercy. You'd have dragged him along and he'd have no company.'

'Yeah,' Ryder said, though he was still half-asleep. The part that was awake was solely for agreeing with his uncle, apparently.

Sawyer couldn't resist a smile. He'd only known Lisa, Byron and Ryder for two years. Lisa had been adopted, but her biological mother was Sawyer's mother. Since their mother had died years before, unfortunately Lisa hadn't got the reconciliation she hoped for. But she'd got him. And his aunt. Though he wasn't sure what that was worth when his aunt had already known about Lisa's existence and had said nothing.

He took a deep breath, hoping to soothe the ripple of anger. He didn't know the details of Lisa's conception, birth or adoption. There could be a reasonable explanation.

Pity he couldn't work up the courage to ask for more than the basic details.

As usual, his thoughts had guilt lining his gut. His aunt had been good to him. She didn't deserve his anger. And meeting his sister, having her in his life, shouldn't stir such negative feelings either.

Another breath, and he was calm.

'Hey, kid, what do you say about pancakes when we're done here?' he asked. 'Add some bacon, maybe some—'

'I don't think you have to convince him anymore,'

Lisa said with a laugh when Ryder visibly perked up. Some of the sleep faded from his eyes.

'Great. Now you just have to beat me on the run today.'

The competitiveness that ran in their family had a fierceness crossing Ryder's face. 'Deal.'

'You sound real confident.'

'I am,' Ryder said proudly. 'You're too old to beat me.'

'Ryder!' Lisa gasped, but Sawyer was too busy laughing to be offended.

'We'll see about that, kid.'

With both their competitiveness adequately flared, the race was interesting. They knew, of course, that it wasn't a real competition. The run was the first part of a charity event that had drawn a large crowd; Lisa and Sawyer had already decided to stick together. Ryder didn't know that, so after a rough start and a quick explanation, they settled into a rhythm.

Sawyer was relatively fit, as was Lisa, but Ryder was a ten-year-old kid who had energy for days. By the end, Sawyer regretted making the bet with Ryder. At least he'd been smart enough to bet food. He wanted pancakes now, too.

And he'd get them, since he lost the race.

'I told you you're too old!'

'Yeah, but what I lack in speed I make up for in strength.'

Sawyer picked the kid up, threw him over his shoulder and enjoyed his nephew's laughter as he spun. But he felt something that made him pause.

His entire skin was prickling, heating. He knew someone was looking at him; he just couldn't figure out why it had such an effect on him. When Lisa returned with water bottles for all of them, he set Ryder down and tried to figure out what he was feeling.

Then he saw her.

His breath left his lungs.

It had nothing to do with the run, or the fact that shortly after, he'd picked up a growing boy. It was entirely her. Her ability, as she'd always had, to take his breath away when he wasn't prepared for how she affected him.

It was as powerful now as it had ever been. She was as beautiful as he remembered. Her twists were tied in a huge bun around her head. Her face was splotchy and red. She stood next to her sisters and two men, neither of whom stood close enough to her to make him think they were with her. Because he knew what it was like to be with her, he knew they'd be hovering as close as possible if she was theirs.

She wore black tights and a loose red top. It showed off the curve of her brown shoulders, which even from here he could see glistened with sweat. A black bra peeked through her top, her sneakers bright red as well. She had coordinated her outfit exactly, and it curved his lips even though it hurt him to see her.

Based on her expression when their eyes met, it hurt her to see him, too.

Chapter Three

One Day, Six Years Ago

'You're both twenty-one now, Zoey,' Grandma Carla was saying. 'I think it's time you and Sawyer get serious about being in a relationship.'

And she thought the worst thing about turning twenty-one was that it had happened a week after her father's death.

Oh, she thought in surprise. That was morbid.

'You don't think we're serious?' Zoey asked, ensuring her tone was light despite the darkness in her brain. 'We've been friends for a long time. Our romantic relationship—' she searched for the right word '—has *blossomed* because of that friendship. And we've been together for over two years. That's plenty serious to me.'

'But *you're* not serious, my dear. Not as serious as Sawyer is.'

Zoey tried to hide her surprise. It didn't work.

'You don't think I see how you play with my boy's heart?'

Completely taken aback by the line of questioning, Zoey searched for Sawyer in the crowd. It was one of his cousin's graduation, which was a big deal. Even bigger was that the cousin was the oldest of Sawyer's cousins, and the first to get their PhD. As dictated by their community, every single person who knew the family was there to celebrate.

Zoey understood the joy and excitement on a theoretical level. In practice, she couldn't imagine celebrating it if it happened in her family. It was likely that that came from grief. If her sisters did decide to plan a party now, for whatever reason, Zoey would have to pretend. She'd have to be the life of the party as everyone expected her to be, despite her grief. So maybe it wasn't that she couldn't imagine celebrating as much as it was she didn't want to.

'He loves you very much, Zoey.' Grandma Carla's voice was quieter now.

'And I love him.'

It wasn't a lie. She loved Sawyer. He was her best friend. He was funny and kind. Caring. Intense, yes. She figured that came from his parents passing away when he was so young. Trauma could do that.

But he was weird, too. She wasn't sure *that* came from the trauma. Trauma couldn't explain why he never wanted her to do anything nice for him. Not fix his tie or help him cook or take care of him when he was sick.

Did she listen to those refusals? No. But now that she thought about it, it *was* weird.

'As much as he loves you?' Grandma Carla asked. 'You don't look at him when he's not looking at you, the way he does with you. You don't search for him when he's not with you. You don't seem to mind it when he leaves.' She reached over, patted Zoey's hand. 'I've always thought you should marry someone who loves you more than you love them. They're more grateful then, and tend to stay that way.' She paused. 'But if you don't at least *think* you love them as much as they love you, perhaps you aren't right for one another.'

With another pat—on Zoey's head this time—Grandma Carla turned and began to talk with someone else. Zoey was dismissed. It took her some time, but somehow through the surprise and wonder and questions, Zoey managed to stand and walk out of the hall. It wasn't the polite thing to do, not saying goodbye, and her mother's voice in her head told her so. But her head also housed her brain, which was surprisingly firm in its desire not to process what had happened. To escape.

From the things Grandma Carla had put into her mind. From the way it seemed like…like truth.

'Zoey. Zo. *Zoey.*'

She should have known he'd come after her. Should have expected it. He was Sawyer. The man who looked for her when she wasn't with him. Who minded when she left.

Shit.

'Zoey,' he said again, this time from her side and not behind her. 'Where are you going?'

'I don't know,' she answered automatically. 'Away. Away from here.'

'Did something happen?' He jogged a few paces ahead of her, stopping so that she'd have to go around him if she wanted to move. So she didn't. 'If something happened, tell me. Was it Phil?' he asked, face growing stormier. 'If it's Phil, I'll make him apologise.'

She shook her head. Sawyer's cousin Phil was supposed to be like a brother to him since they'd grown up together. She supposed Phil's determination to make

Sawyer, and thus, her, feel uncomfortable could be seen as the acts of a sibling. But both she and Sawyer had agreed that it was more the acts of an asshole.

Unfortunately, Phil wasn't the problem today. That would have been much easier to solve.

If it had been Phil, she had no doubt Sawyer would have made him apologise. Her friend wasn't someone who embraced conflict, though he often faced it for her. Because he cared for her. He did things for her. When that boy had stolen her seat on the first day of high school and had taunted her to make him move, Sawyer had pushed him out of the way. That had been the start of their friendship; that's how it had continued.

Two years after they'd become friends, rumours spread about their relationship. Sawyer stood up in the middle of assembly one day and announced they were only friends. A year after that, when Zoey's first boyfriend told everyone she'd slept with him, Sawyer stepped in and soon, her boyfriend was apologising for lying about them having sex.

And then, when they'd found out her dad was sick, Sawyer had taken her to the movies. He hadn't said anything. They just watched the movie. It was a loud action film that masked her quiet sobbing. He sat there, holding her hand, and at the end of it, he told her he'd be there for her through it all. And he had been.

When they got the news her father's brain tumour wasn't shrinking.

When her father had become frailer and frailer.

When they'd buried him a month before.

When she'd celebrated her first birthday without her father the week after.

All through it, Sawyer had been at her side. As he was now, standing in front of her.

'Talk to me,' he said quietly, concern etched into his face. She couldn't remember a time it hadn't been. Not always so deeply, but deep enough that she thought she saw what his grandmother was referring to.

'I think it's time you talked to me, Sawyer.' She lifted a hand, rested it on his chest. 'What are you hiding?'

He blinked. The skin between his brows creased.

'I'm not hiding anything. *You* ran away.'

Without fully realising it, she lifted her free hand and smoothed his frown with a finger. He sucked in his breath, as he had when she'd fixed his tie earlier. With his grandmother's words echoing in her head, she understood his reaction better. Finally, she could see why Sawyer had always been so weird. Finally, she knew why he was always there for her.

He loved her.

'Why didn't you tell me?' she whispered.

When he didn't reply, she thought he hadn't heard her. The night was loud—music thudded in the distance; crickets sounded in the field they were in. But it also felt quiet. It could have been the night sky they stood under. Or the sharp wind that sent a shiver down her spine. The clouds gathering overhead, preparing for the rain that had been forecasted.

Or maybe it was the way he was looking at her.

'I didn't want you to know.'

So he had heard her. And he wasn't offering her excuses. No lies.

Her hands dropped to her sides. His immediately found them.

'This is why,' he said with a sad smile. 'You'd pull away from me. I'd—' His breath hitched. 'I'd lose you.'

For some reason, his words made her think of her father. And that made her think about her family. About how Sawyer was a part of it, of her life. When her world was falling apart, he built a shelter to protect her from the debris. While they waited for the destruction to stop, he started a fire so she could be warm, comfortable. She could turn to him with everything, and she knew he'd make her feel better. Like she was capable of handling things. Like she was *safe*. And he'd make her laugh through all of it. She could never, ever walk away from that.

From him.

She didn't know whether that meant she felt the same way he did. But she did love him, and she was terrified of losing him as she had her father. If she could do it over, she'd never put herself in this position. To lose a man who meant the world to her? Another one?

But she couldn't go back in time and change things. Except…maybe there was something else she *could* change.

'You won't lose me,' she said.

And kissed him.

Chapter Four

One Day, Now

Zoey had never done drugs before. She'd simply never been tempted to. But for some reason, she felt as though she were high.

She considered it for a second. She had just run ten kilometres. Her usual foray into exercising was more controlled—namely, in her room doing yoga or a dance video or something. She was relatively fit, though the run had been pushing it, and perhaps that was it. Maybe she *was* hallucinating seeing the man who used to be her best friend standing metres away.

She reached out a hand, grabbed the front of Parker's jacket. 'Do you see him?'

'What the hell, Zoey?' Sophia said from where she stood next to Parker. 'Why are you touching my boyfriend?'

Her eyes flickered over to Sophia. 'Because we're in love and we're going to run away together.'

Sophia opened her mouth. Closed it. Frowned.

'Seriously?' Parker asked, watching Sophia's reaction. 'You think I'm in love with your sister?'

'No,' Sophia said immediately. Uncertainty flashed across her face before she shook her head. 'No.'

'Soph—'

'Later,' Zoey interrupted Parker, curling her fingers harder. 'Do. You. See. Him?'

'Who is *he*— Oh,' Sophia said, snapping out of the stupor Zoey's teasing had put her in. 'Is that—'

'Oh. That means you see him.' She dropped her hand from Parker's chest. Belatedly, she looked at Sophia. 'I was only touching him because he was closest. He's nice to look at and all, but I have no desire to do anything more than look.'

'Every time we hang out together, you make me glad I'm with Sophia,' Parker muttered.

'Are you sure?' she asked mutedly, her eyes still on Sawyer. 'She's not exactly a catch.'

'Gee, thanks, sis.'

'You're welcome.'

'What's going on?' Angie, their oldest sister, said, re-joining their group as her husband, Ezra, handed out waters. 'You guys look like you were arguing.'

'Not arguing,' Parker informed her. 'Talking.'

'Right,' Angie said with a roll of her eyes. She bobbed her daughter up and down. 'So everything's normal then.'

'Considering Zo's just seen Sawyer, things are definitely normal.'

'Sawyer?' Angie repeated. 'As in, *Sawyer*?'

'Who's Sawyer?' Ezra asked.

'Zoey's best friend,' Angie said. She frowned. 'Well, they used to be best friends.' She tilted her head. 'Why am I only now realising I haven't seen him since I came back from Korea?'

'Because you moved back home, got married and had a baby?' Sophia offered. 'The real question is why, when I asked Zo about why I haven't seen him, she looked like she saw a ghost. Kind of how she looks now, actually.'

Zoey ignored her family. Sawyer hadn't noticed her yet. He was too busy twirling around a kid who looked like he was having the time of his life. The kid looked kind of grown, too. She wasn't good with guessing ages, but that kid was definitely older than two, which was when she last saw Sawyer. So if he'd had a baby when they'd still been...

Well, it would suck. But she was distracted from that thought when a woman joined their group. Sawyer set the kid down and smiled at the woman.

It hit her as hard as if she'd walked in front of a truck. An overwhelming hurt that made her feel as though she were sinking beneath the ocean with no hopes of resurfacing. Her throat got tight, like she couldn't breathe, her heart thumping like it was clinging to its purpose. She felt tears in her eyes. Had no desire to wipe them away. Because if Sawyer had gone on to have a family, it would kill her. But she was also the one who'd handed Sawyer the weapon to do it with.

'Is that Lisa?' Sophia's voice asked somewhere in the distance.

'Yeah,' Parker replied.

'Why is she with Sawyer?'

At that, Zoey turned. 'You know that woman?'

'Yeah, we met a year and a half ago. On the day Parker and I met, actually.' Sophia's mouth curved into the smile she always wore when she referred to the day she and Parker met. Zoey tried not to roll her eyes.

'So you know how she knows Sawyer?'

'No.'

'Oh.'

Their group went quiet for a moment. Zoey's eyes went back to Sawyer.

He looked good. Which wasn't something new. Sawyer was an attractive man. She'd noticed it back when they were friends. Then, it was simply an observation. A fact of life. But things had changed that day his grandmother had told her he loved her. Her eyes had opened, and she'd realised he wasn't only attractive; he was *hot*. Ice-cream-melting, can-I-lick-it-off-your-body hot. Today he wore a cap over the hair she knew to be dark and thick. The back was to the front, something she'd teased him about relentlessly when they'd been friends.

His white t-shirt was wet, probably from sweat, and she should have found it unattractive except it sent a flash of his sweaty bare chest through her mind and her body immediately said *yes, please*. The rest of his outfit was typical for a run—black shorts that were shorter than the black tights he wore beneath them. His sneakers were green and yellow, a bright combination that would have been something else she'd tease him about if they were still friends.

But they weren't anymore. Was it any wonder she didn't want to speak to her sisters about him?

As she was about to turn her head, find a hiding place, he looked at her. His expression changed from open and happy with his…with the child and the woman, to closed. Tight. He'd locked her out so quickly she had to ignore the desire to bang on the door and demand he let her in.

'Zo,' Angie said softly from beside her. She wasn't sure when her oldest sister had come to stand there, but she turned her head, forcing herself to look away from Sawyer. 'Would you hold Cal for me?' she asked. 'Ez and I want to run to the car and grab the energy bars we brought for everyone.'

She nodded slowly, but felt as though she were in another reality. 'Yeah, sure. Of course.'

Angie handed over the baby, who came to Zoey without complaint. The little girl immediately reached up for Zoey's hair, and reluctantly, Zoey laughed.

'No, Cal. It's tied up. Look.' She tilted her head for her niece to see. 'See? Tied up.'

The baby looked at her intently, then shook her head and reached for Zoey's hair again. To distract her, Zoey lifted her into the air, and Cal laughed. It was that free, uninhibited laughter of babies that told her they'd never been hurt before. They didn't know pain. And she would do everything in her power to make sure Cal never did. As unrealistic as it was.

'She's still got it,' Sophia said.

'Who does?'

'Angie. She just distracted you with Cal to keep you from breaking down or whatever.' Zoey looked over sharply. Sophia shrugged. 'It was pretty obvious that you were having some feelings about seeing Sawyer again.'

'I'm not,' Zoey denied. But she stopped lifting Cal and brought her to her chest. Cuddled her in hopes of giving herself comfort.

'So you won't mind joining Parker to go speak with them?'

Her eyes found Parker. He was, indeed, speaking with Sawyer and the woman. She schooled her face.

'I should probably wait here for Angie and Ezra to get back.'

'We're not leaving. We're walking a few metres forward.'

Her hold tightened on Cal. 'Go. I'll wait here.'

'Zoey—'

'Not now, please,' she said, not even upset that she sounded desperate. 'You should go and say hi to your friend.'

Sophia studied her. Reached out and squeezed her hand. Then she popped a finger on Cal's nose, stuck her tongue out, and chuckled as the baby laughed.

Zoey turned before she could look at Sawyer again. She took deep breaths as she rocked Cal. The baby started moaning. After a few moments of readjusting, it became clear that Cal wanted to be on her feet.

'You know you can't walk, right?' Zoey asked her. 'I mean, the thing you call walking isn't actual walking. People who can walk have more than one speed. And they can stand without falling over.'

Unsurprisingly, Cal didn't have an answer, and yet she made the same demands. Zoey sighed, set Cal down and held her hand as Cal did what she considered walking over the grass next to the pier.

Zoey manoeuvred her through the people. There were quite a lot of them, Zoey thought, happy that the event seemed to be such a success already. And she didn't even feel as grouchy about being awake early since the venue was spectacular.

The walk ended at the Sea Point Promenade, right next to the ocean. The salty wind fluttered over her skin, giving her some relief from the exertion of the run. It was already getting warm, a sure sign that it would be a scorching summer's day. Which would be great for the rest of the event since it would no doubt inspire more purchases of liquor and ice cream and the like to cool down. There was a kids' playground a short distance ahead, and Zoey thought Cal might like that, though the baby couldn't use any of the equipment. But she really would have to wait on Ezra and Angie before she did that.

She turned, looked out for them, and once again looked directly into Sawyer's eyes. Except this time, he was in front of her.

He'd have to go speak with her. He had no choice. It wasn't like he could pretend he hadn't seen her, even though that seemed like the preference for both of them. But he'd been introduced to Sophia's boyfriend through his sister, then Sophia had joined and had greeted him warmly—for Sophia—if somewhat suspiciously. Lisa shot him a questioning look, but he shook his head. He'd explain the connection later.

As concisely as he could, leaving out some key facts.

'Hey,' he said suddenly, interrupting the conversation. Four expectant eyes looked at him, and he went blank for a second. Heat rushed into his face. 'Sorry. I thought maybe I could get us some coffee over there.'

'I'd love some,' Lisa said warmly.

'Over there?' Sophia repeated. 'As in, over *there*?'

She gestured toward where Zoey had turned her back to them. She was with her niece—Angie's daughter, he'd been told—and she was walking away from them.

He cleared his throat. 'No. Over there.' He tilted his head to a coffee stand a few metres from where Zoey was.

'Oh, excuse me,' Sophia said dryly. 'In that case, I'd love a coffee, thanks.'

'Me, too,' Parker said, though his eyes were sharp. He could clearly sense something was happening. Sawyer wasn't sure if he knew about his and Zoey's history.

How could he? You're not a part of her life anymore. Haven't been for a while.

'Can I come with, Uncle Sawyer?'

He hesitated, his brain trying to switch gears from that disturbing thought.

'I think Uncle Sawyer should go alone, honey,' Lisa intervened. She gave him a pointed look, one that clearly said *you owe me one.* 'He still has to get over that devastating loss earlier.'

Ryder grinned, and Sawyer walked away. He didn't even pretend he was going to the coffee stand, knowing that if he did, it would give him an excuse not to speak with her. If he didn't speak with her now, he wasn't sure he would.

Unless he sent her an invitation to an event.

But, after two years, would she still be willing to pretend to be his girlfriend?

She looked directly at him as he walked over, and her expression went careful. His heart ached at the difference. At the fake smile that crossed her lips when he got closer. At the fact that it made him miss her even more. At the anger that was there, too.

'Hey, stranger.'

Her voice had always had a husky undertone to it. That wasn't different now. Nor was the way his body reacted to it. It dragged over his skin like a feather, giving him gooseflesh and making him wish he could take her into his arms.

But he was used to ignoring his desires when it came to her. Except for three months, six years ago.

'Hey,' he said, shaking his head to get the memories out. 'I…thought I'd come say hi.'

'Hi.' She offered him a small smile. She lowered, scooped the baby into her arms. 'This is Cal. She says hi, too.'

The baby looked at him. Stared unendingly, as though she knew all Sawyer's sins and was trying to decide what his penance would be.

'I don't think she likes me.'

'She's a little shy when it comes to strangers. Not that you're a stranger,' she said quickly. 'I mean, you are. To her. But not, you know, to me.'

By the time she was done, colour had flooded her cheeks. It complemented the light brown of her skin, dusting her high cheekbones with a charming red. To be fair, he considered most of her to be charming. Even when things were…complicated between them.

'Do you want to help me get coffee?' he asked, lifting a thumb over his shoulder, gesturing to the coffee stand. 'I offered to get the people staring at us some, so we should probably do that.'

Her gaze shifted to behind him. Her smile became more genuine. Oh, he'd missed that smile. The way her full lips curved to spread happiness to everyone who was lucky enough to see it.

'We should stand here a bit longer to mess with them. I'll touch your shoulder. Pretend to laugh.'

The idea of it made him feel embarrassingly eager.

'No,' she said before he could reply. 'They know you. They wouldn't believe you could make me laugh.'

'Excuse me?' He refused the twitch courting his lips. 'I'm hilarious.'

'Who's been lying to you, Sawyer?'

Her question was so serious he couldn't help the smile now. But he didn't show his teeth. On principle.

'Was it, um…your girlfriend?'

The change in the direction of the conversation had him repeating, 'My girlfriend?'

'The pretty lady with the kid.' Her eyebrows rose. 'Did you forget to tell me something when we were in university?'

It took him a while to figure it. He was shaking his head before he started speaking. 'Oh, no, it isn't like that.'

Her eyebrows went higher. A unique skill he'd only ever seen Zoey master. 'No?'

'No.' He ran a hand over his hair. 'No, that's…' He realised as he struggled that this was the first time he was telling someone who knew him before he'd known Lisa that she existed. 'She's my sister.'

Her mouth fell open, but before she could say anything, the baby lifted her hands and pulled at one of Zoey's twists. Zoey didn't have time to do something about it when the baby pulled again, harder this time, and dislodged a twist. It had Zoey's perfect bun shifting to the side of her head, and the exasperated look on Zoey's face was such a contrast to the happy gurgling of the baby that Sawyer couldn't help his smile. With teeth this time.

'Yeah, it's real funny,' Zoey told him, the quirk of

her mouth telling him she wasn't as annoyed as she was pretending to be.

'Hey, I'm just enjoying the entertainment. You're the one providing it.'

'Willingly, as you can see. Will you hold her while I fix this?'

'Er, sure.'

He wasn't comfortable with babies, but he had enough experience with his numerous cousins to know he wouldn't drop them. Cal didn't look thrilled by this new development though. She stared at him suspiciously, then reached out and curled her small fingers over his nose.

'Hey, that's attached,' he said to her, pulling back. Cal made a sound of protest.

'Just let her touch it,' Zoey suggested.

His eyes moved to her. She'd loosened the tie on her thick twists and they cascaded down to her waist. She leaned back slightly, gathering her hair behind her. The move pressed her breasts against her shirt, which was still wet from the run. Her body reacted, and for a moment, he found himself staring at the outline of her nipples pressed against her top.

It gave him another memory, this time of her breasts clad in black lace, those nipples visible beneath the sheer material of her bra.

He looked away, as if doing so would help him pull away from the memory, too. As if doing so would miraculously change how attracted he'd been to her.

His gaze met hers. A thrill went through his body. How attracted he *was* to her.

Chapter Five

One Day, Six Years Ago

This was even better than his fantasies.

He'd never admit it out loud, but he'd thought about kissing Zoey for as long as he could remember. Of course, he knew what it was like to have her lips on his. They'd shared polite kisses before. On cheeks after a long period of not seeing one another. On lips when Zoey got overexcited and smacked hers against his.

There was only one time those kisses had felt like more than what they were. It had been during their first year at university, at a party where someone had asked about their relationship. They were both used to that— had been plagued by questions of what was *really* happening between them since forever—but that night, their acquaintances had refused to believe it. Zoey had kissed him to prove that there was nothing going on.

There was a moment there, as she pulled away, that their eyes met and he thought she felt something. But then she'd gone on as if nothing happened. People had got bored by their lack of passion and moved on. So had they.

Until now. This kiss was definitely *more*.

When her lips touched his, he felt as if he were sinking into his bed after a long day. Her mouth was soft, familiar, comforting. But the movement of it spoke of other things done in bed after a long day. Heat, passion, desire. And all of it for him. From *Zoey*.

She gave a breathy moan into his mouth, and his hands tightened at the start of her hips. At first, he settled them there to steady her. She pressed against his body so fast he hadn't had a moment to think. Not until she looked into his eyes, lifted to her tiptoes, and asked the question he'd fantasised about for years. Now, his hands felt the plush flesh there. His fingers pressed into it, and he was rewarded with another tiny moan. It made him wonder if he was thinking too much during this kiss. And since he was wondering that, he figured he was and gave the reins to his instincts.

The first thing he did was pull Zoey closer. One arm encircled her waist, the other dipped to her butt. He left them there as he deepened the kiss, giving in to the urgency of tasting her. Of answering questions he'd had for much too long.

Yes, she tasted as sweet as he'd always imagined.

Yes, her lips felt like they'd been designed for kissing.

Yes, her tongue was as wicked in his mouth as it was when she spoke.

Yes, she wanted him, too.

He could tell by the way her hands roamed his body. He'd think she was marking him if he weren't already hers. Every laugh she'd given to one of the jokes he'd made for the sole purpose of entertaining her coated his skin. Every tear she'd cried because she was overwhelmed or heartbroken or grieving seared his heart.

Now, every stroke of her tongue disarmed him. The defences he'd built to keep his feelings from stumbling out in front of her, pleading her to feel the same, crumbled. The fear of it almost overwhelmed him. Would have, if he didn't have her mouth against his, her hands on his body, his hands on hers.

If this was all he had, he would use it. The hand on her butt tightened, lowered until he could cup her, pressing her against the evidence of what he felt for her. She gasped, but didn't stop kissing him. Instead, she plastered her body against his even more. She pulled at his shirt. As soon as it was out of his pants, she slipped her hands beneath the material to touch his skin.

'Have these also been here?' she asked, her husky voice adding another layer of desire to the spell that surrounded them.

'My muscles?' He chuckled when she nodded. Hissed when she gently scraped her nails over his abs. 'I believe so.'

'Impossible,' she purred. Her hands still caressed his skin. 'Surely I would have noticed.'

'You haven't,' he replied softly. She stilled. He brushed her forehead, her cheek with a kiss. Ran a thumb over her lips. 'But that's okay. You've noticed now.'

'I have,' she said, her eyes shining up at him. She leaned up, pressed a kiss to his neck, right where his pulse throbbed so erratically. 'I suppose we'll have to make up for lost time now.'

'Here?' he asked in a strangled voice when she nipped at the skin she'd kissed.

She laughed throatily. 'Why, Sawyer, I didn't realise you were the kind of person who got turned on by doing it in public.'

'I'm not. But I am the kind of person who's turned on by you.' His voice lowered. 'Whatever the hell you want, I'll give you.'

Her eyes widened. The surprise reflected the part of him that had retained his sanity. That part of him couldn't believe he said what he just said. Couldn't believe he was being honest with her, finally. But her surprise didn't allow that part of him to take control. The remainder of him was too big—and it liked the freedom. It was like a beast that had been hiding its entire life and was no longer being hunted by the townsfolk.

'I don't know this part of you, do I?'

'No.'

'Should I be afraid?'

He didn't answer her. He did lean forward and kiss her softly.

'Hmm,' she said when he pulled back. 'I'm taking that as a yes.'

'You don't have to be afraid of me.'

'I'm not.' Her words were earnest. 'I'm afraid of how this will change things.'

'Do you want them to change?' he forced himself to ask.

'Depends.' Her eyes twinkled. 'Does change mean we get to make out some more?'

She didn't want to answer him. Fair, since he didn't know whether he wanted an answer. It wasn't the best approach. Zoey was spontaneous, passionate. She did what felt good in the moment. He imagined she was leaning in to that now, after her father's death. The best approach then would be if *he* took a step back. Thought things through.

Except he could really only think about her. Everything that had happened in the last twenty minutes demanded he only think about her. Accepting it—despite the faint unease that decision came with—he smiled.

'Absolutely.'

Her lips claimed his before he could finish the word. They demanded his attention, and he obeyed. His tongue swept into her mouth, tangled with hers. He slowed the pace, then sped it up. He tasted her and teased her. Worshipped her. Pleased her.

She shivered beneath his touch, against his body. And the passion he hid from her for years took over his hands. He traced the outline of her body. Lingered on the spots he'd admired for years, but forced himself not to. The cinch of her waist, the flare of her hips, the curve of her butt. He wanted to lift her up, have her link her legs around him, get better access to the heat of her centre. But part of him was aware they were in public. In the middle of a field next to the hall where his cousin was celebrating her graduation. Where his family could see them.

'Maybe being in public isn't such a good idea,' he said, shades away from panting.

She laughed. 'Maybe. You never know when Grandma Carla might try to find us. I doubt you'd want her to find you like this.'

She tilted her pelvis forward, pressing into his arousal.

He groaned. 'Why would you even say that?'

'Because it was funny.' Her eyes sobered. 'To give you a chance to slow down.'

'I don't need to slow down.'

'You say that now. Until you wake up one day and realise I'll be your responsibility.'

A tiny frown knitted her brow. He pushed a kiss to her forehead to smooth it.

'You say that like it's a bad thing.'

Her face softened. 'You've never had a problem with it, have you? With helping me, I mean.'

'Why would I?'

She cupped his face between her hands. 'You wouldn't. Because you're the best man I know.'

I love you.

He almost said it. Caught himself in time. Comforted the need with his next question.

'Ready to leave?'

'What about your family?'

'What about them?'

'You're not thinking clearly.'

'I'm thinking more clearly than I ever have,' he said with a smile. 'And if I'm not, I like it.'

'Did I put a spell on you?'

'Since I met you.'

She stared. Shook her head. 'How did I not see this?'

'You see it now,' he repeated.

There was a pause. 'I do.' Another one, shorter this time. 'So let's get out of here.'

Chapter Six

'So, a sister, huh?' Zoey said, taking Cal from Sawyer. She tried not to notice how good he looked with a baby in his arms. Tried to ignore the way her ovaries exploded and begged him to save the eggs that were released in the carnage.

Okay, that response was probably a sign she had to stop looking at sexy men on social media. Or maybe it was a sign that she should look at *more* men on social media so real-life men didn't look so appealing.

That's how it worked, right?

'Yeah.' His expression was unreadable. 'I can't believe it myself, most days.'

'How long have you known?' she asked, hoping it didn't sound like an accusation. Once she'd got over the initial shock that he had a sister, she'd been able to hide her reaction more easily. The disappointment that he didn't tell her. The inexplicable betrayal attached to it.

But she was well aware that she was the reason for their estrangement. They hadn't seen one another in two years. That had been at his request, but still, it was *because* of her. The four years before that, they'd seen

one another four times. After the three months they'd
been… After those three months, she'd thought it best
they didn't stay in contact.

Then an event had appeared in her calendar, as it
always had when he needed his pretend girlfriend. She
couldn't ignore it. Self-preservation and reason told her
she had to, but she couldn't. His family knew nothing about what happened between them. They'd have
suspected something was off if she hadn't gone. She'd
have disappointed Sawyer, too. So she'd gone because
of…obligation. Duty to the man who'd been there for
her through the worst time of her life.

It was a slap in the face when he told her he no longer needed her to fulfil that obligation, that duty. But
she'd expected it. She didn't fit into his ideal world
anymore. She simply didn't fit with him.

'I found out about her shortly after the last time we
saw one another, actually. So about two years.'

'And you two are…close?'

He looked over at the group of both his and her family. The little boy—his nephew—waved. Sawyer waved
back. 'We should get the coffee.'

'Sure.'

They walked to the coffee stand in silence. Cal was
content since Zoey had left out two twists for her to
play with. She waited to the side as Sawyer placed
the order, then plastered a smile to her face when he
joined her.

'Yes,' he said after a few seconds. 'You asked if Lisa
and I were close. We are.'

'Good.'

It was all either of them said for some time.

'I can't believe your aunt didn't know,' Zoey said,

the awkwardness driving her crazy. 'Or your grand-mother.'

His expression went unreadable, and again, she felt like he closed the door on her.

'We don't know what Grandma Carla knew,' Saw-yer said primly. 'She's not here for us to ask.' He said nothing about his aunt.

Her instinctual reaction was to apologise. But what for? For the fact that he had a sister no one had told him about? That clearly his aunt had deliberately kept that information from him? Or the fact that his grand-mother had died?

She focused on the last one. Enough to say screw it. She'd been there after his grandmother had died. She'd supported him and he'd asked her to leave him alone. So though her heart ached because she knew this in-formation about his sister must have killed him, she didn't apologise.

'I know how much family means to you,' she said instead. 'I'm... I'm happy you found your sister.'

So many emotions ran across his face. She didn't react to any of them, calling on every inch of her self-control not to. Things had changed so damn much be-tween them. If they hadn't, she would have been able to reach out and hug him. Comfort him. Or at the very least, ask him why he needed comfort.

It frustrated her that she didn't know. It frustrated her that he'd discovered he had a *sister* and she hadn't known about it. She wished he'd called. She wouldn't have asked questions. Not many, anyway. She would have bought him alcohol because sisters were *hard*. Having two herself, she was quite certain about that.

Or maybe the alcohol would have been champagne, to celebrate that he had a sibling.

Maybe she just wished he hadn't iced her out of his life.

But how could she blame him? *Her* decisions had brought them here. And how could she justify them being in one another's lives with their history? That would have been painful. Rather ice then. It cost her less. Though she was doubting that now.

'Thank you.'

It was all he said before he turned back for the coffees. She offered to put Cal down to help him, but he rejected, pointing to the cardboard holder they gave him for the eight coffees.

'Pride is one of the deadly sins for a reason, you know.' Saying the sulky comment helped her get out of her head. Or rather, her emotions.

'Good thing I didn't decline your offer because I'm too proud to ask for help.'

'Just stubborn then? Cool.'

'Neither,' he said with a laugh. 'I was imagining how you'd walk all the way to our family holding Cal *and* carrying one of the cartons.'

'Oh,' she said, frowning. 'I said I'd have put her down.'

'And held her hand, presumably, which would have likely led to half of the coffee being spilled over you.'

She waited a beat. 'Good points.'

'That was painful, wasn't it?' he asked with a grin.

'No.'

He laughed. 'Proud and stubborn. I definitely think one of us has those characteristics.'

Refusing to let him have the last word, Zoey

bounced Cal on her hip. 'Are you going to let this man you've just met talk to you this way, Caleah?'

Cal gave the most perfect gurgle in response. Zoey looked at Sawyer smugly. 'You've hurt her feelings.'

He laughed again, shook his head. 'You're lucky I'm an easy-going guy. Otherwise, this might have annoyed me.'

'Don't underestimate my ability to annoy you.'

She stuck out her tongue.

He was still chuckling when they reached the group. It now included Angie and Ezra, and Cal immediately reached for her father.

'Hey,' Angie said, accepting the coffee from Sawyer with a smile, but directing her words to her child. 'You realise I make the food around here, right? Not your father.'

'But I'm the fun dad,' Ezra said, spinning Cal around in a circle. He was rewarded with a giggle from Cal and a look from Angie.

'Let's see if you say that when she's sixteen and wants to go have fun with someone else.'

'Why would *you* say that?' Ezra asked, bringing his daughter closer to him as if protecting her from her mother's prediction. 'You're speaking it into existence.'

Angie rolled her eyes, but the annoyance was all fondness. Not for the first time, Zoey felt a pinch of jealousy. As always, she shut it down. Took a long drag from her coffee and hoped the burn of the too-hot liquid was enough to shame her for her evil thoughts.

'Thanks for this,' Parker told Sawyer. 'We need to get going. We need to get back to Kirstenbosch and have to shower first. Then pick up my mom.'

'Sure,' Lisa said. 'We'll see you later.'

'You will?' Zoey said, realising it was the first time she was speaking to the woman. 'Sorry. I'm Zoey.' She hesitated before saying, 'Sophia's sister.'

There was a part of her that wanted to introduce herself in relation to Sawyer. But she couldn't do that anymore, could she? She no longer had the right. And if she was being honest, she wasn't entirely sure of their status.

'Lisa.' Lisa took Zoey's outstretched hand. 'I'm Sawyer's sister.'

'So he said.'

'We didn't know you had a sister, Sawyer,' Angie interjected with surprise.

'Neither did I,' he said with a half-smile. 'It's a long story.'

'Why didn't you tell us, Zo?'

It was an innocent question. So again, Zoey reached for her fake smile and told her sister, 'I didn't know either.'

Realisation flashed in Angie's eyes, followed quickly by an apology. Zoey shook her head. She didn't need an apology. She needed to get out of there.

'You need my help, too, don't you?' Zoey asked Parker. She gave him a pointed look. If he wanted her to help him with Sophia's proposal, he would help her with this.

'Er, yeah, sure,' Parker said after exchanging a look with Sophia. 'We should get going now.'

'Of course.' She turned to Angie and Ezra. 'I'll see you guys at the concert.' She blew a kiss to Cal, which made the baby smile. 'It was nice meeting you,' she said to Lisa. 'Maybe we'll see one another later.'

But not if I see you first. In which case, I will run

in the opposite direction and hope it doesn't happen again.

Then she turned to Sawyer. 'It was…good seeing you. We should catch up some time.'

She moved forward, aware of all the eyes on her. Knowing she'd be asked about it if she didn't, she moved forward and hugged Sawyer. Her intention was to keep it short. They'd both run a ten-kilometre race. Hugging was the last thing they should be doing, really.

But the moment his arms closed around her, her throat tightened. It was so familiar and comforting. There were sparks of more, too, feeling his body against her. She resisted the urge to close her eyes and press her face into his chest. When his hands touched her waist, she resisted the desire to ask them to linger, so she could feel the heat they'd once shared such a long time ago.

She shut that part of her off after they ended their romantic relationship. Particularly because those desires had been part of why she started that relationship—and ended their friendship.

Now with his arms around her, his hands on her body, she remembered. Every kiss, every stroke, every murmur against her skin. He would touch her lightly, trail his fingertips over her body, as if he couldn't believe she was laying naked in front of him. And then he'd press his lips along the trail he'd created, torturing her with the sweetest pleasure as she welcomed his worship…

She pulled back, her cheeks burning. But rather that than tears, which she knew were as close to the surface.

'Bye,' she murmured, refusing to meet his eyes. Instead, she followed Sophia and Parker to the car. When they were an appropriate distance away, Sophia waited for Zoey to catch up, and took her hand.

'Should I ask?'

She took a ragged breath. 'Not yet.'

'Okay.'

The rest of the walk was silent, but when they had the car in sight, Sophia said, 'Was Sawyer always that hot?'

A strangled laugh escaped her throat. 'Pretty much, yeah.'

'I guess things are tainted when you're older.'

'Oh, please, you're one year older than us.'

'But years and years wiser.'

Zoey laughed again, though this time it was freer. 'Is that what you tell yourself?'

Sophia bumped her hip against Zoey's. 'You know it is. My head isn't this big genetically.'

Another laugh. Zoey squeezed Sophia's hand. 'Thanks for distracting me.'

Sophia winked.

'So, are you going to tell me what happened back there? Or am I going to have to wait until Ryder has kids to find out?'

Sawyer kept his eyes on the road. 'It's been all of twenty minutes since we left the Promenade, Lisa.'

'Yeah, but it's been the longest twenty minutes of my life.'

He chuckled, and tried to figure out how to tell his sister about the woman who'd been the most important person in his life for seven years. Did he tell her Zoey was the first person to make him feel as though he belonged? Growing up with his aunt and uncle and cousins had been good, but he always felt outside their unit. Probably because of that conversation he'd over-heard between his aunt and uncle about taking him in. It hadn't been their first choice. So having some-one choose him like Zoey had was important to him.

More so because of who she was: a vivacious, happy woman. And she'd chosen *him* to be her friend. A lit-eral piece of sun had deigned him, a dark crevice in a cave somewhere, worthy of shining her light on. Zoey wasn't lacking in options. She attracted people with her carefree attitude. Her laugh was infectious, and when she walked into a room, she made people smile.

He'd been in love with her for almost as long as he'd known her. But he couldn't sacrifice her light for his love. So he'd kept his feelings to himself, even when it was hard to, because he loved her as a friend, too. He couldn't lose her.

Until that one night when everything changed. Things had snowballed, rolling at high speed, until predictably, they'd crashed. He and Zoey had crashed. Absently, he rubbed his chest at the pain that still flared when he thought about it.

Did he tell Lisa that, too?

'Zoey and I used to be friends.'

'The one with the big bun?' Lisa asked. 'Or the one with the baby?'

'Bun,' he said, his heart thudding at the idea of Zoey having a baby. He knew there was a possibility she'd moved on in the two years since they'd last seen one another. He was grateful it didn't seem like moving on entailed a new relationship. A family.

Selfish, an inner voice taunted.

'Okay, so you were friends,' Lisa said. 'Was there some big fallout?'

His hands tightened on the wheel. 'I guess you could say that.'

'I am saying that. There was enough tension between the two of you that I thought about flagging a police officer in case they needed to intervene.'

'Funny.' He slanted her a look. 'It's a long story.'

'Isn't it lucky we're going to breakfast then?' Lisa asked slyly.

He sighed. 'I don't really want to talk about it.'

He could feel Lisa studying him, so he kept his eyes on the road. It was busy. He expected as much with the event closing off some of the roads. He ran through the options of where they could go for breakfast, and settled on the Waterfront. It was easy to get to, and they could wait the traffic out there without too much hassle. Also, he figured they all needed as much air as possible since none of them had showered yet. He made a mental note to find a restaurant outside.

'It's funny that in the two years we've known one another, you haven't once mentioned Zoey.'

He didn't reply.

'Obviously, you two were close friends. And maybe something more, because the way she was looking at you—no, the way *you* were looking at *her*—was pretty hot.'

'I was not looking at her in any way.' He resisted for all of a beat. 'Was she looking at me?'

Lisa gave a delighted laugh. 'I'm not leaving this car until you tell me what's going on.'

'Where were you going to go?' Sawyer asked under

his breath as they crawled through traffic. He cleared his throat. 'Ryder, you okay back there?'

When he got no answer, his eyes slipped to the rear-view mirror. Kid was fast asleep.

Lisa smirked. 'So much for using my son as a distraction.'

He sighed in defeat. 'What do you want to know?'

'When did you meet?'

'Our first day in high school.'

'How long were you friends?'

'Seven years.'

'Did it ever become romantic?'

He hesitated. 'Yes.'

'Really?' Another squeal of delight. His mood darkened a shade. 'Why did it end?'

'We were better as friends.'

'But you're not friends now.'

The piece of his heart that had broken off when he and Zoey ended their relationship peeked out from the box he shoved it in. He kicked it back ruthlessly.

'No, we're not.'

'What happened?' Lisa asked softly.

'A lot. Too much to tell you.'

Too raw to tell you.

He didn't say the words out loud, but Lisa must have sensed it because she stopped the interrogation. She was sensitive like that, a fact he never before appreciated as much as he did now.

It was interesting when they first met and he realised it. It seemed to be a genetic trait since he shared that sensitivity. Which told him now that she was hurt he didn't want to tell her more, but she was putting his feelings ahead of her own.

For the most part, things were fairly easy between him and Lisa. They were both extraordinarily happy that they'd found one another, and bonded immediately. Lisa had her adopted parents, but she'd always felt a little out, though she assured him they hadn't made her feel that way. He could relate. Plus, they were both the other's connection to their mother. Sawyer didn't remember much about the woman, so he couldn't talk to Lisa about it. It was both a blessing and curse, because it removed any jealousy that might have existed for Lisa at Sawyer getting to spend time with their mother. But it meant neither of them had learnt about her by knowing her, which sucked.

There were moments when navigating the relationship with Lisa was tricky. Mostly because his aunt had known about her, and hadn't said anything. And so had his grandmother. But these women were his family, too, and he refused to engage with Lisa's anger about the situation. Hell, he refused to engage with his own anger about the situation. So, tricky.

This was another tricky moment. But he couldn't condense what had happened with Zoey into one conversation. Or he didn't want to. It felt like he was dishonouring what they'd shared. Even though things hadn't ended well between them, to him, the years when things *had* gone well hadn't been negated by that.

He played around with it in his mind as they waited in traffic. By the time they reached the open road, he'd decided on an abridged version.

'Zoey and I were inseparable for years. She was… family. Sometimes more than the Steinbergs because she chose me, you know. She didn't have to choose me.' He shook his head when it didn't sound entirely sensical to him. But Lisa didn't interrupt. 'Anyway, everything was great until one night we kissed. And then things…went further.' He left the description of their romantic relationship at that. 'It was a mistake. By the time we realised it, it was too late. There was nothing to salvage.'

Lisa didn't respond until they reached the parking lot. When he pulled into an empty space, her soft voice said, 'It didn't look like there was nothing to salvage, Sawyer. It looked…like you both regretted what happened.'

He swallowed. 'Yeah, I think we both do.'

Chapter Seven

One Day, Six Years Ago

'You want me to go in there?' Zoey asked. 'I refuse, sir.'

'On what premise?'

'On the fact that it looks like that.'

She gestured to the cabin. It was on a dark estate that required them to drive an incline in the middle of the night, which had a lot to do with Zoey's feelings.

'What is "that" exactly?' Sawyer asked. 'Because I see a beautiful cottage a short distance away from a vineyard in the middle of gorgeous trees and fynbos.'

'I see a location a serial killer stops at for a quick kill.'

He chuckled, but his next question was sincere. 'Do you want to leave?'

'No,' she said without hesitation. She put a hand on his thigh. His muscles clenched beneath her fingers, and she felt a rush at the power. She didn't stop to examine it. 'If a serial killer does make this their next stop, I'll push you ahead of me as I run away into the gorgeous trees and fynbos.'

His laugh was louder, and the contact she had with

him had the vibration going through her. It made her immeasurably happy, an emotion that had kept its distance since her father's death. Since long before that, if she was being honest. Daniel Roux's brain tumour had made the decline of his health difficult to watch.

She contrived a lot of her happiness during that time. For the sake of her father, who looked at her to cheer him up whenever he was going through a particularly rough patch. For the sake of her sisters, who were falling over themselves to make sure everything else was fine. For the sake of her mother, who would collapse whenever she'd see their father.

It wasn't for herself, she'd discovered after the funeral. The emotion had hit her hard and fast after that. The exhaustion of pretence along with the grief. She struggled against it at first. Hell—who was she kidding? She was still struggling against it. So this happiness? It was a relief. And this...whatever was happening with Sawyer, a welcome distraction.

She thought back to his kisses in the field. Shivered.

A *very* welcome distraction.

'Are you planning on getting out any time soon, or are we going to stay in the car?' Sawyer asked.

'Can we make out in the car?'

His eyes widened, and she laughed at his surprise. In all honesty, she wasn't sure what was going on between them. Everything had shifted, turned on its head, but had stayed the same. Sawyer was the same person who held her as she cried after her father's death. He was her rock, her best friend in the world, and she couldn't imagine her life without him.

But suddenly that life looked different. It wasn't all talking to one another over the phone at night; it was spending the night together. She didn't want to call him when she wanted to talk with him; she wanted him there. She wanted to look at him and enjoy those muscular rifts of his body. The broad shoulders, the perfect pecs, the ripped torso. She wanted to run her hands over the thick black strands of his hair, and run her tongue along his full lips.

It was hard for her to believe all this had come from something his grandmother had said. Somewhere between that moment and the moment she'd leaned in to kiss him, she'd realised that the feelings stirring inside her weren't new. They had always been there, simmering, and maybe that's why she didn't care that things had changed.

She ignored every inkling that suggested otherwise.

'I'm going to take that as a no,' she said when he didn't answer her. 'Such a pity, really. I'm quite flexible.'

With a wicked grin, she got out of the car. She made it all of three steps before an arm snaked around her waist and Sawyer pulled her against him. Their lips met as her brain registered what he was about to do, and she clasped her hands around his neck as their tongues mingled.

She never expected him to taste this good. Or to be quite this good at kissing, frankly. His tongue teased hers as though they were old duelling partners. He was a skilled swordsman who knew when to attack and when to draw back. And she let him lead, trusting his skill, his intuition as the sensuality of the moment sent a thrill from her head down to her toes.

It took her a while to realise that that thrill wasn't entirely from his kisses. Because minutes later, another went through her. Then another, followed by a lot more in quick succession. She pulled away and looked up, laughing when she realised it had begun to rain.

'I thought the shivers going through my body were because of you,' she told him, lowering her arms to wrap them around his waist. 'When really, I was getting cold.'

'I'd like to think some of those shivers were because of me,' he said with a half-smile. Which was so sexy that it did send another shiver down her spine. 'Come on, let's get you inside. I'll put the fire on.'

'No,' she said. 'Kiss me again.'

His eyes searched hers and then his head dipped. He softened the kiss, and her stomach flipped over itself. Then it melted, pooling into a lazy heat that settled between her legs. As if sensing it, Sawyer ran his hands down her back, settling them on her butt to cup her cheeks, then lifting her up so she had to wrap her legs around him.

It brought her in contact with the hard length of him, and she rubbed against it tentatively, uncertainty creeping into her as she realised the enormity of what could happen between them. He groaned, his hands tightening. He pulled away, grazing her bottom lip with his tongue, before his head dipped back. After a moment, he straightened, looking at her. *Really* looking at her, seeing her. It was part of what had made her friendship with Sawyer so special.

'We don't have to do this,' Sawyer said, searching her face.

'I know.'

Streams of water ran from that gorgeous black hair down over his face. She brushed it away with her fingers.

'Nothing that happens tonight is irreversible, Zo,' he said. 'We can stop now. I'll take you home and we'll go to the new superhero movie tomorrow as planned and pretend it didn't happen.'

'But it did happen,' she said with a small smile. 'I appreciate the offer, but I don't want things to go back to what they were.' And despite what he said, she knew they wouldn't. Couldn't.

'But you're not ready for us to sleep together either.'

She rested the hands that had been playing with his hair at the base of his neck. 'I don't know.'

'Which means no.' He gave her a chaste kiss on the lips, then set her down. 'Until you can give me a definitive yes, I won't do anything more with you.'

She took a few moments to process. 'But you'll still kiss me.'

He laughed lightly. 'I'll still kiss you. If you want me to.'

'*Yes.*'

She kissed him again, her heart fuller than it had ever been with a man before. Oh, she realised suddenly, even as their mouths were moving. Maybe because their mouths were moving. She *had* felt this way before with a man; she'd felt it with him.

It hadn't been anything more than affection then, but there were countless times during their friendship where she felt a wave of gratitude at having Sawyer in her life. It stemmed from the fullness, that wave. Because Sawyer meant the world to her. Sawyer *was* the world to her.

Beneath the night sky full of clouds. As the rain poured over them and they got soaking wet. With the trees around them rustling in the slight wind, and the earth coating them with its signature scent of rain hitting soil. Each of those things seared this moment she and Sawyer were sharing in her brain. It would become one of her forever memories, she knew. One of those defining moments where she looked back on and thought, *Oh. That's when it happened. That's when I realised I want to spend my life with him.*

Oh.

Oh, she thought again. And pulled back from his embrace.

Chapter Eight

One Day, Now

'I'm not telling you how to do your job, Ricardo,' Sophia snapped. 'I'm telling you that if you say it's a "gourmet" meal, you *cannot* offer your customers a cheese sandwich. *And it's not even toasted, for heaven's sake.*'

'Soph,' Zoey said, intervening. 'Maybe you should take a walk.' She looked at Parker. 'Parker, maybe you and Soph should take a walk. You know, get some air. Walk off the frustration.'

Parker's brow knitted tighter, though she didn't know how. He'd been drawn to the commotion because of Sophia's obvious frustration, but he hadn't said anything to the chef. Zoey couldn't figure out if he was distracted by the event; worried about his mother, since Evie had called before they could pick her up to say they'd come on their own since his mother was having a 'stubborn spell'; trying to get a handle on his frustration with the chef; or if he was nervous about his planned proposal.

Perhaps all of them? Who knew?

He and Sophia were the perfect match because they were both pretty hard to read. Although her sister was being transparent today, particularly with the 'a gour-met meal is a normal cheese sandwich' chef.

'Parker?'

His eyes flickered to Zoey. She gave him a look. He shook his head. 'Come on, Soph. Let's go get a drink.'

'It's eleven in the morning.'

'I didn't mean alcohol.'

'Then I'm not sure I want to go with you,' Sophia grumbled. But straightened her spine. Looked at Zoey. 'You better have a plan with this guy, or I'll make sure he'll regret taking this job.'

With those words, she walked away. Zoey spent a few seconds looking after her, then she looked at Ricardo.

'She's a lot, isn't she?'

'If you want to call her that, yeah.'

His expression told Zoey he had another phrase in mind for Sophia. She thought it best they stuck with hers.

'You've got to admit she has a point,' Zoey continued conversationally. 'I'm not sure I've ever gone to a restaurant serving gourmet food and been offered a cheese sandwich.'

'What do you want me to do, lady?' the man asked, his body language screaming impatience. 'There are going to be hundreds of people here today. I can't serve them chicken cordon bleu. I need something that's gonna be fast and easy.'

'I get it.' She waited a moment. 'You can't expect them to pay gourmet prices then, can you?'

He opened his mouth, but she spoke before he could say anything.

'Look, Ricardo, honestly, I do think you could do

more than a cheese sandwich and variants thereof. Use the bacon for the cheese and bacon sandwich, wrap it around some cheese sticks, fry them, and boom, there's something interesting.' Zoey searched her mind for more ideas, but she wasn't a cook. She settled for straightforward. 'Or maybe chicken mayo. Add some chips. Or toast the damn sandwich.'

'You're not much better than she is,' Ricardo said after a pause.

'Yeah, I am, and we both know it.' She didn't wait for confirmation. 'My advice? Remove the gourmet food from your sign. Price the sandwiches more reasonably. If you can't be creative, that's the minimum you can do.'

He released a breath. 'Fine.'

'Thank you.' She took a step away, then turned. 'Oh, and you know your contract was specific with the terms of the agreement. You knew there were going to be hundreds of people here today. You're supposed to be serving what you told the organisers you would be serving. So, if you don't do your job properly today, I'll make sure the contract is voided and you don't get paid.'

His face got red. 'I'll sue.'

'You're overcharging people for cheese sandwiches,' she replied. 'We both know you can't afford to sue us. But we can sue you for breach of contract. We won't, if you do your job properly. Which, luckily for both of us, you've already agreed to do.' She gave him her best smile. 'People will be here in an hour. Get going.'

She didn't wait for a reply, though she knew she got one. Probably in the form of a silent curse or a rude hand gesture at her back. She didn't care. She was an events manager for a corporate company, and while she didn't have much to do with this event—the charity had their own events coordinator—all contracts were pretty standard. And because this wasn't her job where she'd get in trouble with legal for making threats, she embraced her freedom.

There was just something about being a bitch for a good cause that sent a surge of adrenaline through her body.

'Your expression is pretty fierce. Everything okay?'

That adrenaline spiked her heartrate, although it wasn't because she'd just been a bitch.

'Sawyer.' She frowned. 'It's too early for you to be here. They're only letting guests in from twelve.'

She knew because she'd intended on hiding from that time on. There were plenty of places obscured by trees in Kirstenbosch. She wouldn't have to see anyone she didn't want to. And she didn't want to see Sawyer and be reminded of their awkward reunion earlier that day.

Or what she knew she'd have to do if they reunited again.

'I guess we got special treatment because Lisa and Parker know one another.'

Sawyer gestured to his left, where Lisa was speaking with Parker. Her kid wasn't with her this time, though there was a tall, wide man standing next to her. He looked like he could lift a car if he wanted to. Zoey wondered if he ever had the urge.

'Is the world really that small?' she asked, the silly question giving her a reprieve from the more serious questions floating around in her head.

How are you?

Do you miss me?

How did we mess things up so badly?

'You mean, so small that you're forced to see the man you've been avoiding for six years because your sister's boyfriend happens to know my long-lost sister?'

She gave a surprise laugh. 'Excuse me? I have not been avoiding you.'

'We haven't seen one another in two years.'

'Because you told me it was no longer necessary for us to pretend to be in a relationship for your grandmother's sake since she'd…you know.'

It felt too cruel to say died, especially with the heat she'd been speaking with. She was familiar with death, of course. Her father had been dead for seven years now. But Sawyer's grandmother had only passed away two years before, and there'd been no warning of illness like with her dad. She passed away in her sleep at the age of eighty-six, which, all things considered, wasn't a bad way to leave the earth.

Not that Zoey knew how Sawyer felt about it.

Again, the frustration at being cut out of his life vibrated inside her.

'I'm sorry,' he said with a wince. 'I shouldn't have said that.'

But he had, which made her think two years—and the four years before that, when she'd spent a total of four days with him—had changed him.

Or had simply brought out a version of him that had always existed.

'No worries,' she said easily, though her last thought confused her. 'Look, I should get back to Soph. She's not dealing with this day well, and I'm trying to support her.'

The slight curl of his lip told her what he was thinking. *Not avoiding me, huh?* He didn't say it. Which she mentally congratulated him on, because her own filter was dangerously close to breaking.

'You and Sophia seem a lot closer than you used to be.'

She angled her head. 'We've always been…fine with one another.'

'The dynamics have shifted,' he replied, ignoring her comment.

Because he knew her well enough to know the nature of her relationship with her sisters. So maybe he hadn't changed that much. She studied his expression, tried to figure out if it was true. Got nothing more than what he wanted to show her.

Which was a good enough change in itself.

'Maybe,' she acknowledged. 'The entire family's dynamics have shifted. Angie left us after Dad died and that changed things. Which you know,' Zoey said, face burning since their romantic relationship had started after that. 'While she was gone, things changed. She came back, met Ezra, had a baby. Sophia met Parker, which changed her. All of those things shifted.' She shrugged. 'It's the nature of family. Things will change again, I'm sure. Actually, as soon as Parker proposes—'

She froze. Tried to think through her options. She could pretend like she hadn't said anything. Play it off as normal and hopefully he wouldn't notice. Her other option was to beg him not to say anything. He would only have to keep the secret until the end of the day.

The look in his eyes told her the second was more likely.

'You can't say anything.'

His lips curved. Slyly, she thought, her brain scrambling. But Sophia and Lisa were walking toward them now, and she only had time to say one thing.

'If you say something, I will tell your sister about how much you love the English Royal Family.' She narrowed her eyes. 'You must be thrilled with the latest news. You've always wanted them to be more open-minded.'

His smirk disappeared, but his eyes glinted. 'I am, and I'm not ashamed of it.' At her raised eyebrows, he relented. 'Fine, I am. But I don't care if Lisa knows it.'

'Okay, then I'll post it on your social media. On your work profile that you keep so clean even I can't tell it's you.'

'How did you know I have a work profile?' he hissed.

'Because I'm excellent at stalking people on social media,' she snapped back, and turned to their sisters with a smile. 'Hi! Are you looking for us?'

He didn't believe Zoey would stoop that low. Revealing one of his biggest secrets? Although…it wasn't anything to be ashamed of. So what if he liked the Royal Family? If he rooted for the princes to find happiness and love? If he'd told a couple of co-workers he couldn't join them at a rugby game because he wanted to watch the Royal Wedding instead? If he'd lied and told them his sister needed him, which was why he couldn't go…

Okay, she knew where he was weak. But two could play that game. He wouldn't tell Sophia her boyfriend was going to propose, of course. The fact that Zoey thought he might told him all he needed to know about the state of their relationship. It awoke strange emotions inside him. And made him petty. He wouldn't tell Sophia about her boyfriend's planned proposal—but Zoey didn't know that.

'Parker went to get his mom and Evie at the entrance,' Sophia said to Zoey.

'They got here okay?' Zoey asked. 'Ms Jones is feeling better?'

'I'm not sure. I guess we'll find out.'

Zoey's eyes met his. *I'll explain later*, they said. He nodded. Looked away when their wordless communication made him feel linked to her. But they weren't *linked*. Their previous conversation had proven that.

Hadn't it?

'Parker seems like a cool guy,' he said to Sophia.

'Depends on who you ask.'

He tilted his head. 'His…girlfriend?'

Sophia met his gaze. Amusement sparkled on her face, a stark difference to how she looked after Zoey's question about Parker's mother.

'I guess he's okay,' Sophia allowed.

'She adores him,' Zoey interrupted.

'Clearly,' he replied dryly.

'No, I've seen it,' Lisa said, smiling. 'This is just a part of what they do.'

Sophia rolled her eyes. 'I don't *adore* him. But… he's a cool guy.' She directed those words to Sawyer.

'I think he thinks you're cool, too.'

He could feel the panic radiating off Zoey. He fought to keep his face straight.

'Of course he does,' Sophia responded with a frown.

'Just confirming it for you.'

Sophia gave him a puzzled look. It was edged with something that told him she thought he was an idiot.

Fair, he considered. But he was willing to look like an idiot if it meant riling up Zoey.

'Lisa,' Zoey said very deliberately. 'Who was that handsome gentleman I saw you with earlier?'

'Byron?' Lisa beamed. 'He's my husband.'

'The cute kid's dad?' Zoey asked. She shook her head immediately after. 'Not sure why I asked that. Please ignore me.'

Lisa laughed. 'He is the cute kid's dad. And he's trying to find me something to drink.'

'It's none of my business.'

'I don't mind answering your questions.'

Zoey turned. Tilted her head. Then nodded. 'You're wondering if I'll return the favour.'

Lisa's eyebrows rose. 'I am indeed. How did you know?'

'Your expressions are similar to your brother's. I used to be quite good at reading them.' She looked at him, then back at his sister. 'Seems like I still have some of that talent.'

He didn't react to that. Put it in the box where he kept all his other memories of her. Slid the box back into the recesses of his mind, where it had been before he'd seen her that morning.

He ignored the mocking laughter in his head at the lie.

'What do you want to know?' Zoey asked.

'Seriously?' Lisa gave him a look of glee. 'I can ask you questions?'

'Sure.'

'And if she won't answer them, I will,' Sophia said with a small smile, though she was staring in the direction of the entrance. 'He spent enough time at my house that I'd know some of the answers.'

'What was he like when he was younger?'

'Kind,' Zoey said immediately. 'Generous. Loyal. He put people he cared about above himself all the time.'

'So, the same as he is now then,' Lisa said with a smile.

'Okay.'

Zoey sounded sceptical.

Because she doesn't know you anymore.

'Any memorable girlfriends?'

Zoey's eyes shot to his. A range of emotions rushed onto her face; his own emotions went haywire in response. But his mouth responded to the panic Zoey was expressing. He was opening it to tell Lisa to leave it be when Sophia said, 'Oh, I can answer that. Sade. When he was fifteen.'

'She wasn't his girlfriend.'

'She wasn't my girlfriend.'

He and Zoey said it at the same time. A blush stained her cheeks. She dropped her head, making her twists— which were loose now—hide her expression. His fingers ached to touch them. To push them away so he could see the hue on her face and brush a thumb over her skin. He wanted to tell her she had nothing to be embarrassed about.

The urge was so strong he stepped back.

'Maybe I should find Byron,' Sawyer said, looking at Lisa. She gave him an apologetic look. He'd accept it more formally later. 'He's been gone awhile.'

'Sure.' Apparently, Lisa was eager to give him an

escape since she put him in the position to need one. 'He went in that direction.'

With a cursory nod at the Roux sisters, he began to walk in the direction his sister had pointed. A few seconds later, he heard his name. He stopped.

'Thank you for waiting,' Zoey said.

She didn't say anything else until he asked, 'Why did you ask me to?'

'I'm sorry. About back there.' Her face was pink again. It was still adorable. 'I shouldn't have encouraged Lisa.'

'It's fine,' he said curtly. 'She likes to know things about me. It's harmless.'

'Oh. Okay.' Again, he heard what she wasn't saying. *It wasn't harmless back there.* 'Okay then.'

'Okay,' he repeated, and took a step away.

'No, wait.' She put a hand on his arm. His body instantly went warm, then iced when she dropped her hand. 'Sorry.'

He shrugged.

'There's something else.'

A long time passed before she continued. When she did, he understood the pause. The hesitation.

'I was wondering whether… I mean, I think it's time…' She released a harsh breath. Squared her shoulders. Looked him right in the eye. 'I think we need to get a divorce, Sawyer.'

Chapter Nine

One Day, Six Years Ago

Sawyer was hopelessly in love with her. This wasn't news to him. As he lay on the fluffy carpet in front of the fire in his aunt and uncle's cabin, he felt it more than ever. She lay next to him, wearing a robe he'd found in the master bedroom's cupboard. He'd called his aunt, told her he was safe, and asked if he could sleep in the cabin for the night. She hadn't given him too much drama, though he had to promise to clean up after himself and, in her words, 'be responsible.'

He'd cringed appropriately at that.

But he didn't care now, looking at Zoey. She was laughing at something she told him. Her cheeks were flushed from being so close to the fire. Her hair was loose, sprawled across the white carpet like rays of the sun. The perfect description for her, he thought with a smile.

Like a cat seeking heat in the winter, he was drawn to her. Not only to the beauty her high cheekbones, her full lips, her eyes that were deep and warm and full of light created. It was that happiness that spilled out of her like champagne from a bottle that had been opened. And as with the alcohol, her burst of happiness spread to others.

Most of the time.

She'd lost some of her natural bubbliness since her father's death. Since his illness, too. She'd hidden it, but he'd seen her struggling. He would have done anything to help her with it. He had.

'Sawyer.'

His eyes met hers. 'What?'

'You're not listening to me.' There was a soft smile on her face. 'What are you thinking about?'

'You.'

She laughed. 'I'm right here. You don't have to think about me.'

She reached out to take his hand, curling her fingers between his. The gesture warmed him from the inside out. There was an abandon in it, in the realisation. A freedom in not having to hide his feelings; not having to ignore them because they weren't appropriate. And to have them *reciprocated*. He didn't know which gods were looking down on him, but he thanked them. Even if it wouldn't last.

'I can't help it,' he said, ignoring that last thought. 'It's not a choice for me.'

She turned to him. 'Why didn't you say anything?'

'I told you. I didn't want to lose you.'

'But you don't know that you would have.' She tapped her fingers against his knuckles. 'I feel…things for you.' She said it shyly. This confident, full-of-life woman was shy because of him. Fondness bloomed in his heart. 'I felt them before, too, even if I didn't know it.'

He thought about it. 'What do you feel now?'

Her lips parted, but no words came out. He waited. Wondered whether it was purely selfish of him to want to know, or if there was a reason he asked. By the time he concluded it was both, she was speaking.

'Lucky.' Her words were barely louder than the crackling fire. 'So damn lucky to know you.' She shifted closer. 'You're the best man, Sawyer. And I'm not saying that because I care about you. I just...' She trailed off, smiled at him. 'You always take the shopping bags when we leave the grocery store. You let me go ahead of you whenever there's a line. You open doors for me and get me drinks at parties. I've never asked you to do any of that, but that's who you are.'

'How do you know I don't just do that for you?' he asked gruffly, not sure what to do with the emotion her words brought.

'Because I've known you for seven years. You don't do it for recognition. You do it because you're a gentleman. And you're kind. You defended me in high school even though I was a stranger. That first day, I mean.'

'I know.' He waited a beat. 'Maybe I knew then already I wanted to be with you.'

She laughed. The husky sound of it caressed his skin. 'Again, I've known you for seven years. Your game isn't *that* good.' When he didn't reply, she looked at him. Whatever she saw in his eyes made her inhale. 'Did you know?'

He waited awhile before he answered.

'The first time I saw you, you were laughing. The girls around you were laughing, too, probably at something you said, but you were the one I noticed. Immediately. I... I didn't have a choice.' He chose his next words carefully. 'Magnets are attracted to one another, right? Except they have to get close enough before they pull together.' He untangled their fingers so he could cup her cheek. 'That's what it was like for me. When I saw you laughing, when I got close enough to see it and hear it, I knew I needed to be with you. That didn't happen to you. At least not then,' he said when she opened her mouth. 'It might be happening now.'

'Might be?' she asked, turning her head to kiss his palm. 'There's no might about it when you woo me so smoothly, Wilson.'

'Did you say "woo," Roux?'

She laughed. 'Did you rhyme, Wilson?'

He thought back. Laughed. Zoey shifted onto her back, looking at him so trustingly his heart ached.

'I don't think you've always felt this way about me, Zo. I'm fine with that. Seven years isn't that long if it helped you see you can trust me with more than your friendship.'

'Seven years is an eternity.'

'I would have waited longer for this.'

He leaned forward and pressed a kiss to her chest, over her heart, keeping his gaze on her face. Her expression softened. Something equally soft entered her eyes. She slid a hand through his hair, gliding it over his scalp until she reached the base of his neck. She pulled his head down and their lips met.

He felt the softness in her kiss. She didn't demand anything with the movement of her lips. When her tongue touched his, she sighed. The ease, the sweetness of it filled his blood with his love for her. It pulsed heavily in his veins, heightening his arousal. Her hand slid down his chest, over his abdomen, and rested at the evidence of that arousal. He groaned as pleasure spiked through him; moaned when she squeezed lightly and need joined. Then she moved. Before he knew it, he was on his back, Zoey on top of him.

'Are you su—'

She cut off his question with a kiss. Since her legs were on either side of him, her heat pressing against his erection, he wasn't in the position to complain. No, this position was distinctly for other things. She ground against him and he moaned. She pulled her lips from his, opened the top of the robe he wore, pressed a kiss to his neck. Repeated it on the other side. Used her tongue in the valley between his neck and his collarbone.

'Have you always tasted this good?' she asked as she leaned back.

The grin that took over his lips came from pure enjoyment of her seduction. 'No. While you were in the bathroom, I put on edible cream.'

She blinked, the hazy pleasure in her eyes eclipsed by confusion. 'Really?'

He chuckled, and rediscovered the use of his hands. He stroked her thighs, enjoying the softness of them. 'No, Zo. But was I supposed to say yes?'

She rolled her eyes. 'Do you know how dirty talk works, Sawyer?' She didn't wait for an answer. 'You're not doing a good job of it.'

'Makes sense since I've never practised.'

She frowned. Straightened, though her hands remained on his chest. 'You've never talked dirty during sex?'

'I've never had sex, so no.'

'You've…' She trailed off. 'What about Chandra?'

'No chemistry.'

'Alicia?'

He shrugged. 'Same.'

'How did I not know this?'

'You never asked.'

'Because I assumed…' She shook her head. 'Shame on me, I guess.'

He pushed up on his hands, looked into her eyes. 'Is this a judgement of my skills?' he asked lightly. 'Because in all fairness, you haven't given me the opportunity to show you.'

'If I used your skills as a basis for judgement, I'd have thought you were more experienced,' she told him without heat.

She linked her hands around his neck. The movement parted her gown at the front, revealing the start of the curves of her breasts. He allowed himself a moment to stare before tearing his eyes away. Her lips were curved when he looked at her.

'They're right there,' he said with a grin. 'I'm a mere mortal.'

'Why didn't you tell me?' she asked with a shake of her head, though the curve of her lips had widened. 'That you didn't sleep with them, I mean.'

'Why would I?'

Curiosity joined amusement in her expression. 'You're not ashamed, are you?'

'What do I have to be ashamed about?'

'Nothing,' Zoey said with a laugh. 'This is why I love you, Sawyer. You're so unapologetically yourself.'

He waited before he reacted to her words. Waited for her to realise what she said. When she did, her cheeks flushed and she bit her lip. He opened his mouth to tell her that it was okay, he knew what she meant, but she shrugged.

'You know what? Screw it. I do love you, Sawyer. I've loved you as a friend for a long time, but today is the first time I think I'm *in* love with you, too. Although,' she said, leaning forward, 'I don't think today's the first time I've felt it.'

His eyes flickered up. She was inches from his face.

'I love you, too. I'm in love with you, in case you need that.'

She trailed a finger from his forehead down, over his cheek, but her gaze never left his. In it, he saw certainty. Affection. And, he was quite sure—and amazed to see—love.

'I don't,' she said simply.

He believed her.

'Okay.' He moved forward to kiss her, but she leaned back before he could. 'What?'

'Were you waiting for me?' she asked quietly, searching his face. 'To have sex, I mean.'

Her blush deepened, as if she couldn't believe she asked it. He would have found it charming if he weren't so perplexed by her question.

'No,' he said with a shake of his head. 'No, of course not. I just wasn't attracted enough to any one woman to be interested.'

'You weren't… You've had enough girlfriends that that sounds like a lie.'

'I didn't say I didn't find them attractive. But that doesn't mean I wanted to have sex with them.'

'Chandra's breasts were the best I've seen,' Zoey said, unconvinced. 'Alicia had sex appeal galore.'

He chuckled. 'Sex isn't only about the physical, Zo.'

She still looked unconvinced. He sighed. Forced himself to ask.

'You're telling me you've slept with men when they haven't made you feel beautiful? Or worthy? I'm not asking to judge you,' he clarified quickly. 'I'm asking for comparison purposes.'

'Well, then, if it's only to compare,' she said dryly. Then she bit the inside of her bottom lip. 'No. I haven't. But that has nothing to do with them, really. More with me.'

'Okay,' he said gently when her cheeks went redder. 'Hey, you don't have to be embarrassed. Your sexual history is none of my business.'

'Is that why you've never asked?'

'You mean besides the fact that I was utterly in love with you so it wasn't information I wanted to know?' he teased. 'Yeah, I guess so.'

'And I guess maybe I never offered it because I didn't want you to think differently of me.'

'I don't care about who you've slept with.'

'I know. But I wasn't talking about that.' There was a long pause. 'You know how in love my parents are? Were?' she corrected, with a quick shake of her head. A shadow crossed her face, but then she shook her head again. 'Anyway. They met each other at university and they were always so in love…'

He slid an arm around her waist, rubbed her back in comfort.

'What I'm trying to say is I was waiting.' She released a shaky breath. 'I was waiting until I felt what I saw between them before I took the plunge, so to speak.' She smiled. 'Actually, before, I was waiting until I got married to do it. But when I got older, I realised that might not be possible, and I figured as long as I could find someone I shared something special with, I'd be lucky.'

'Okay,' he said slowly. 'But you've never really dated anyone for long. Not that that matters, but…' He trailed off at the look on her face. 'Oh.'

'Yeah.' She laughed. 'Oh.'

'Why were you giving me such a hard time then?'

'I wasn't the one giving the other a *hard* time.'

He stared. 'This is why you'd never make a good comedian. Your jokes are terrible.'

She smirked. 'Good thing it was never something I seriously considered.'

'Are you going to answer my question?'

'Oh, right.' She tilted her head. 'I guess I thought you'd be different. You were in actual relationships.'

'So were you.'

'And yet I can't remember one of my boyfriends right now.'

'Dan.'

'Came up with that one quickly, didn't you?' she asked with a quirk of the brow.

'He was a dick.'

'Which is why I'm not sitting on his lap in nothing but a robe and my underwear.'

'You're not wearing a bra.'

'Underwear refers to more than bras, Sawyer,' she admonished lightly. 'And really, you're stuck on *that* fact?'

He laughed. 'Sorry. I've been wanting to say that for a long time.'

'That I'm not wearing a bra?'

'That Dan was a dick.'

'I believe you did say that. As soon as we were over.' She narrowed her eyes. 'I also believe I asked you why you'd waited so damn long to tell me.'

'I don't remember my answer, but I know it wasn't entirely truthful,' he said wryly. 'The entire truth is that I couldn't give my opinion on your relationship because I didn't know whether I was being objective.'

'So you just let me date dicks?'

'Dick, singular.' Honestly, the things this woman got him to say. 'The rest of them were…okay.'

'Do you need some water?'

'Why?'

'I thought you'd like some, what with you choking on those words.'

He flipped her onto her back—gently—and she laughed.

'You think you're real smart, don't you, Zoey Roux?'

'I don't *think* it,' she replied with a sweet smile. 'Anyway. You say the rest of them as if there were hundreds. I don't remember anyone. Besides Dan, who told everyone I slept with him—'

'—dick—'

'—I don't remember the rest of them because dating wasn't important to me. When my dad got sick…' Her smile turned shaky now. 'It seemed trivial.'

'He would have wanted you to live your life.'

'Yeah. That's what he told me all through his treatment.' Only the side of her mouth was lifted now. 'And before he… At the end—'

She broke off. Lines appeared between her eyebrows. They tightened and relaxed, twitched with the frequency of those movements. She cleared her throat, but Sawyer knew she was trying to clear her emotions.

'He, er, he said a twenty-year-old should be dating.' She spoke determinedly. 'And I told him I'd be twenty-one soon, so I was glad I didn't have to worry about that.'

He chuckled, but pulled her in tighter.

'He would have been annoyingly happy about this, you know.' A tear slipped down her cheek, but her eyes were amused. 'He always liked you.'

'I liked him, too.'

They were quiet for a long while before Zoey said, 'I'm sorry. I didn't mean to make things awkward.'

'You don't have to be sorry for grieving.'

'I'm tired of it.' She let out a mocking laugh. 'It's only been a month and I'm tired of being sad.'

'It's been years of expecting it to happen though. Hoping it wouldn't.' At her blink, he continued. 'You had to grieve the man you used to know when your dad couldn't do the things he used to do while he was sick. You had to grieve the life you had before he was diagnosed.' He brushed a thumb across her cheek, wiping away the tears that had slipped past her guard. 'You've been grieving for a long time.'

The crackling fire was the only sound between them for some time.

'You always see, don't you?' Zoey asked quietly.

'You're the world to me, Zo.' He could say it now, so he did. 'I pay attention because if I didn't, one day, the ice caps might melt and I'd cease to exist.'

'Are you comparing me to global warming?'

He wrinkled his nose. 'I think I am. Sorry.'

Her laughter was void of the sadness she had minutes ago. Zoey never dwelled in darkness for long. One of the most remarkable things about her was her ability to move forward.

'I think I found it,' she whispered later when she rested her head on his chest.

He stroked her hair. 'What?'

'What my parents had.' While his brain scrambled to process, Zoey kissed him. They were breathless when she leaned back and said, 'Let's get married, Sawyer.'

He thought he might stay breathless forever.

Chapter Ten

One Day, Now

She'd said it. Finally.

I think we need to get a divorce, Sawyer.

Damn, but it hurt.

Not only saying the words, but seeing Sawyer's expression. It was necessary though. They'd been married for six years. After their initial months together as husband and wife, they'd seen one another all of four times in those six years. Five, if she counted today. But she didn't, because today she was finally putting on her adult panties and taking responsibility for a mistake she made when she was young and in love and foolish. So foolish.

'I'm sorry,' Sawyer said, his expression showing none of the turmoil it had moments ago. 'Could you repeat that?'

'You heard me.' She cleared her throat when the reply came out soft and husky. 'I want a divorce.'

Before Sawyer could reply, Lisa's husband interrupted them.

'Sawyer,' he said, slapping Sawyer on the back. Zoey was surprised it didn't hurtle Sawyer forward.

'Good to see you, man. Thanks for being here for Lees. You have no idea how much it means that you do things like this for her.' He turned, as if noticing Zoey for the first time. 'Hey, I'm Byron. This guy's brother-in-law.'

'Zoey.' She took the massive hand he offered. He shook hers gently, as if aware of his strength. It was kind of nice that he knew he had the power to kill and took it seriously. 'I'm this guy's—' She stopped herself when she didn't know what to say.

'She's an old friend,' Sawyer supplied, eyes boring into hers.

'Actually, I'm Parker's girlfriend's sister,' Zoey said, purposefully distancing herself from him. It was what was best for both of them. For him. 'And I need to find Parker in case he needs help. We'll talk later, okay?' she told Sawyer. 'And nice to meet you, Byron.'

She walked away before they could respond, though she felt Sawyer's eyes on her. She needed a place to shield herself from his view. From the view of anyone who might care for her, actually. They couldn't see her fall apart. They'd want to know what was wrong and she couldn't tell them without telling them she married Sawyer six weeks after their father's death. She could feel it coming on, the roll of panic and grief and disappointment. She didn't have much time. And the only place she could hide was…

She looked around. Saw nothing. Even the trees that were everywhere seemed too far away. She broke into a run, not caring if Sawyer was still watching her. Actually no, she did care. So she stopped, and looked around again as emotion tumbled toward her. This time, there was something. She ducked under the tent of *Ricardo's Food* and braced on her knees.

'Excuse me—'

She cut him off by putting one hand out. 'Give me a second here.'

'But you can't just—'

Her head snapped up. 'I'm having a moment,' she growled. '*Let me have my moment.*'

He didn't say any more. Silently, she praised him for it; loudly, she tried to get her breathing right. Oh, this was embarrassing. But she was so damn sad. The loud breathing now came courtesy of tears, which ran down her cheeks without any obstacle.

Zoey let herself feel the feelings. The grief counsellor she'd seen after things ended with Sawyer had told her avoiding feelings wouldn't help her. In fact, she'd insisted it would hurt Zoey. Since avoiding her feelings about her father's death had resulted in her marrying her best friend, Zoey agreed.

Still, when their marriage ended, she'd tried to fight her sadness. At the end of their friendship *and* their relationship. At losing him and her father. It had made her bitter and tense, and she couldn't cope. One day she broke down. Sophia was at work; her mother out for a church luncheon. Zoey had cried. Cried and cried and cried until she'd needed to drink water because there was no more hydration in her body. She'd felt better after that, and had seen it as a lesson. She needed to feel to get through it. Even if, at the time, the feelings sucked.

When she was done, she straightened, but closed her eyes. She opened them to a bacon covered—she supposed it was a cheese stick, since Ricardo was offering it to her.

'What's this?' she asked, grabbing a couple of serviettes from behind him and blowing her nose.

'It's the bacon-wrapped thing you told me to make.'

The way he stood made her think he wanted to shift his weight between his legs. She bit her lip to keep from smiling.

'Is there a particular reason you're giving it to me?'

'To cheer you up? I figured you must like them if you suggested them.'

Though the logic needed some work, Zoey accepted the peace offering—or was it a comfort offering?—and bit into it. Salty bacony cheesy goodness melted into her mouth, and she gave a groan of pleasure.

'This is really good, Ricardo,' she said. 'Like, super good.'

He smiled. 'Thanks.'

'See what you can do when you put your mind to it?'

'You sound like my mother.'

She paused halfway to her mouth. 'Not that I have anything against your mother, but if you're hitting on me, that's really not the way to go.'

'What? No. I'm definitely not hitting on you. I'm happily married.' He took a step back from her as if to emphasise the fact.

'Did you compare your wife to your mother when you married her, too?' she asked innocently, eating the rest of the bacon-wrapped cheese stick as she watched him.

He stuttered, and made excuses, and didn't see her smile until he was done.

'You're pulling my leg.'

'I am. And along with the food, it's really cheered me up.'

He studied her. 'You're lying.'

She gave a startled laugh. 'Not entirely. I do feel better. Though cheered up might be a bit of an exaggeration.'

He nodded. 'Look, I gotta keep prepping. I have a couple of workers coming in soon, and the place opens in thirty minutes.'

'Yeah, of course. I'll get out of your way.'

'But I wanted to tell you,' he said, as if she hadn't spoken, 'that you sounded heartbroken. I'm not the politest guy. I could do some work on my business persona. But if you want me to kick his ass, I will.'

Her face split into a grin. 'For me?'

'For any woman who came into my tent crying.'

'Why, Ricardo, I didn't know you cared.'

'Get out,' he said with a small smile.

She laughed. 'You want cash for the bacon?'

'Consider it making amends. Now seriously, get out.'

She laughed as she made her way out of the tent, but turned before she left completely. 'Nice pivot with the food, by the way.'

'Thanks.'

'And…thank you.'

'You're welcome.' She turned. Turned back when he said, 'Hey, kid.'

'Yeah?'

'You know where to find me if you decide to take me up on the offer.'

She was smiling when she walked away.

'Why does it feel like I chased your girlfriend away?' Byron asked, staring after Zoey with Sawyer. It snapped him out of his stupor.

'She's not my girlfriend.'

'Obviously, if she's running away.'

'She's my wife.'

There was a stunned silence.

'Did we know you were married?'

'You're the first person I've told.'

'Oh.' Byron paused. 'Lisa doesn't know?'

'You're the first person I've told,' he repeated.

Byron rubbed his beard. 'I guess what I'm trying to figure out is why you decided to tell me?'

'Because you're here,' Sawyer said. 'She just asked me for a divorce. I'm processing out loud. And…and you happen to be here.'

Byron nodded, as if the information wasn't new and Sawyer wasn't having a breakdown. And maybe he wasn't having one. Maybe he *was* simply processing. Yeah, that was it. All these emotions filling him up were nothing to worry about. They were part of processing. The fact that despite them filling him, he felt empty, was probably part of it, too. Her words slamming a gong inside him, having reverberations echoing through him, speaking to a hollowness and an anger and betrayal that had been there for a long time… It was all completely normal.

Nothing to see here, folks, he told the panic circling those thoughts like a vulture hovering over the almost dead. *This is all processing.*

'Sawyer.' Byron was suddenly in front of him. 'Let's get a drink.'

'I don't need a drink.'

'Yeah, well, I do,' Byron said, flinging an arm around Sawyer's shoulders. He took out his phone, pressed a couple of buttons and put it to his ear. 'Babe,

Sawyer and I are going for a drink.' Pause. 'Nah, everything's fine. We're bonding.'

He slapped Sawyer on the back. Hard.

Did his brother-in-law want to kill him? Probably not. He likely didn't know his strength. No—that was bull. Byron was exceedingly gentle when he needed to be. So this might have been an attempted murder, after all. On the upside, it would solve a lot of his problems.

'Everything's fine, babe. Are you going to be okay?' He laughed. 'Sorry. Call you when we're done.' He put his phone away. 'She says I was supposed to bring her something to drink, not take you out for one.'

'We don't have to do this.'

'I think we do,' Byron said cheerfully.

They didn't speak the rest of the way, and walked up the incline of Kirstenbosch to the restaurant that sat at its very peak. Another time, Sawyer would have appreciated the bright flowers and stretches of green. He wouldn't have been annoyed with the number of people dodging him. Part of the gardens was still open to the public, and since it was a weekend on a summer's day, the place was full. Some of the visitors looked at Byron in wonder. Occasionally, they'd say his name, wave or take his hand. Only two people asked for a picture, which Sawyer had to take. He did so without comment.

After the second picture, Sawyer asked, 'This doesn't bother you?'

'I'm used to it,' Byron said without pausing. 'You know how people feel about rugby in South Africa.'

'Sure. But I'd feel differently if I was the one being stopped every few minutes.'

'Part of the job.'

When they reached the restaurant, the head waiter's

eyes nearly popped out his head when he saw Byron. Another waiter had to dig an elbow into the man's ribs to get him to seat them. They were given a prime spot on the terrace overlooking the garden.

'I see there are some privileges though,' Sawyer commented wryly.

Byron laughed. 'All part of the job.'

They ordered a couple of beers. Byron sat back in his chair, his massive biceps crossed over his chest.

'I'm not usually one for feelings unless they're Lisa's,' he said slowly. 'But something tells me you have a lot of them, and I happen to be the only one who knows why.'

'Again, not sure I want to do this.'

The waiter brought their beers. Sawyer took a greedy gulp. To do something other than share this mortifying conversation with Byron *and* hoping the alcohol would numb him. After a second gulp, he re-alised he'd need stronger alcohol for the latter. Then Byron started talking, and he thought he'd need it for the former, too.

'Fine, you don't have to talk,' Byron said. 'We can enjoy the beers in silence.'

'Cool.'

For about fifteen minutes, Byron kept his word. Their beers were done, the bill was asked for, and as they waited, Byron said, 'I have one thing to say to you.'

'What's that?'

'You know Lisa's older than me.'

'Yeah.'

'I found out about Ryder when I was twenty-two. I was at the peak of my career. I didn't want to be a father.'

'What happened?' Sawyer asked in spite of himself.

'I broke up with her. Told her I'd take care of them financially, but I couldn't make any promises about the emotional stuff.' Byron's lips curved at the memory. 'I believe I called it "the mom stuff," which is such bullshit. Except I was a kid myself, and didn't know any better.'

'She couldn't have been happy about that.'

'She wasn't. But she told me that she didn't want her child to be around someone who didn't want to be around him. She accepted the break-up. We both tried to move on.'

'And?'

'It took me a month to realise I'd made a mistake. I went back begging for another chance.'

Sawyer smiled, imagining it. 'Please tell me she made you crawl.'

'Metaphorically,' he said with a quick grin. 'I spent the rest of her pregnancy trying to prove I deserved to be in their lives.'

'And it worked.'

'Yeah, it did.' Byron grew serious. 'Because I wanted it to. Lisa was the best part of my life. I needed that break-up to realise it. I don't regret it because I wouldn't have known I wanted a future with her otherwise.'

'You're saying I need to ask Zoey to take me back?'

The scoff was on the tip of his tongue when Byron said, 'I'm saying that however long you two haven't been together should have given you a chance to realise what you want. If it's your wife, you better tell her.'

He opened his mouth, sure he'd respond with that scoff. He didn't. He made no sound, said no word.

Because he realised he didn't know *what* he wanted with Zoey.

He wasn't used to that feeling. For the majority of their friendship, he knew he wanted her in his life. He knew he was sacrificing his love for her to have that. When things had changed between them, he knew he wanted them to love one another for the rest of their lives. But then things had ended, and he'd stopped thinking about what he wanted.

Or had he? He'd continued the charade of their fake relationship for four years. He'd ignored why then, but now he could see he wanted to see her. To still have her in his life. Even after he said they needed to end the pretence, he still wanted that.

Why else hadn't *he* asked for a divorce? Why hadn't *he* ended things properly?

Despite everything that had happened between them, he couldn't imagine not being linked to her. That was what he was processing now. That was why her request for a divorce had sent him into turmoil. He was in this situation because of his indecisiveness, his desires, however hidden. And now she was acting because he hadn't.

Knowing this, and knowing Byron was right and Sawyer should know what he wanted, meant he should be able to act now, too. Except he couldn't. Because he'd spent the last six years actively trying *not* to think about his marriage. He'd been clinging to her even then, and he hadn't known it.

The waiter arrived, and Sawyer couldn't articulate any of it to Byron.

'Your bill has already been taken care of, sir.'

'By who?' Byron asked. The waiter pointed at a

group of women a few tables away, all wearing the jerseys of Byron's rugby team. Byron grinned. 'There are definitely more privileges than downsides to this job, Sawyer.'

He didn't answer.

Chapter Eleven

One Day, Five Years, Eleven Months Ago

'We have champagne. Strawberries dipped in chocolate. A variety of foods I don't particularly care about because there are strawberries dipped in chocolate and champagne.'

Sawyer laughed. 'Impressive, babe.'

'Thank you.' Zoey gave a mock bow. 'As a wife, it's my responsibility to take care of my hu—'

She broke off when he kissed her. Lost her thoughts as he teased her with his mouth. Her body went lax with pleasure when his hand found her breast, his fingers grazing her nipple.

'What was that for?' she gasped when he pulled back.

'You're my wife, aren't you?'

'As of eleven this morning, yes,' she said with a smile, hooking her hands around his neck. 'So you're just happy I'm your wife?'

'Yes.'

He nuzzled her neck. It was part pleasurable, part ticklish. After a moment, it became only ticklish and she put a hand on his chest to stop him.

'We should have something to eat.'

He stuffed his hands into his pockets, as if that were the only way he wouldn't reach for her again. 'Sure.'

'We have to celebrate,' she said, walking over to the kitchen island and pouring them both champagne. She handed a glass to him. Lifted her own. 'To a bright new future as mister and missus.'

'Cheers.'

He tapped his glass on hers and took a big sip. 'Have you spoken to Sophia?'

'Yeah,' Zoey said, sliding a butt cheek onto the kitchen stool.

'Yeah?' Sawyer sat opposite her. 'You told her about this?'

'Hell, no.' Zoey shook her head vehemently. 'She'd give me an earful about my choices.' She waved a dismissive hand. 'I won't let my wedding day be tarnished by such blasphemy.'

He smiled at her, but something flickered across his face that had a part of her looping around itself.

'You'll have to tell her eventually, Zo.'

'Yeah, but not now.' She narrowed her eyes. 'But based on your reaction, you must have told *your* family.'

He blushed. 'I didn't. But only because I want to tell Grandma Carla first, and face-to-face.'

'She's in Canada visiting your uncle.'

'For the next couple of months, yeah.'

'Convenient.'

'Accurate.'

She eyed him suspiciously. 'You don't plan on telling anyone for at least a few months and you're being sanctimonious about my decision?' She took a strawberry from the tray. 'It's sweet you've already embraced your role as hypocrite. I mean *husband*.'

He stole the strawberry from her before she could put it into her mouth.

'Don't eat my food, wife.'

She aimed a glare at him, but let him have it. She took another.

'Besides,' he said when he was done chewing, 'you know your family needs the contact more than mine does. I tell them I'm fine, they leave me alone for days. You tell Soph you're okay, and she checks in again hours later. How are you going to explain you've moved in with me?'

'I'm not going to explain anything,' she said simply. She had it all figured out. 'I'm going to call and tell her I'm safe every day, but she doesn't have to know where I am.'

'Zo—'

'No,' she interrupted him. 'They're still grieving. I'm not going to upend their lives with this news, too. I don't want them to worry.'

'Why would they worry?' His voice was careful.

'They always worry about me,' she answered flatly. 'I'm their baby sister. The one who was close to Dad and who cheered him up. Made him laugh.' She was still exhausted from pretending everything was fine back then. From forcing cheer and happiness when they were the last things she felt. 'They'll think I'm acting out because I don't know how to deal with…'

She took a deep breath.

'This is special to me. It's my wedding day, and it's our marriage, and it's *you*. I don't want them to spoil it.'

'Zoey,' he said seriously. 'Are you acting out?'

'No. Of course not.' She slid off her chair. 'And if your next question's going to be whether I'm sure I wanted to do this—too late, love. We're already married. I have the certificate to prove it.'

'We could have it annulled.'

'Seriously?' When he didn't reply, her jaw locked. 'Sawyer, I've had two weeks to think this through. I married you because I want to be married to you. I love you. If you want an annulment, fine, but don't do it on my account.'

Her chest was heaving when she was done, her throat thick. She moved toward the bathroom, but Sawyer stopped her before she could.

'Wait, Zo, I'm sorry.'

She didn't turn around, but she didn't keep walking either.

'Zo.'

His voice was closer now. She dropped the hands she folded at her chest to her sides. As she expected, his arms circled her waist.

'Look, I'll admit there's a part of me that believes this is too good to be true.' He spoke softly. 'And maybe I am using your family as an excuse not to face that. But—' he gently turned her around '—this is my dream come true. Literally. I've spent seven years wanting you and now I have you. It feels like it should be a cruel trick.'

'It's not.' She put her hands on his chest. 'I'm your wife, Sawyer. Get used to it.'

'Done.'

It made her smile. Damn it. 'Just like that, huh?'

'Just like this.'

He took her hand in his, rubbed a thumb over the

ring he'd got her. A small diamond, classic cut. She'd
loved it immediately.

'You know what usually happens at weddings?' he
asked, wrapping his arms around her.

'What?'

'First dances.'

He began to sway.

'There's no music, Sawyer.'

'Are you sure?' he asked. 'I'm certain I hear it.'

She felt his hum before she heard it. She rolled her
eyes, but her lips were curving at his silliness, her heart
soaring at his sweetness. This was why she wanted to
be with him. He made the small moments special. He
tried to make everything special for her. He tried, period. She felt lucky and happy, more than she had in
a long time.

When her father had been diagnosed, it had felt
as though there was no more luck in the world. Before then Zoey had been a strong believer in the more
mystical parts of life. Luck. Karma. The fact that the
universe knew exactly what to give her when. But her
father's illness changed all that.

With Sawyer though, she was beginning to think
that maybe the magic in the world hadn't completely
vanished. It was merely waiting for her to see it again.

'This song must be the longest ever recorded,' she
murmured as they swayed.

'According to that clock, it's been going on for two
minutes.'

She pulled back. 'Two minutes? And this is a fake
song? How the hell do people dance to real songs at
their weddings? It's *forever*.'

'If I were someone else, I'd be offended by this re-action.'

'But you're not someone else,' she said, standing on her tip toes to kiss the end of his nose.

'Hmm.' The sound was dry. 'I also happen to agree with you.'

'*Right?*'

'Remember how it was at Shelly's wedding?'

'Oh, that dance took forever. The part they choreo-graphed at the end didn't help at all.'

'Of course it didn't help. Everyone kept staring at them. Who chooses the extended version of a song to dance to at their wedding?'

She laughed, then took Sawyer's face between her hands and kissed him. She intended for it to be an *I enjoy you* kiss but something changed halfway through, and suddenly she was pulling back, panting.

They stared at one another. Zoey's body didn't enjoy the reprieve. It made demands in the silence, telling her to jump the gorgeous man she married. But the hesi-tance inside her was still there. She knew things would irrevocably change once she and Sawyer made love.

And they haven't changed already? a voice in her head asked. *He's your* husband.

'What are you thinking?' he whispered, his hands perfectly still where they touched her.

'That I'm very attracted to you.'

His mouth curved. 'That's it?'

'No.' She chewed on the inside of her cheek, delib-erating. It took a moment to decide to be honest with him. 'I'm a little scared of—' She hesitated, felt her face go red because of it.

'You never have to be scared with me.' He let go of

her hand to lift her chin. Her gaze reluctantly lifted. 'It's me, Zo. Your best friend. You don't have to be scared.'

'You don't even know what I'm scared of.'

'You're afraid of your feelings for me,' he said confidently. 'I feel the same way.'

A gasp of laughter escaped from her lips. 'I think I've already dealt with those fears. I'm sorry you haven't.'

He frowned. Because Sawyer was all confidence most of the time, the frown made him look damn cute.

'I… I guess I've always been afraid of my feelings for you. That hasn't changed because we're married. Shifted maybe, but it hasn't changed.'

'We should talk about that.'

'Oh, no,' he said with a shake of his head. 'You're not going to distract me with this.'

'Are you sure?' She fluttered her lashes. 'A healthy relationship is built on communication. Mostly with a man communicating his fears because that's important.'

'Zoey.'

'Fine,' she said with a harsh breath. 'I'm talking about…' Why was this so hard? The man already knew all her embarrassing secrets. 'Well, Sawyer, I'm scared of making love with you.'

He froze, but not before she could see the panic running wild across his face. Then he was stammering, which amused her. He was trying to comfort her, but she apparently fried his ability to speak properly and it came out in a jumble of words and stop/start sentences. Eventually, he fell silent.

'Done now, are you?'

He nodded.

'This is why I didn't want to tell you, by the way.'

'No.' His voice was gruff. 'Please don't do that. I'm glad you told me. I was processing. That's why I sounded—'

'Like a machine malfunctioning?'

He sighed. 'Why does it feel like I've just given you something to hold over my head?'

'Because you have,' she said with a smile. 'But that's not important now.'

'No, it isn't.' There was another stretch of quiet. 'I love you, Zoey. That won't change, even if you don't want to be physical with me.'

'Wait—when did I say that?'

Again, folds creased the skin between his brows. 'You said you were scared—'

'Of making love with you. We've been plenty physical in the last two weeks. Or have you forgotten?'

He shook his head slowly. She took pity on his incoherence this time.

'Are you telling me you're not scared, Sawyer? It'll be our first time together. It'll…it'll change things.'

He took her hands, brought them to his lips. 'I'm ready when you are.'

'You're not answering my question.'

He searched her face, brought her to the couch. When they both sat down, he said, 'I'm not scared of that. Nervous, maybe, but not scared.'

'You're that confident in your skills?'

'Is that what you're worried about?' he asked, frown deepening. 'That you won't know what to do?

'I mean, that's part of it.'

'Is any other part of it emotional?'

'Yes.'

'Most of the rest of it is emotional, isn't it?' he asked after a moment.

'Yeah.'

'Yeah,' he repeated. 'Because you know we'll figure the physical stuff out.' He traced the curve of her face. 'It'll be a fun new thing to explore.'

'Are you calling my vagina a thing?'

His laughter relieved some of her tension.

'You have such a knack for making intimate conversations less awkward.'

'This is less awkward?' she asked, amused despite herself.

'Yeah, it is. And you know what you're doing, too. Distracting us both from the fact that you're nervous about the emotional connection we'll share after being intimate.'

'You sound like such a dork.'

'But I'm right.'

She sighed. 'You're right.' After a moment, she let her fears spill out. 'I'm scared it's going to make things so much more intense between us. And since things already are intense, I'm worried I'll never recover.'

Chapter Twelve

One Day, Now

'Sophia, can I talk to you for a minute?' Zoey asked her sister.

She'd called Sophia when she was sure the traces of her tears were gone, trying to figure out where her sisters were. When she arrived at the spot, she saw Sophia and Parker, Angie and Ezra, Parker's mom, Ms Jones, and Evie, her companion. Pretty standard, she thought, and greeted everyone. Except minutes later, Lisa joined their group. Apparently, she'd been to the bathroom, which was why Zoey hadn't initially seen her and hightailed out of there. Lisa had smiled, told her Byron and Sawyer would be joining soon, and Zoey asked to speak with her sister.

Sophia stared at her. Zoey prepared herself for the quip she knew was coming, but Sophia didn't say anything. She only got up, and went to stand next to Zoey. Once she had, Zoey realised she hadn't thought this part of her plan through. She couldn't say what she wanted to say here, so she scrambled.

'I need to speak with you in private,' she whispered into her sister's ear. 'Obviously, I can't say that out loud without worrying or offending anyone, so please pretend I need your help with something.'

Sophia slanted her a look.

'You can drop your laundry off at Mom's house for the next month.'

'So you can turn my white clothing into tie-dye masterpieces?' Sophia said in a low voice. 'No, thank you.'

'Please. Please don't be difficult about this.'

'Okay,' Sophia said after studying Zoey. 'I'll go on one condition. You tell me what's going on.'

Zoey gritted her teeth. 'Why do you think I'm asking to speak with you in private?'

'Hey—are you two okay over there?' Angie asked, her older sister's concern clear on her face. Also, her frustration at their lack of manners.

'Yeah,' Sophia said in a loud voice. 'Zo just needs my help with something. We'll be back in a few minutes.'

Sophia turned. Before Zoey could follow suit, Parker widened his eyes at her. She shook her head—she wasn't about to tell her sister about the proposal, for heaven's sake. She could keep a secret. Except with Sawyer, apparently. But Parker didn't need to know that. She was fairly certain Sawyer would shut his mouth. Partly because she'd tell his colleagues about his Royal Family obsession, and partly because she was keeping a much bigger secret. Neither of them wanted their marriage coming out to the entire world.

'Okay, out with it,' Sophia said when they were far enough away from the group.

Zoey glanced back, saw that if some of the guests angled, they would still be able to see them. She pushed Sophia behind a tree.

'What the—' Sophia broke off with a sharp breath, as if she didn't want to swear near the flowers. Zoey wanted to point out that she'd already done so countless times that day. She chose not to. 'Okay, Zoey, you better have a damn good reason for—'

'Sawyer and I got married.'

Sophia's eyes nearly popped out their sockets. Zoey could see her sister visibly pulling herself together, but it took time. Zoey gave it to her.

'What did you just say?'

'After Dad died,' Zoey said, tired of the secret. 'We got married. And we kind of, sort of, never got divorced.' She exhaled. 'But I asked him for one today, and I'm a little freaked out by it because it's final, isn't it? A divorce. And I'm not sure I want it to be final. Not our marriage. No, that was over a long time ago.' She swallowed. 'I mean, me and Sawyer. There'd be nothing linking us together anymore. And I'd never see him again if we did this. Sure, we haven't really seen one another in the last six years. But we still had this deal, right, where if Sawyer had a big family function, I'd be his date. Like we did before we got married. So I got to see him four times, and that was kind of nice. No—really nice. But I can't see us still having that deal when we're divorced. But Sawyer needs to move on, right? He's the kind of guy who should have a family and a wife and just thinking about it makes me a little sick.'

She was pacing at the end of it, her breath shallow. Although honestly, that last part wasn't a surprise. Since she and Sawyer had ended things, her lungs had given up some of their capacity. No matter how hard she tried—meditation, yoga, kickboxing—she couldn't regain full lung capacity.

Unless she counted that morning, when she was talking with him again. Then she could breathe fully just fine, and damn if that didn't make things worse.

'Would you hold on one moment?' Sophia asked.

'What? Why?'

Sophia held up a finger, then disappeared behind the tree. Zoey stared after her, then resumed her pacing. She thought she was okay after the crying stint, the bacon-wrapped cheese stick, the affirmations in the bathroom. But nope. She was not. Not if she was telling her sister the truth. No doubt Sophia was disappointed in her. She'd tried her utmost in the last year and a half to get her shit together. No more being taken care of. No more being a burden. She would look after herself, make better decisions. She wouldn't disappoint her family anymore. And then Sawyer had walked into her life and reminded her that it wasn't possible. Not until she sorted things out with him.

'Zoey.'

'No,' she said when she heard his voice. 'No, I can't do this right now.'

'What are you talking about?' Sawyer asked, his hands in his pockets. 'You said we have to talk.'

'Yeah, but I didn't mean now.'

'Would you like to give me a time that would be more convenient for you then?' he asked dryly. Out of the corner of her eye, she saw Sophia. Turned.

'You told him I was here? After I told you what happened between us?'

'You told her?' Sawyer asked. At the same time, Sophia said, 'No.'

'Then what is he doing here?' Zoey asked, not answering Sawyer.

'I was heading to my family,' Sawyer offered. 'Since you were alone, I thought it would be a good time to talk.'

'She's not alone,' Sophia said, stopping slightly in front of Zoey.

Seconds later, Angie joined, effectively forming a shield in front of her. A massive lump grew in her throat. Her eyes began to burn. She should have taken allergy medication that morning.

'Full disclosure,' Angie said easily. 'I have no idea what's going on, but I agree with Soph. Zoey isn't alone.'

Her allergies did something again. She sniffed.

Sawyer's eyes slid past both her sisters and rested on her.

'We have to talk, Zo,' he said softly.

He walked away.

Her sisters didn't leave their post until he was no longer in their sight. They both turned to face her at the same time.

'Okay, that was *tense*. And not something I expected between you and Sawyer, Zo,' Angie said. 'What did I miss?'

'A lot, apparently. And not just you,' Sophia said. 'Do you want to tell her, or should I?' She directed the question at Zoey.

Zoey released a breath. 'We're married.'

'I'm sorry—what?'

'Apparently, our baby sister mourned Dad's death by getting married to her best friend.'

'Don't say it like that,' Zoey snapped at Sophia. 'It wasn't a mourning thing.'

'Wasn't it?'

'No.' Her anger fizzled. 'Okay, fine, some of it might have been because losing Dad was hard. And it made me see things differently.'

'Like your best friend?'

'Like our relationship, yes.'

'I'm sorry, I'm still trying to wrap my head around the fact that you're married,' Angie said.

'Longer than you and Ez have been, too, Angie. You could ask Zoey for marital advice.' Sophia smirked. She sobered quickly though, wrinkling her nose. 'Or maybe not, since Zoey's asked him for a divorce.'

'*You're getting a divorce?*'

'Angie, shh.' Zoey looked around to check if anyone had heard. No one was looking at them. 'Why did you bring her?' Zoey asked Sophia. 'You knew she'd react this way.'

'Reinforcement,' Sophia said with a shrug. 'I don't know how to tell you this, Zo, but things are kind of a mess. Angie's a good cleaner.'

'You make me sound like I'm a domestic worker,' Angie interjected. 'Although I am a good cleaner, both literally and figuratively.' She sighed. 'Okay, we need a plan, right? You asked for a divorce, so we need to get you a lawyer. Ezra has a friend who—'

'No,' Zoey interrupted before her sister could continue. 'No, this isn't why I told you, Sophia. It's not why I told you either, Ange, though that part was coerced.' She shot Sophia a look.

Sophia ignored it. 'Why did you tell us then?'

'Because I'm freaking out, okay? And I needed support, or whatever.'

'Support,' Sophia repeated. 'From me?'

'Yes. Just like you needed support today. And last

week, when you were freaking out about Parker being distant.'

'Parker's being distant?' Angie asked, turning to Sophia. 'Why didn't you tell me?'

Sophia glared at Zoey. 'It's not a big deal. I'm sure he's distracted because of the event today.'

Or because he's about to propose.

She didn't say it.

'It must be a big deal if you told Zoey.' Angie frowned. 'Look, I get that I wasn't around for you guys after Dad—'

'It's not that,' Zoey and Sophia said at the same time.

'Yeah?' Angie asked, her voice soft. 'Then why does it seem like you two are confiding in one another and leaving me out of it?'

'Cal,' Zoey said, at the same time Sophia said, 'The baby.'

'What?' Angie's expression was shrouded in confusion.

'You have Cal to look after now,' Sophia said after a quick glance at Zoey. 'I didn't want to add to that.'

'And I didn't want you to feel like you have to clean up my messes. Especially with the baby. Actually,' Zoey said in full confession, 'I didn't want either of you to feel that way. I thought Sophia would be less likely to, although you've both set boundaries in the last couple of years, so I'm not sure why I thought Sophia would be better.' She frowned. 'What does it say that you both reverted to trying to fix things for me despite those boundaries?'

Angie and Sophia exchanged a look.

'Habit,' they both said.

'I would have felt bad about it once I got home. That I did it, I mean,' Angie said.

'I would have got angry,' Sophia said.

Zoey looked from one sister to the other. 'Good thing I didn't accept then.'

'Yeah,' Sophia said. 'That surprised me.'

'You haven't noticed I've been trying to take responsibility for my actions lately?'

'I have,' Sophia said apologetically. 'I guess I have more habits I need to break than I even knew about. Sorry.'

'How do you need us to support you?' Angie asked into the silence that descended on them.

'Keep Sawyer away from me.'

'Not possible,' Sophia said. 'Lisa's Parker's friend, and he's the only person she knows here.'

'You mean besides her husband and brother?'

'She's here because of him,' Sophia told her bluntly. 'It would be rude to ask her to leave because you want to avoid your husband.'

'And avoiding your husband is not a viable solution to your problems,' Angie jumped in. 'Sawyer's right, the two of you are going to have to talk. Even if it's for the sake of your divorce.' She cleared her throat. 'Did you, um, sign a pre-nup, Zo?'

'We were both twenty-one, Ange,' Zoey said, defeat slowly making its way up her spine. 'We had nothing. Why would we need a pre-nup?'

'For six years later when you want a divorce?' Sophia suggested.

Zoey tilted her head back. 'Maybe I should let you guys fix this.'

'Too late,' Sophia said. 'You're already one of those people who takes responsibility for their actions.'

'Speaking of… I'm sorry I forced you both to do that for me when we were growing up.'

Sophia and Angie didn't reply. Too stunned to, it seemed.

'Isn't this what you advised me to do with Sawyer?' Zoey asked a little dryly. 'I distinctly remember you both saying I can't run from it. And since I am trying to be more responsible, and since you're both here… I am sorry. I'm sorry for what it did to you when Dad died, too. Neither of you were responsible for me, and I let you think that you were. I'm a lot like Mom that way, aren't I?'

'No,' Angie said, taking her hand.

'Yes,' Sophia said with a quirked brow at Angie.

'Well, you're not anymore, are you?' Angie said, narrowing her eyes at Sophia. 'Although, to be fair, Mom's been a lot better since Dad died, too. Anyway,' Angie continued, 'we were just as much to blame as you were. We didn't let you take responsibility for your actions. We did it for you. Of course you wouldn't feel like you had to under those circumstances.'

'That,' Sophia said, 'I agree with.' She tilted her head. 'And yeah, the other stuff, too. You might have been like Mom, but you're not anymore. Neither is she, entirely, either, I guess,' Sophia conceded. 'But it's part of life, figuring this stuff out.'

'You're both being a lot more forgiving than I anticipated,' Zoey said, tension she hadn't known existed easing in her belly.

'We're well aware of growth,' Angie said with a

small smile. 'Sometimes, we need to go through things and meet certain people before that happens.'

'And if we didn't forgive you, we can't expect you to forgive us for the things we did. Or any of what happened when we were figuring things out. Or whatever,' Sophia added with a roll of her eyes.

Zoey squeezed Angie's hand. Offered Sophia a small smile. Then sighed.

'I guess I have to go take responsibility for another of my actions now.'

'Go clean up your mess,' Sophia suggested.

'Nothing wrong with being a domestic worker,' Angie said.

There was a beat of silence, and they all laughed.

If nothing else had worked out, Zoey thought, at least she had that. Them. Her sisters.

Pity it had taken a parent's death, a doomed marriage and decades of their lives for that to happen. But like Angie said: they'd had to go through all the drama to get to this place. It was one thing—perhaps the only thing—she was grateful to the drama for.

Chapter Thirteen

One Day, Five Years, Eleven Months Ago

'Are you just…not going to say anything for the rest of the night?' Zoey asked. Her voice was disembodied in the dark, the hoarse tone of it as much natural as it was from concern.

'I've said things.'

'Yeah, but not about what I said about us making love.'

He winced, grateful she couldn't see it in the dark. 'I don't have anything to say about that.'

'No?' she asked. 'You don't agree or disagree that making love would make our relationship…more.'

He did have an opinion on it, but he didn't think she wanted to hear it. Not really. Her entire approach worried him. What if they made the wrong decision when they got married?

If his opinion had anything to do with an answer to that, it might have been that *he* didn't want to hear it.

When she suggested marriage, he couldn't help but think they were fulfilling the future he always pictured for them. He had been concerned about whether they were moving too fast, but it was a small concern. What difference did it make if they married now or in ten years? If they married now, they'd be a family sooner rather than later. Not in the having kids sense, but in the being a unit of their own sense. He'd finally have a unit of *his* own. He wouldn't be a part of someone else's family because a legal document said so; he'd have created his own. Creating it with Zoey meant he had all the things he ever wanted for his life.

Except…maybe they should have waited. Maybe she wouldn't feel as uncertain if they waited. She was going through a lot, and he understood that she was processing. If he could do it over, he wouldn't have told her about his feelings so soon after her father's death.

But when Zoey had asked him about it, he couldn't lie to her. He hadn't chosen this now. It had simply happened. The universe had designed it that way.

It didn't matter that he'd never believed in the universe's powers before. No, their marriage was meant to be. Things wouldn't have happened this way if it hadn't been. He wished she could trust that. He wished she'd trust *him*, and not be scared of their connection growing. There was nothing to be afraid of. He'd always be there for her.

But he wasn't going to tell her all that and make it seem like he wanted to have sex with her. Because— duh, yes. But more importantly, he didn't want to push her. If she came to this decision, it needed to be for her own sake. Because she was ready. Not because of him.

'Sawyer, I can hear your brain working.'

'Can you hear what it's saying, too?'

There was a movement on her side of the bed. Seconds later, the light went on.

'Maybe I should sleep in Kurt's old room.'

'He took everything when he left,' Sawyer said, his heart thumping in protest at her suggestion. He didn't say anything. He wasn't going to force her to sleep with him if she didn't want to. It worked in both ways, he thought, darkly amused.

'I guess that's karma for giving him two weeks' notice to move out because you wanted to share this place with me.' She paused. 'Which you're probably regretting anyway.'

He sat up. Took a moment to gather his thoughts.

'Kurt's fine. It gave him and his girlfriend a reason to have the "next level" talk, and they moved in together. I spoke with him a couple of days ago. He has no hard feelings.' He did ask Sawyer if he knew what he was doing. To which Sawyer had replied, multiple times, that he did. He wasn't so sure now. 'And if you want to be alone, you can. I'll sleep on the couch.'

'No.' Her hand gripped his wrist. How had she moved that fast? 'I don't want you to sleep on the couch. I... I thought you might appreciate space since I clearly upset you.'

Her eyes were big, showing him every thought in her brain. He knew that brain worked overtime. He also knew that the uncertainty and self-consciousness she was displaying was a sign she was scared. She told him as much, so he wasn't surprised. It broke his heart that she felt that way.

'You haven't upset me.'

'Sawyer. I know you as well as you know me. You can't hide your feelings.'

'Okay.' He took a breath. 'I'm upset, but not at you. At myself, for pushing this when you weren't ready.'

'What did you push?' she asked, shifting so she

faced him. Her legs were curled under her. Her night-dress lay partially over her thighs. It was silk and summery—the nightdress, not her thighs—revealing smooth brown skin and curves of breasts and—

He was getting distracted.

'If I remember correctly,' Zoey was saying, 'I've been here every step of the way. Making decisions with you.'

'Would you have made the decision if you didn't know how I felt about you?' He didn't wait for an answer. 'I shouldn't have told you about how I feel about you.'

'Technically, *you* didn't.'

'What?'

'Grandma Carla said some things that made me think some things.' She played with the hem of her nightdress. 'If she hadn't said it, I would have never asked you how you felt about me. And you would have never told me.'

So his grandmother, not the universe, was the reason his romantic dreams had come true.

'I would have told you some day.'

'Maybe. Or maybe you would have waited until my wedding to someone else to tell me the truth. I wouldn't believe you—because why would you only tell me at my wedding? Why wait?' She paused only long enough to take a breath. 'You'd spend the entire night thinking about it, and then you'd realise that if you didn't speak now, you'd have to hold your peace forever. Boom!' She clapped her hands. 'You're kicking open the church doors and proclaiming your love for me.'

He stared at her. 'And apparently waiting for an ambulance to fix my broken leg.'

'You're fine.' She waved a hand. 'It was an old church. The doors were basically falling apart anyway.'

He smiled and took her hands. 'I adore you.'

Her smile was there, but reluctantly. 'Even when I'm being dramatic about sleeping with you?'

'It isn't an easy decision.'

'You're my husband.'

He tugged her toward him. She came willingly. A few short moments later, they were curled into one another on the bed.

'We can have the marriage annulled,' he said quietly, wanting her to have the option.

She turned to him. 'I don't want that.' Pause. 'Do you want that?'

'Of course not.'

'Why do you keep suggesting it?'

'You know why.'

'I don't regret marrying you.'

'Okay.'

'Sawyer.'

'Zoey.'

'Don't be like this.'

'I'm a little confused as to how to be, honestly,' he said, veneer cracking. 'I'm trying to support you and give you what you want, but you don't know what you want. It complicates things.'

'So tell me what *you* want.'

'What I want?' he repeated, laughing. 'I have everything I want, Zoey. I'm trying to give you what you want because what I want is simple. And I have it.'

'Me?'

'You.' He let out a breath. 'I have a future with you. I have the present. I get to look at you in a nightdress and enjoy how beautiful the moon makes your skin look. I get to listen to your anecdotes about me stopping your non-existent marriage and bask in the beauty and light of your brain. I have what I want. And I just want to give you what you want so you'll feel the same.'

There was a deliberate silence after he was done. She moved out of his arms. He was mentally preparing to get up to sleep on the couch when she switched the lights off and plunged them into darkness. Her body was back against his seconds later; then, so were her lips.

He fell into the kiss before his brain could stop him. His body took over from there, remembering the two weeks they'd spent doing everything but making love. Desire demanded he kiss her below her ear since she trembled whenever he did. He obeyed, and she shook in his arms. His hands trailed over the skin at her chest, lightly, because he knew it would make her hair stand on end and her nipples harden. When they did, he brushed a thumb over one of their tips. He pulled his mouth off hers and bent to lick her other nipple. Her sharp intake of air went straight to his groin. Pleasure added to the pressure building in his body as he teased her with his tongue.

It was a long time before he lifted his head. When she looked at him, her eyes were glazed. There was no small amount of pride that he'd been the one to cause it. Then his brain finally caught up and he rested his hand on her waist, bracing himself above her.

'You're trying to distract me,' he said.

'Is it working?'

She smiled. It was sweet and somehow laced with

an edginess that sent desire spiralling through him. He laughed, low and husky.

'You know it is.'

She cupped his face, her eyes going serious. 'You'll catch me if I fall, won't you?'

'Always,' he said, though he wasn't sure what she was talking about.

'Okay.' Her eyes swept across his face, then she brushed her thumb over his lips. 'So let's make this marriage official. Well,' she said, her eyes crinkling with amusement, 'in the biblical sense, I guess, since legally it's about as official as it can get.'

'Say it,' he whispered, needing to hear the words.

'Make love with me.'

'Zoey—'

Her thumb pressed against his lips again, silencing him. 'This is what I want, Sawyer. Give it to me. Please.'

So he did.

It was the most remarkable thing he'd ever experienced. Not because it was perfect—it wasn't. Neither of them had done it before. It wasn't as smooth as he'd hoped. He was overwhelmed by having her, by feeling her, by exploring her. Though he'd had a taste before, knowing there were no restrictions heightened the stakes. It made him…nervous.

But she was Zoey, his Zoey. She teased him. Laughed. Gave gentle instructions that helped him use his tongue on her. Then she tapped his head. When he looked up, she tilted his chin between her fingers.

'You're thinking too much. This is supposed to be fun.'

He opened his mouth but she cut him off.

'Don't you dare apologise,' she added. 'We'll work out the kinks. But you've done this before. Just do what you—'

She broke off when he kissed her inner thigh before moving back between her legs. He kept the strokes of his tongue soft. Concentrated on where she'd always guided him to in the weeks before. Her breathing came faster; so did his. When he slid a finger inside her, and another, she pulled his hair. He hadn't even known she was holding on to it.

'I'm…sorry…for…'

She stopped with a hoarse cry. A primitive satisfaction pulsed through him as her hips ground against him. Her cries grew louder, before tapering off.

'What were you saying?' he asked when she was done, straightening beside her.

'Hmm.'

It was all she said for a moment. He waited.

'I think I was going to apologise for making you bald.' She turned, her smile gratified. 'Not anymore. I think you could pull it off.'

'I'm sure you'll give me plenty of opportunity to find out.'

'Damn right.'

She pulled him back, kissing him before he could protest. Part of him wanted to offer to wipe his mouth. It was still wet from her. He loved it, and it turned him the hell on that she didn't seem to care, but surely that was the gentlemanly thing to do? Except she didn't care that he was a gentleman. When they were together like this, she was so free. Unrestrained. Uncaring about things he thought he should offer her.

So he didn't care, too.

He welcomed her seduction. Focused on her body beneath his hands, his tongue. Thought about the fact that he had her. That she'd lost control against his mouth. When he finally slid inside her, he had to stop moving altogether.

'What's wrong?' she asked, voice breathy.

'I'm giving you a moment to adjust.'

'I thought you'd done that earlier.'

She tilted her hips. He sunk deeper. Mentally, he went through the alphabet.

'You know, with the copious amounts of foreplay. With how you went back down on me, how you made me—'

'I get it.'

She smiled. 'You're very good at that, by the way.'

Her voice was husky, like she'd spent a solid portion of her day shouting.

To be fair, she kind of had.

'It's your first time.'

'I'm fine,' she said softly. 'It feels good. Sawyer.' Now, her voice was firm. 'I'm fine.'

'Are you sure?'

'Yeah.' Her eyes searched his face. Understanding lit her eyes. 'But this is your first time, too. This must be, um, hard for you.'

'Are you making fun of me *while* I'm inside you?'

'Never.' There was a small smile on her face. 'But I get it.' She paused. 'You already know this is perfect, right?' She brushed his face with her hands. 'Everything about it is perfect. That isn't going to change because you don't give me a third orgasm tonight.'

'I'd like to,' he said, even as he tumbled more in love with her.

'Okay.' She pulled her lip between her teeth. It made her look sexier. He almost groaned. 'But how about we save that for later?' she whispered.

She tilted her hips again, setting his brain on fire. Ashes flew around his skull, so he closed his eyes, and groaned out loud when she kissed him.

It was soft and gentle, as were the movements of her hips. She was encouraging him to move, telling him it was okay to, and something switched off in his brain and turned on in his heart. Love and lust and desire and respect had him sliding in and out of her, slowly, as her tongue teased his, and he didn't try to stop himself as he fell over the edge.

Because just as he would catch her, he knew she'd catch him.

Chapter Fourteen

One Day, Now

It was good to know that after six years, he hadn't changed as much as he thought he had. Good was a relative term, of course. It was *good* that he hadn't sworn at Zoey's sisters as they formed a protective circle around her. It was *good* that he hadn't told them *he'd* been there for her when they weren't around. When they'd thought she wasn't capable. So the fact that he described getting up when Zoey made eye contact with him when she re-joined their group as *good* should be taken with a pinch of salt. Especially after the years he'd tried to forget her and her power over him.

Still, he walked toward her. Because like he'd told her before they got married, she was a magnet. He couldn't help it.

Footsteps sounded behind him, then passed him. It didn't bother him until he realised the man was running toward Zoey. He sped up, but then realised the man was Parker. Not that Parker's expression did anything to soothe Sawyer's concerns.

'Zoey?'

'What?' she asked, eyes widening as Parker gripped her arm.

'The horse and carriage. They're here. Now. The guy got the time wrong or something, and he's here.'

'The horse and carriage,' Zoey repeated.

'Yeah, the one that was supposed to take Sophia and me from here to a restaurant at the beach for a meal.'

'You hired a horse and carriage for that?'

'Yes.'

'Are you proposing to *Sophia* Sophia? As in, my sister?'

Parker gritted his teeth. 'Yeah.'

'The sister who used to read fairy tales to me, then laugh?'

'I realise now it wasn't a good idea.'

'Okay,' Zoey said after a moment. 'What do you want me to do?'

'Get it away from here.'

She blinked. 'How do I do that?'

'I don't know,' he said. He looked around, seeming to only notice Sawyer then. 'Take him. The two of you can talk about the good old days as you ride to the beach.'

'Oh, I don't think—'

'Great, we'd love to.' Sawyer spoke over Zoey's protests.

'Yeah?' Parker's expression brightened. Then he straightened. 'How much of our conversation did you hear?'

'Enough to show you how well I can keep a secret.'

Parker studied him a moment, then nodded. 'I appreciate your help.'

'Woah, wait. I didn't say I'd do this.'

'But he—'

'Doesn't speak for me.'

'You said you'd help.'

'Yes, me. Solo.'

'So go by yourself. No, don't,' Parker added almost immediately. 'I don't want you to go alone.'

'I can take care of myself.'

'Yeah, but with him you won't have to.'

She released a breath. 'So what are we supposed to do? Sit at the back of the carriage until we reach the beach, then come back?'

'Have the meal I planned,' Parker said. He shook his head. 'You're right, Zo. Soph would hate all this.' He sighed. 'Please do this for me. Get the horse and carriage the hell away from here. Take your payment in the form of a meal.'

'You know,' she said sourly, 'when you said you needed my help, this wasn't what I pictured.'

'Please.'

She bit her lip. 'Fine. But you owe me.'

Parker kissed her cheek, then gave her a gentle push. 'You need to get out of here. *Now.*'

Zoey gave her future brother-in-law a look that would have destroyed a lesser man. But Parker stood there like a tank, waiting for her to move.

'Come on.'

Sawyer assumed those words were directed at him. Soon, they were heading down the path to the front gate, walking past the guards and against the crowd. They paused when they reached the front and the horse and carriage were right *there*. People looked at it in confusion, some whispering about whether it was part of the show.

'Maybe it's for one of the performances?' someone asked.

It spurred Zoey into action.

'We better get in before it creates more unrealistic expectations.'

He followed her into the carriage, and moments later, they were trotting off into the road. Trees lined either side of it, tall and thick. Light peeked between them. There was nothing disrupting nature's silence except the clacking of hooves. It was perfect for an honest conversation.

'You hate this,' he said, trying to keep his voice light and ease them into it.

'What?'

Her voice was flat. He might need to ease harder.

'Being trapped with me in a carriage.'

'Not exactly the reunion I pictured, I'll admit.'

'What did you picture?'

He tried not to get hung up on the fact that she'd pictured a reunion at all.

'Something with a few more exits.'

He laughed lightly, unable to help himself. 'Your sense of humour is still intact then.'

'It does tend to stay over time, a sense of humour.'

'Really?' he asked. 'Mine hasn't.'

Though she kept looking out the window, her head shifted at his comment. It was almost as if she were physically resisting turning to him.

'No, I don't imagine it has.'

He waited a beat. 'Is there more to that then innuendo?'

Now she did look at him, to give him a sickly-sweet smile. 'No.'

He sighed, looked out his own window when their eyes locking seemed like unnecessary torture. No cars passed them since the road was closed for the event. He wished it hadn't been. He could have used some good old Capetonian traffic anger to distract him from the tension.

From the other anger burning in his gut.

'We need to talk,' he said when he grew tired of it.

'Yeah.'

She didn't say anything else.

'You're the one who brought up a divorce, Zoey. You must have more to say on the topic.'

The silence lingered for long enough that Sawyer thought he might need to prompt her again. As he was about to, she spoke.

'We've been married for six years, but we spent three months together.' She shifted. For the first time, she looked at him properly, her body facing his. 'That was in our first year. Since then, we've seen one another four times. You can't tell me a divorce hasn't crossed your mind?'

He didn't reply. Because it hadn't. Despite the hurt she'd left behind when she walked away from him, he hadn't once considered reaching out to her about getting divorced.

Now he knew he should have. Considered it, at the very least. The fact that he hadn't—and his conversation with Byron—told him he'd contributed to the current state of their relationship. The confusion, the uncertainty. The loyalty, too. He hadn't considered divorce because it felt like betrayal. After all they'd been through together, betrayal was the last thing he wanted to do to her.

He still remembered how she stood up to his cousin when Phil tried to bully him. It had taken a month of her visiting, watching Phil give him a hard time, before she had. When he asked her why, she told him he didn't deserve it. That his cousin was being a loser. Her fourteen-year-old vocabulary wasn't as colourful as it was now, he thought. He barely resisted the smile.

Then there were the days he got made fun of because he didn't have parents. It had somehow got out after a parent/teacher conference that his aunt and uncle were raising him. Kids, being as cruel as they were, called him an orphan. A loser. Unwanted. It had stung, mostly because it hit close to home. But Zoey walked with him in the passages, head held high, holding his hand, too. She glared at anyone who dared to call him a name. Got right up in their faces if she had to. Eventually, the next scandal happened and people forgot about him. But he'd never forgotten about it. So he couldn't betray her.

Even though she betrayed you?

The anger burned in his gut again. He tried to ignore it.

'What did you think was going to happen?' she asked softly. He met her gaze and he realised that she'd seen some of the emotions on his face. She'd always been able to see. 'Our marriage was doomed from the start.'

'No,' he disagreed. 'It wasn't.'

'We got married for the wrong reasons.'

'Really?' he asked. 'Strange you say that. I recall giving you plenty of opportunities to back out. I told you that if you were getting married out of some twisted sense of loyalty to me and to what I felt for you, you shouldn't. And you know what you said, Zoey?'

She shook her head. He didn't know if it was in answer to him, or because she didn't want to answer at all.

'You said "I do."'

'That's not fair.'

'No?' He sat back against the plush velvet of the carriage seat. It occurred to him that he was more comfortable there than he would have been at the back of a car. Not that that was important. 'What *is* fair then?'

She released a harsh breath. Seconds after she answered.

'I can't deny that I married you because I loved you.' She spoke slowly, her words dancing over the piece of his heart that broke when she said *loved*. 'But I lost my father, Sawyer. I lost another man I loved and maybe I couldn't bear to lose you, too.'

He looked out the window. Something moved in the greenery that gathered around the trunks of the trees. The wind fluttered at the same time, sending a gentler disruption through the leaves and branches.

He wanted to say it reflected what was happening inside him, but there was nothing gentle about that. His feelings were sharp and destructive. Words of a similar nature whipped through his mind.

You know you shouldn't have married her. She wasn't ready. She was grieving. You took advantage. Your marriage was a sham.

The disappointment washed over him in waves. Judgement. Anger. Even though he'd considered it before they'd got married, hearing her say it was crushing. At the same time, he wondered what more he could have done. He'd asked her, checked in with her. He'd done it too many times to remember. And she'd been insistent, as she was now, that she wanted a marriage.

Maybe they should have waited longer. They should have, he thought with more certainty. And he should have urged them to. He'd known Zoey for a third of his life then. He knew that she was spontaneous and passionate and she rushed into feelings. She enjoyed them and celebrated them. Until she realised they weren't right, and she course corrected. He usually helped her come to that realisation. Helped her move to the right path. But with this…

His feelings had obscured the truth. He'd ignored his instincts. So he didn't know where to direct his anger. At her, for marrying him, then leaving him? At himself for letting love get in the way?

'I thought about that,' he said slowly, still looking out the window. 'I asked you about it.'

'Sawyer—'

'But I should have known I couldn't trust what you were saying.'

'What do you mean?'

He looked over. 'You say things now and you don't mean them later.'

Her expression went blank. 'Are you saying I lie?'

'No. I think you genuinely believe them when you say them. But that changes so quickly, sometimes it gives me whiplash.'

'I don't… I mean, I was…' She trailed off, her face now contorting in concentration. 'Are you saying I did this before my dad died?'

Instead of giving her a direct answer, he said, 'You didn't go to classes for months after your dad died. Did you believe that was the right decision then?'

Her cheeks flushed. 'I needed…time.'

'Did you end up finishing your degree?'

She gave a curt nod.

'What about that time you gave away all your pants because you said they reminded you of the patriarchy? Didn't you end up buying new pants a month later?' He didn't give her a chance to answer. 'And remember when you—'

She cut him off flatly. 'I get it.'

'You asked,' he pointed out. 'I'm not saying this is your fault. I should have known better, too.'

She studied him. Seconds later, her eyes went sharp. 'Yes, you should have.'

He looked up. 'Excuse me?'

'I can hear you're blaming me for this—'

'I'm not blaming you for anything.'

'My mistake,' she said primly. 'Is there some other way I should interpret you outlining my flaws as reasons for why you should have known better than to marry me?'

His fingers curled into fists. 'I'm saying we both need to take responsibility for what happened.'

She gave a hoarse laugh. 'Is that what you're saying? Because all I hear is you telling me *I* need to take responsibility for what happened. And I get that. I know who I used to be. I know it as well as I know the people around me enabled me.' She let it linger. 'You *know* there was more to you marrying me than the fact that you loved me. Not that it matters now.' She said it as easily as she'd dropped the bombshell right before it. 'We're righting the mistakes of the past. At least, I'm trying to.'

* * *

Zoey hadn't intended on calling Sawyer out. Frankly, she hadn't even known the ability existed inside her. But she wasn't enjoying him pointing out her faults when she was trying to be better. She especially didn't enjoy that he was framing their marriage as a mistake he'd made because of *her*. Because she was grieving and he should have known better. Not because he had an idea of who he wanted them to be, and it had contributed to them marrying as much as her grief or their love for one another had.

They'd both made a bad decision. It had been obscured by love and their own personal issues, but it had been bad. She could see it. Probably because she'd done a lot of work on herself in the years since their marriage had ended. Clearly, Sawyer hadn't. Which was fine. Everyone went at their own pace. She shouldn't be frustrated that he was blaming her then. He was still in denial. So why the hell *was* she so frustrated?

Could frustration make a space stuffy? Clearly, since she was desperately wishing she could open a window. Or was that because she suddenly felt claustrophobic? Either way, they were in a carriage—a literal carriage—and she had no choice but to suck it up.

It boggled her mind that Parker thought this would be a good idea for Sophia. Sophia, who, like with laughing at fairy tales, had refused to watch any movie with a prince and princess because 'real life wasn't like that.' Parker knew Sophia well, but this was a mistake. The whole proposal thing was clearly freaking him out. Zoey wondered what Sophia would say when she found out this was why he was acting weird.

Probably something with expletives, she thought,

amusing herself as her eyes swept through the carriage. In the opposite corner stood a small cooler box. It was on Sawyer's side, but since she wasn't talking to him—or he wasn't talking to her—she stretched over and tried to get it.

She lost her balance almost immediately.

Strong hands caught her before she could topple over and bump her head. Determined not to let her clumsiness deter her, she pulled at the cooler box, shifting it closer. But she couldn't pick it up without losing her balance again, and the longer Sawyer's hands stayed on her waist, the more she was reminded of how good he was at touching her. Their marriage might have been short, but they'd made the most of it. The thought had her scrambling back on her chair.

'Would you, um, get that, please?' she asked, breathless because she'd basically contorted herself in front of him. She'd blame that and not her dirty memories for the state of her breathing.

'You could have asked me in the first place,' he said under his breath.

'Yeah, well, maybe I didn't want to deal with this mood you're in. But thank you,' she added, when he put the box on her lap. She opened it, and nearly cried when she saw a bottle of wine and cheese and crackers.

'I've never seen someone so happy to see wine before.'

'I know that's a lie because this is how I respond to wine every time I see it.'

'You weren't drinking wine so much when we were still…' He hesitated. 'Friends.'

'Hmm. Our friendship must have sparked my drinking habit then.' She took out the bottle and examined the label. 'Oh, it's the good stuff. Do you want a glass?'

His face was doing something weird. She replayed the last minutes and realised what she said.

'I was kidding, Sawyer. I mean, I did start drinking more after we ended things, but it didn't have *that* much to do with our marriage.' She winked. He didn't even crack a smile. 'Really? Your sense of humour's changed so much you don't find my wit amusing anymore?'

'Maybe I never did,' he grumbled. 'Maybe I was faking it.'

'And maybe I was faking my orgasms.'

She blinked, not sure why she said that. She shouldn't be alluding to their sex life. That was one part of their past that needed to stay there. If it didn't, she might be tempted to revisit it in the present.

'You weren't faking your orgasms.'

His deep voice was full of—deserved, sure, but still annoying—pride.

'But how can you really know, Sawyer?'

'You couldn't get away from me quick enough when I touched you just now.'

'Because you were touching me.'

'Yes,' he said dryly. 'That is what I said.'

'No, I mean—' She broke off. Clenched her teeth. 'I didn't want you to touch me because we're not on good terms.'

'Which makes your attraction to me even more inconvenient.'

'Have you always been this cocky?' she asked, turning. 'Or is that something you've developed over the last couple of years?'

'Was *cocky* really the best word to use in this conversation, Zo?' he asked conversationally, taking the bottle from her and pouring wine into a glass. She had no choice but to let him, since she was pretty much frozen by the seductive tilt his demeanour had taken.

He handed her the glass. 'I thought you might need some help since you stalled for some reason.'

Oh, man. She didn't ever remember him being this self-satisfied. It was irritating, but that arrogance looked *really* good on him. Sexy.

She shook her head. This was what thinking about orgasms got her.

'Thank you,' she said, taking the glass from him and drinking. She closed her eyes when the flavour coated her tongue. Gave a little moan of pleasure for good measure. When she opened her eyes, his own were brighter than they'd been before. She smirked. 'Something wrong?'

'You don't want to play this game with me, Zoey.'

His voice had somehow got deeper.

'Oh, but I do.' She leaned so far forward their noses were almost touching. 'You started it. You don't get to call a time out because you're losing.'

His expression tightened. With a smile, she reached a hand behind her, resting her weight on it as she studied him. She drank her wine slowly, enjoying his anger.

'Look,' she said easily. 'You're out of your league here. I've played this game before.'

'Yeah, you have,' he replied after a moment. He took her glass, downed the wine, then set it in the cooler box with the bottle. 'With me.'

'I was drinking that.'

'And if I recall correctly,' he said, ignoring her

words, but pulling her onto his lap, 'we both ended up winning.'

Her breath caught the moment he touched her. When he pulled her onto his lap, she lost it altogether. Now she was straddling him, her face centimetres from his, and she forgot about something as insignificant as breathing. There was only him. His brown eyes that were shining with lust and something darker, heavier. The dark of his brows, the furrow between them. He'd grown a beard since she'd last seen him—kissed him— and it looked good on him. It was short, full, highlighting the sensual curve of his lips.

Lips that inched up as she studied him.

'Got nothing to say now, gamemaster?'

'Say, no.' She let the seconds tick by before she lifted her gaze. 'Do, maybe. That depends on you.'

Another sheath of darkness slid over the lust in his eyes. There was plenty of it she couldn't read, but two things were clear: hunger and need.

'Say yes,' she told him, her voice a rasp. 'Let me kiss you.'

'It's a bad idea.'

'Really? You're listening to that voice in your head *now*?'

'Maybe if I'd listened to it before, we wouldn't be here.'

It was torture having this discussion in this position. She could see him fight with every word, could see his resistance in the coiling of his muscles. She could also feel his arousal, which undermined everything he said, though she appreciated the effort. But she wouldn't force him to do something he didn't want to do. Only…if she moved, she would be giving in, or turning him on, and neither option seemed desirable.

'You can do hypotheticals all you want, Sawyer, but we can't go back to the past and change things.'

If they could, she would have stopped their wedding herself. Not because she regretted it, but because its end seemed inevitable now. She hadn't anticipated that. Not for their marriage, and sure as hell not for their friendship. And that was why him saying all these things hurt so deeply.

Taking responsibility for your actions is going to be painful, she gave herself a mental pep talk. *But you can only take responsibility for your own actions*, another voice in her head said. Logically, she knew it was her own mental voice. But in this situation, where logic had taken vacation—she was sitting on her estranged husband's lap, after all—she thought her gut was trying to tell her something.

'I know,' he said, watching her. 'But you can't say there isn't a part of you that wishes we could.'

'There's a bigger part of me that wishes you and I could have kissed without the walk down memory lane.'

'You can't ignore what happened between us.'

'I'm not. I asked for a divorce. Now I want to remember some of the good things, too.'

'I thought you were faking it.'

'Not all of it. I liked how you kissed me.'

'But that's it, right?' he said. 'You didn't have feelings about my hands?' He rested them on her thighs, then slid them up to cup her butt. He used the position to thrust her forward, against his hardness. She let out an involuntary gasp.

'None,' she said breathlessly. 'No feelings about them at all.'

'Not even when they did this?'

He moved his hand under her shirt, pulling her bra down and touching one of her breasts. Seconds later, his thumb found her nipple. He caressed it slowly, just how he knew she liked. Bent forward to take it in his mouth through her top. Scraped his teeth lightly over it as he leaned back.

'Technically, that was your finger,' she pointed out stubbornly. 'Then your mouth.'

'If you're caught up on technicalities, you know you're losing.'

'Didn't you say we both win in this game?'

'Shut up.'

It was the last thing he said before his mouth found hers. Immediately, she pressed herself forward, trying to get as much of him as possible.

It had been years since she'd kissed. She'd chosen not to break her vows with anyone else, despite the dubious state of her marriage. But that meant no one had sated her needs in years. Though she thought, as Sawyer kissed her, that no one besides him would have been able to.

His tongue was a worthy opponent to hers. They tangled like enemies, full of passion and lust, though not bloodthirsty. Then the rhythm changed to that of lovers: exploratory, languid, like someone finding sun on a cold day. She missed the way he tasted; like wine now, but more. Like trust and steadiness. Like heat and passion and the first and only man she ever loved.

She pushed that thought away by touching the skin under his shirt. A simple grey one that made her mouth water even when she refused to admit it. It clung to his muscular body much like she currently did, the heat of his skin creeping under hers and setting every part of her on fire.

The heat all pooled between her thighs, a place conveniently located against his erection. She moved her hips slowly first, grinding against him, and was rewarded with a guttural moan. She did it again and again, positioning herself so that she'd get the most pleasure from it. Not once did her mouth leave his. She'd starved herself of his kisses for too long. And she was good at multitasking; she could use his body and his mouth at the same time. It was one of her gifts.

She chose not to think about what this meant. Or how her emotions were screaming for joy, rejoicing that they'd finally returned home. *We've been so lost without you*, they told Sawyer. *Thank you for finding us again.* She ignored them. Shoved them aside, in truth. She couldn't afford not to. She asked him for a divorce, for heaven's sake. There was no home. Not after that.

'Zoey,' he said, pulling away from her. 'We need to stop.'

'Why?' she asked. 'Is it your conscience again? It'll go away. Okay, it'll come back later, but by then, you and I will be done with this and at least we'll have that.'

His face was light with amusement. 'No, it's not my conscience. Although it's making me very aware of how bad of an idea this is. But that's not it.'

He gently extricated her hands from his body. Then, he lifted her from her lap. She moved accordingly, until she was sitting next to him and no longer on him.

'Are you going to tell me why you stopped us?'

'Look outside.'

She did, and saw that they were heading toward a path that had people on it. It cut through the forest, which she had some thoughts on, mainly regarding serial killers, but at that moment, she could only think of one thing.

'How did you know they were there?'

'I looked.'

'Your eyes were open?' she asked. He nodded. 'I read somewhere that only psychopaths and sociopaths kissed with their eyes open.'

He chuckled. Reached out to take her hand.

'Also people who want to memorise things.'

'Like what?'

'Like how you look when I kiss you.' He brushed a thumb over her wrist. 'How turned on you are. And sexy.'

She didn't interrupt him.

'Most importantly, I wanted to memorise how you look when you aren't faking, so I know when you are.'

She narrowed her eyes. 'Who says I wasn't faking it now?'

It shut him up long enough to soothe her discontentment at being stopped.

Part Two

'I've broken you.'

Chapter Fifteen

It was the most insignificant thing that sent her spiralling. A line from a movie. But then it wasn't insignificant anymore. Then it was her entire world—her family, her marriage, her mental and emotional health—that was falling apart, its pieces crushing the denial she'd been in for the last three months.

She was making dinner for her and Sawyer. He was still at work. An internship with a logistics company formed part of his degree and kept him busy until late. He earned some money from it, but not enough to maintain a household. His aunt and uncle paid for his flat since he'd got a scholarship for his studies, so they were okay for now. She suspected that wouldn't be the case when his family found out they were married.

Which was fine. She was a term away from graduating, and then she could find a job, too. Granted, she hadn't gone to class or done any assignments or tests since things with her dad got intense. But it would sort itself out. It usually did.

She had the TV on in the background. An old movie that had recently been remade was playing. Then came the line. The infamous one about being late for an important date. She realised *she* was late. For her period. Which, since she was in no way ready to start a family, was a pretty important date, too.

Her brain went blank. For a full moment, she thought nothing. Did nothing. Then, slowly, she set down the knife she'd been cutting with. Her legs walked to the bedroom; her hands grabbed her coat. An amount of time later—she would never know what that amount was—she was buying three pregnancy tests. Instead of going back to the flat though, she went to the mall across the road and peed on a test in a nondescript stall.

It wasn't the story she wanted to tell her kids— *hey, Mom found out about you on a Thursday night in a dirty toilet*. She couldn't figure out why she didn't want to go home though. Was it because the very idea of children had her heart and lungs acting as if they had no idea what they were doing? Or was it the fact that she couldn't conceptualise having Sawyer catch her peeing on sticks and realising what was happening?

In truth, *she* wasn't quite sure what was happening.

The first test was negative.

She stared at it for a while. Then she left the bathroom, bought a bottle of water. After she downed it, she waited on a bench until it worked through her body.

The second test was negative, too. But it was the third negative test that sent a rush of emotion through her body. Relief. Emptiness. As if the idea of this child had filled her up and finding out she wasn't pregnant had drained her.

It made no sense. She wasn't planning for a family. Hadn't thought about it at all. Largely because for the last few years, family had meant something difficult. Something painful. Then Sawyer had offered her a different definition of it. He offered her peace and safety. He offered her a reprieve from grief and pain. She grabbed on to it like a dying woman. Which, in truth, she thought she was. Not her physical being, but her mental health. Her emotional health. Her father had got sick and then he'd died, so yes, sure, her emotional and mental health had died, too.

She was in no state to plan a family. The possibility of a pregnancy showed her she wasn't even ready to think about it. Hadn't she, minutes before she realised her period was late, thought about how her problems would sort themselves out? Deep down, she knew she believed her family would. She was avoiding her sisters, her mother, but she was still counting on them to figure out her mistakes.

A gush of air escaped through her lips. She was *avoiding* her family. That's why she didn't want to tell them she got married. That's why she wouldn't answer any of Sophia's questions when her sister asked where she was. It wasn't entirely that though; she wasn't lying when she told Sawyer they'd think she was having some sort of mental breakdown. But avoiding them— their grief that would remind her of her grief, or force her to act bubbly and happy when she wasn't—was part of it. It made her wonder if she *was* having a mental breakdown. What would happen if she added a baby to that? How could she look after a child when she couldn't even take responsibility for herself? All the responsibility would shift to Sawyer. The father. Her husband.

She was thankful she was still in the bathroom stall. Thankful no one could see her bottom lip quivering and her chest heaving in and out as if someone were pushing against it.

She got *married*. To avoid her family and her grief, she got married. If she doubted she wasn't responsible before, this would prove it. She wanted people to fix things so badly that she got married so Sawyer could fix her grief. He allowed it because he'd always been willing to fix things and she would always let him.

But what would their future look like if they continued that way?

She'd seen her sisters' responses to looking after her. It consumed their lives. After their father's diagnosis, they kept the house running. But Angie's daily routine revolved around doing so. Sophia stopped dating her boyfriend, stopped going out. It was like the entire world existed in their household. Zoey had never realised it before, probably because she was part of the problem.

How could she do that to Sawyer, too? The man she loved beyond reason? Who, after all he'd gone through with his parents and his aunt and uncle, deserved to have a stable family? A *healthy* family?

He deserved more than her. His feelings had led him astray. Feelings for her; feelings about what he knew he deserved. She was sure he wanted a healthy, stable family. So much so he thought he'd get it if he married her. He wouldn't—she was neither healthy nor stable— which proved to her he'd been led astray. And one day, he would see. She wasn't the person he made her out to be. She wasn't able to give him what he wanted or needed. They'd break up and he'd grow resentful and hate her because of it. Because she couldn't offer him a place to heal from his past when she was still healing from her own.

It was official: she couldn't avoid the consequences of her decisions anymore. The last three months as Sawyer's wife had been a reprieve from her life. From Angie constantly asking if she was okay. From Sophia constantly checking in with blunt questions about practical things. All of it was designed to show how Zoey was coping, and she hadn't been. Pretending she was was exhausting.

But so, she realised, was pretending her marriage would last.

She made it home minutes before Sawyer did. She picked up where she left off; she was slicing an onion when he walked through the door.

'Hey,' he said. When he saw the tears falling down her cheeks, his expression went from fatigued to alarmed. 'Everything okay?'

'Fine.' She forced a smile. 'It's just the onions.'

He stopped in front of her. Studied her. She did her best to hide what she'd gone through that day. She didn't know what she was going to do about it. She wanted an opportunity to figure it out.

But his eyes were sharp. They saw. She went willingly when he pulled her into his arms. Barely caught her sob when she realised he hadn't thought the turmoil he saw was because of him. Them. It was selfish to accept comfort when she knew the truth, but she would be selfish one last time before she did the right thing.

It was becoming abundantly clear what the right thing was.

Chapter Sixteen

One Day, Now

'We're supposed to eat here?' Zoey asked, her head lifting as she looked at the tall building.

'I believe so, ma'am,' the driver of the carriage said. He'd been relatively unobtrusive throughout the experience, probably because he couldn't see them. The carriage only had windows on the sides. Good thing, too, or the make-out session with Zoey would have been awkward. Sawyer would rather it only be a bad idea. 'I was hired to bring you here.'

'Here?' Zoey said again. 'It looks expensive.'

'Ma'am?' the driver said, brow knitting.

Zoey shook her head. 'It's fine.'

'If we're here, this is probably where we have to be,' Sawyer said.

He hoped.

'Will you be waiting?' Zoey asked the driver.

'No, ma'am.'

'Great.' Zoey sighed. 'Thank you.'

'You're welcome.'

They waited for the driver and carriage to leave.

'We should get inside,' Sawyer said. Zoey nodded.

He wanted to reach out and take her hand so they could cross the road together. It was instinct when he was with her. He crushed it. His instincts could no longer involve caring for her. They were going to get a divorce. Their make-out session didn't change anything. It was simply…a release of tension.

He kept lying to himself as they made their way into the building. Then he stopped himself mentally, shifting gears. There were things he didn't have to lie about to remind him things wouldn't change because they kissed. Like how she slowly pulled away from him a couple of weeks before their marriage ended. His instincts were nowhere to be found then. Or perhaps they were; he simply didn't listen to them. Work had complicated things. He'd been working on a big project at the company he was interning at. He had a small role in it, but he was determined to prove himself. If he did, he would get a job offer. He'd be able to provide for his wife. Their family.

But when the project was done, his job offer hadn't mattered. His marriage was over. Now Zoey was implying he'd had something to do with that. Except he hadn't been the one to pull away. He hadn't walked out.

Yeah, those were pretty good reminders why a kiss wouldn't change things.

He kept his head down and followed Zoey into the building. It was all gloss and sleek lines. The tiles made him worry he'd slip with each step. He couldn't figure out if the trees were real or fake. His initial impression was the building was a corporate headquarters of some kind; according to the receptionist, it was a hotel. He wasn't an interior designer, but that didn't seem right.

Shouldn't guests feel welcome when they walked in, not repelled?

Things were better at the rooftop restaurant they were sent to. A wall of glass shielded patrons from some of the wind, though the roof was open. He could smell the salty air of the ocean just metres away, and occasionally, he could feel its coolness. They were led to a small table with a white tablecloth. Candles flickered at its centre; long-stemmed roses lay across each setting. Champagne chilled in a bucket nearby, but the server still offered them wine.

'This is probably going to cost an arm and a leg,' Zoey said as she picked up the menu after the woman left. 'Especially since the menu has no prices. That's never a good sign.'

He picked up the menu, looked for himself. 'It's a set menu, Zo.' He frowned. 'What did you think—they only had three options for each course?'

'Fancy places like this do,' Zoey defended herself. 'But I wasn't paying that much attention, to be honest with you.' She put down the menu. 'I was thinking about whether I could get our end-of-year function held here. It's not a bad option, this room. Exorbitant, likely, but if we reached our targets this year, the company might be willing to make an exception.'

He studied her, though the animated tone of her voice already told him what he would see. 'You enjoy your job.'

'I do,' she said with a small smile. 'I mean, it's a nightmare sometimes. I have to deal with executives who think that because my job is to arrange events for the company, I can do so for them, too. One of them once asked me to arrange a romantic dinner for their girlfriend.' She dropped her head. 'He was married.'

'Ooh,' Sawyer said, wincing. 'How did you handle that?'

'I told him I'd be happy to give recommendations, but I don't arrange personal functions for executives.'

'He was fine with that?'

'No, but I think he knew he crossed a line. Fortunately, my manager is pretty good with keeping the execs on their toes. When he has the time, of course.'

She paused when the server poured their wine. They chose their options from the set menu, and then she was gone again.

'What about you?' Zoey asked hesitantly. What did it say about how he'd been treating her that she was nervous asking him a simple question? A spear stabbed through his heart. 'Did I hear you moved to an automotive company?'

'Five years ago.' *A year after you left.* 'The mechanics of the job is pretty much the same everywhere, I admit. Fortunately, those are the parts I like.'

'You always were a nerd,' she said slyly.

'Didn't I hear you work for an IT company?'

'Touché.'

'I can't imagine that's the most interesting place to work at.'

She thought about it. 'It's not uninteresting. The people are challenging. Mostly because everyone thinks they know better than you do, even at your own job.'

'You should fit right in then.'

'Ha,' she said, then gave a genuine laugh. 'Actually, I do. I have power there. I can make people smile because most of the time, they don't. It's fun to play around with what makes different people tick.' She blushed. 'Sorry. That probably wasn't interesting to you.'

'No,' he said slowly. 'I don't mind it.'

It was an understatement, but he was playing it cool. She sounded like the old Zoey. Before her father's illness and death had robbed her of some of her spark. He'd never thought about how much he missed it until now; even before they ended things. Not that he should have thought about it. She'd been going through a lot; thinking how he missed who she was before that was selfish.

But he still felt it.

You know there was more to you marrying me than the fact that you loved me.

Had he thought their marriage would bring her spark back? Had he only wanted to bring the old Zoey back with their relationship?

No. No, of course not. But Zoey's voice was still echoing through his head, making him wonder whether there *was* more than love in his desire to marry her, after all.

'I like hearing about your work,' he said, trying to distract himself. 'It's nice to see you passionate.'

'Because I wasn't before?'

'It wasn't a criticism.'

'No. You were being honest.' She didn't seem upset. 'A lot of things have changed. I'm not… I'm not that person anymore. I care about things beyond myself these days.'

'I never thought otherwise.'

'Never? Not even when I told you I couldn't be your wife anymore?' When he didn't answer, she continued.

'My life used to be centred around me. I didn't realise it until—' She broke off, reached for her wine. She took a deep sip. Looked out at the ocean.

She was avoiding him.

'What changed?'

His voice was low. Probably because he was trying to hide the desperation.

'A lot of things.' She set her glass down and looked at him. Her expression gave nothing away. Things had changed, he thought for the millionth time that day. 'In quick succession, too.' There was a beat. 'Loss can open your eyes if you let it.'

Losing your father or losing me?

He refused to ask the question. He didn't need the answer. Or he shouldn't need it.

He reached for his own wine, frustrated that he *did* need it. He blamed Byron. If his brother-in-law hadn't put it in his head that having Zoey in his life again was an option, he wouldn't be thinking any of this. Hell, his conversation with Byron was probably the reason he'd had his hands all over her in the carriage. Why he'd used his mouth to taste her, his tongue to tease her...

The server arrived with their starters, the perfect distraction while his brain gave him a stern talking to.

Boundaries. Protection. You need the first for the latter since you're hopeless around her.

But he couldn't blame himself. She was still witty, quick on her feet. And how could she think she hadn't cared about those around her? She pretended to be okay throughout her father's illness because she hadn't wanted her grief to sadden her family. She pretended to be his girlfriend at big family events, even after they split, because she made a promise and she was loyal.

She was sacrificing her own feelings about being on a date with her estranged husband because her sister's boyfriend asked her to. The fact that she was helping Parker was easily something he could picture her doing before.

Did she really think she'd changed? Why couldn't she see who she was, even before? Or had he created a version of her that didn't exist?

Boundaries. Protection.

'So.' The word drew him out of his thoughts. She was cutting a piece of carpaccio. She added a shaving of parmesan to it before glancing up slyly. 'You have a sister.'

From one easy topic to the next.

'Yeah.'

'What happened? Did she force you to take a DNA test in front of a live audience?'

He laughed, not sure how he felt that she'd been able to make him laugh. 'No. She kind of…pitched up at my door.'

'Oh.'

'Don't sound so disappointed,' he said dryly.

'I'm not disappointed. I'm surprised. I thought it would be more eventful.'

He lifted his eyebrows. 'Like me taking a DNA test in front of a live audience?'

'Exactly.' She grinned 'Fine. Maybe I am a little disappointed.' She paused. 'I *am* glad it wasn't disruptive.'

'I didn't say that.' He ate his buttered parmesan crostini, not tasting it. Sipped his wine. Tried to ignore her expectant expression. Failed. 'She hired a private detective. It was a closed adoption, but the detective was shady—Lisa's words—and she found out my mom gave her up.'

'How old was your mother?'

'Seventeen.'

'Wow,' Zoey said. 'You couldn't have known? Aunt Pat did though, right? Grandma Carla?'

'I didn't know. My aunt did.' His chest burned. He put it down to indigestion. 'And Grandma Carla knew everything.'

'Not everything,' Zoey disagreed after a moment. 'She never knew we were faking it. Or that we got married.'

'Actually, she knew both.'

'*What?*'

'She told me she knew about the fake relationship at one of the events we attended together. After, I mean.'

She seemed to understand he was talking about after their marriage.

'What did she say?'

'Something about neither of us looking happy.' He shook his head. He couldn't dwell in it. 'She wasn't upset we were conning her though.'

Zoey's forehead creased. 'She must not have known for long.'

'She said she knew it the entire time.'

'But… That night at your cousin's graduation. She told me you had feelings for me.'

'Her matchmaking skills were more advanced than either of us could have anticipated.'

Zoey gave a slight laugh. 'We never stood a chance.'

His lips curved. 'No.'

'What about our marriage?' she asked after an awkward beat of silence.

'I told her the truth. She already guessed something happened.'

'You told your grandmother we were married?'

'You told your sisters.'

'I'm not judging you. I'm wondering how the rest of your family don't know.'

'She seemed to think the two of us being unhappy was enough reason to keep it to herself.' He paused. 'She gave me advice. It was part of the reason I... thought it was best for us to stop pretending.'

'Did she give you any more advice?'

'No. We never spoke about it again.'

'Pretend it didn't happen. Make it go away,' she commented coolly, drinking her wine.

He waited until the server cleared their plates before he spoke. It gave him an opportunity to let the indignation dissolve.

'You must have pretended it didn't happen, too. We haven't been together for six years.'

'I know.' She was all ice. 'I still kept my vows.'

'Really? What do you tell people when they ask you about your husband?'

Her cheeks flushed. 'I didn't say I told people about you. But I haven't forgotten I'm married. There've been no new partners, no crossing the line with anyone.' Somehow, her cheeks became redder. 'I'm very aware I'm married.'

'What does that mean?'

'I don't know. I've been saving.' The colour on her cheeks went past red to maroon. 'I buy stuff.' She muttered the last words, but he heard it.

'Like what?'

'Stuff we didn't have,' she said impatiently now. He

couldn't tell if it was directed at herself or him. 'Remember how we always wanted good coffee, but only had instant? I bought a coffee machine.'

He didn't know what to say. His brain was finally overloading with the information she offered. She said there hadn't been anyone else in the last six years. It stunned him. He hadn't expected her to keep her marriage vows, but he hadn't known she wanted to. She had options; men were drawn to her. He'd experienced it himself. Still was, if he was honest.

How could he not?

She'd thought there were things wrong with her, so she'd done something about it. It indicated courage. He'd always known that courage was there, but he didn't think she had. The fierceness in her eyes told him she knew now.

Did that mean she *had* changed? It bothered him that he didn't know. He hadn't ever thought to ask her what she thought about herself when they were friends. Now, he couldn't tell if that change was because she saw her perceived faults, or because she was doing something about it. He could only trust what she was telling him, and while he wanted to, he still didn't think she saw herself clearly.

Or was it that *he* didn't see her clearly? That he hadn't?

Was the fact that she didn't seem to need him now making him think that she'd never needed him? Had he simply created that narrative for himself, or was it the truth? And if she didn't need him, she must have wanted him. But why didn't that feel right to him? Especially after she told him she was buying things for their life together. Didn't that mean she might *still* want him?

'Oh, no,' Zoey said softly. 'I've broken you.'

He took a deep breath. 'Yeah, I think you have.'

'So let's change the subject,' she offered a little too brightly.

'Okay. Answer me this though.' She gave a nod of acquiescence. 'You sound fine? About this. About everything.'

'Do I?' She brought her glass to her lips. Before she drank, she said, 'I must be a better actress than I thought.'

She wasn't sure what it was about the last few hours, but she'd lost her ability to filter. She was saying things and doing things that were better left unsaid, undone. And sure, she didn't regret what she and Sawyer had done in that carriage. Her body had been curiously dead since the last time they'd been together. It rarely paid attention to things sexually, except to tell her that she missed the intimacy of sex. With him. The carriage had proved it. She was both alarmed and relieved at that fact.

But it was easier not to regret that than what she said to him. That was more complicated. She hated that he wanted to pretend their marriage hadn't happened. That he assumed she did, too. But part of her wished they'd waited. Maybe if they'd married now, she'd still have her best friend. She was different now. More aware of her faults. Of his, too, which surprisingly made her feel more confident things would work between them.

If they married now, she could have kept herself from expecting him to take care of her. That day she thought she was pregnant wouldn't be marred with fear and heartbreak. She wouldn't suddenly have realised she was incapable of being responsible because she would have been.

Or maybe not. She had to go through what she went through with him to realise she was selfish. Just like she had to have the argument with Sophia to realise thinking about changing wasn't the same as changing.

The day Cal had been born, she and Sophia had argued about how Zoey saw Sophia. Before then, Zoey thought she was doing well. Making atonement to her sisters for forcing them to care for her when she was younger. But that argument had shown her good intentions meant nothing. It opened her eyes. Forced her to try harder. She didn't know if she was succeeding.

Would her marriage have suffered because of that, too?

Their marriage, however short, had been the start of this journey she was on. She could face her shortcomings. She *wanted* to be a better person, a better version of herself. And maybe she was working so hard so she could prove it to Sawyer, too. Maybe she wanted him to know how much she'd achieved for herself, for them, so he didn't think she gave up. Maybe she wanted to prove she could be a good wife.

Why had she asked for a divorce then?

'What?' Sawyer asked, breaking into her thoughts. 'Is your dessert not good?'

'No.' She cleared her throat. 'It's excellent, actually.'

'Why do you look like you've bitten into a lemon?'

Because I had an epiphany about our marriage and I'm freaking out.

'I was thinking back on our conversation.'

Sawyer's lip curled. 'It was disturbing.'

She couldn't help the slight laugh. 'I was talking about your sister. We didn't finish.' She took another bite of the white chocolate cheesecake. It was actually tasty. 'It must have messed with your head.'

A muscle twitched in his cheek. 'It wasn't great to find out my mother had some wild days in her youth, no.'

'We all did.'

He gave her a look that said, *Not me.*

'You got married,' she pointed out bluntly. The look disappeared. She bit her lip to keep from smiling.

'I guess I was more surprised she gave her child up for adoption,' he said after a while.

'Why?'

'Because it was her child?' Sawyer answered. 'My grandmother knew. She encouraged it. Considering how she felt about family, it's…strange she made that choice.'

His hesitation said more than his words could.

'She probably thought she was protecting your mother. *Her* child.' She shrugged when his expression went tight. 'I'm not offering judgement. I'm saying think about it from your grandmother's perspective. Her daughter, still a teenager, falls pregnant. If your mother was wild, the father of that baby might not have been reliable.' She paused. 'Does Lisa know who her father is?'

His face twisted. 'Yeah.'

'I'm assuming he wasn't what she expected.'

'He's in prison,' Sawyer said. 'On manslaughter charges. She doesn't talk about it. Frankly, I don't need the information, but best I can glean is that she isn't interested in knowing more about him.'

'Not even if she has another sibling?'

'Like I said, she doesn't talk about it.' He took a sip of water. 'She needs time. Finding out her biological mother's died, and that her family knew about her existence... It's a lot.'

She was unsurprised by his intuition.

'So, knowing that her father's a criminal, do you understand why your grandmother and mother did what they did?'

He blinked. She almost saw the gears shifting in his brain.

'You're saying an unreliable father is an excuse to give away your child?'

She didn't think he realised it, but every time he spoke, anger lined his voice.

'I'm saying a teenage pregnancy with someone you don't trust warrants some understanding from your family.' She waited for him to reply. When he didn't, she softened her voice. 'Your mother, your aunt, your grandmother... They're still the people you know. Love.'

'Are they?'

Such anger, she thought, her heart breaking.

'Look... I'm not saying you have to forgive them. But—'

'I don't want to talk about this anymore.'

'Sawyer—'

'Zoey, please.' His voice was pleading. 'I don't want to talk about this.'

She studied him. Realised, again, that Sawyer had his faults. His idea of family was so...rigid. She got it. If her parents had died when she was younger, she, too, might have turned them into perfect mythical creatures. It might even have led her to create the concept of a perfect family. Where two people chose to marry, where they chose to have a child, chose to live happily.

But her parents hadn't died, so she knew there was no such thing as perfect family. Parents were human; imperfect humans who made mistakes. Sometimes, there was no choice involved in family. Sometimes, brain tumours were thrust upon a family and the family just had to deal.

The fact that Sawyer couldn't understand that made her believe she'd been right all those years ago. He would have expected her to conform to that rigidness, that perfection, too. Look at the standards he was holding his mother, grandmother and aunt to. She couldn't live up to that. Not even now.

So she nodded. 'Sure. If you don't want to talk about it, we won't.'

'Thank you.'

There was a long moment of silence.

'We should probably talk about something safer,' she said. 'Like the years we've spent apart despite being married. Or the end of our friendship. Maybe the terms of our divorce.'

His forehead was creased when he looked at her, but it smoothed when he saw her expression.

'You joke, yet somehow I think it is safer.'

'Give it time,' she said, and winked.

Chapter Seventeen

One Day, Five Years Ago

Sawyer wasn't sure she'd come.

In all honesty, he was stuck on the fact that he invited her. It had just…happened. He'd been working late. After a final read-through, he'd emailed his supervisor, and clicked on his calendar. There, in red, was the reminder of his cousin's wedding two weeks away. Without a second thought, he emailed Zoey an invitation.

It was something he would have done before, when they were still friends and their agreement was still in place. But they weren't friends anymore. Weren't lovers. He hadn't heard from her in seven months. Yet he was conditioned to include her in his life. Which meant he actively had to condition himself out of it, too.

Unfortunately, that realisation hadn't come before he sent her the invitation.

He hadn't heard back from her, which he took as an answer. Still, he hoped. He waited outside the church, greeting his family, avoiding questions about Zoey when they inevitably came. His grandmother wasn't as easy to dodge. He hadn't seen her in a while. He'd pretended to be busy with his final year, with his internship, with anything else he could use as an excuse. He felt bad, but she'd ask him about Zoey, and what would he say?

So when he saw Grandma Carla now, he hid next to the church. Paced. When he saw his bride-to-be cousin drive into the church lot, he realised he couldn't wait anymore. Uncertainty was replaced with resignation: Zoey wasn't coming.

As he turned the corner of the church he saw her.

He couldn't describe what it was like. This was the longest period of time they'd been apart since they met. It was worse now; he knew what it was like to be with her every day. To come home to her and enjoy her beauty and her light, her compassion and wit.

He knew how much he was missing out on.

She looked amazing. A dress in a shade of green that reminded him of the mint sweets his grandmother would sneak him when he was younger covered her curves. Her hair was in twists, long and flowing down her back. She'd tied some of it up. It highlighted her defined cheekbones, dusted with a light pink colour. It matched the pink of her lips; highlighted the dark liner she'd lined her eyes with.

He absently rubbed at the ache in his chest.

'Hey,' she said, when she saw him, relief all but pouring from her. 'I thought you'd gone in. Or you weren't here at all. And the second part made me doubt the first part, so I was just waiting. But your cousin's here—' She broke off with a shaky smile. 'Sorry. Nervous.'

'I, er—' he cleared his throat '—I was waiting for

you. Around the corner. I was hiding from Grandma Carla.'

'Why?'

'She would have asked about you. I didn't want to lie.'

'Oh.' She shifted her weight from one foot to the other. Her gaze slipped past him. 'We should go in. They're waiting for us.'

He turned to see his cousin and uncle giving them a pointed look.

'Yeah.' He offered her a hand. After a brief hesitation, she took it.

They were met with looks of approval and familiarity as they walked in and took their seats. He wanted to point at it as the reason he invited her. His family expected her to be there. With him. But he knew that was a lie because he was imagining what it would be like if they were still together. How much it would mean to be there with his *wife*.

Except she wasn't his wife. Not in the ways that mattered. Not anymore.

The music began to play and they stood, waiting for his cousin to walk down the aisle. A part of him wondered if things would have turned out differently if this was the wedding he and Zoey had had. A small sound at his side drew his attention.

'Zo?' he whispered when he saw her rummaging around in her bag. 'What are you doing?'

'Tissue.' She gave him a watery smile. 'Sorry.'

This time he hesitated, but he took her hand. 'I'm sorry.'

She gave him a strange look. 'About what?'

'This. I should have given you this.'

Her frown deepened, then she shook her head. 'That's not why I'm upset.'

The ceremony began, so he couldn't ask her what had upset her. At least not then. He had no intention of letting it go, even if things weren't good between them. An hour later, they stood outside, waiting for the newly married couple to exit the church.

'Are you going to tell me what upset you in there?'

Her eyelashes fluttered. 'What?'

'You thought I was going to be polite and forget,' he said. 'Sorry. I lost some of that ability the last seven months.'

'That quickly.'

It wasn't a question.

'It was long enough.'

She didn't reply immediately. With a sigh that was filled with sadness, she said, 'I was thinking about my dad. How he'll never get to walk me down the aisle.' She paused. 'It has nothing to do with how we got married. It's…a grief thing, I guess.'

He took her hand, not caring that they weren't together. 'It's getting worse?'

'Sometimes. Some days, I can't believe he's gone. Others, I can function normally and not even think about him. There's always a little feeling in my chest though. I've got used to it mostly.'

'It gets easier,' he said. 'You slip into a routine and that routine helps you find your new normal. Maybe that doesn't mean easier,' he corrected thoughtfully. 'Simpler might be a better word.'

'Simple isn't exactly what I'd use to describe grief.'

'Not now, no.' He squeezed her hand. 'But years from now, it will be. Simple in its awfulness.'

His cousin emerged from the church, and they were distracted by rose petals and bubbles. They wished the couple well, and his cousin told Zoey it would be her turn soon. Zoey smiled, but Sawyer could tell she was uncomfortable. But by what—his cousin's assumption that she wanted to get married? By the fact that they were already married? Or that he was there to witness his cousin's harmless comment? He couldn't tell.

They didn't speak much as the day went on. Or they didn't speak as they used to. Apart from the discussion outside the church, things remained superficial. Great dress, she told him about his cousin's gown. He agreed. Lovely décor. They were graduating soon. How were their families? None of it mattered, yet he couldn't bring himself to ask her about what did.

His grandmother summoned Zoey over the moment she saw her. Zoey went willingly, smiling and laughing as though Grandma Carla was her own family. Technically, he supposed she was. Through marriage, but also the years they spent together as friends. Grandma Carla might not have known the nature of their relationship, but she welcomed Zoey regardless. It was nice to know that hadn't changed. Even though everything else had.

'I better get going,' Zoey said later that evening. 'I have work tomorrow.'

'Work?'

'I… Um, I got a job. Small,' she clarified. 'An event coordinator's assistant.'

'That's great, Zo.' He paused. 'Why didn't you tell me earlier?'

'It feels weird.'

'Why? You used to tell me these things all the time.'

'Yeah, but then we were—' She broke off when she

caught the eye of his aunt. 'We probably shouldn't talk about it here,' she said after a quick wave.

'I'll walk you out.'

His mood had taken a nosedive at some point during the cordiality. They were married, but they were acting like acquaintances, for heaven's sake. And before they were married, they'd been friends. Good friends. He hated that they messed that up.

Except…he didn't regret it. The three months they spent together had been the best of his life. He loved having a reason to come home in the afternoon. He'd walk into his flat, see her there, and his day would get better. She was his, and he was hers, and they were a unit. A family.

It felt as though his heart had stepped between the closing doors of an elevator.

'This is me.'

'Whose car is this?'

'Sophia's. She let me borrow it for tonight.'

'You need one of your own.'

She laughed. 'I can't afford one of my own. I'm an assistant.'

'Doesn't that mean you have to have a car of your own?'

'Yeah. Soph, my mom and I figure it out. Sometimes my boss lets me use his.' She released a sigh. 'It's not ideal, but it is what it is.'

'You know you could use mine. Drop me at work in the morning and use it as much as you'd like.'

'Sawyer—'

'We're married, Zoey.'

'In name,' she said firmly.

'In more than name,' he scoffed. 'We were living

together for three months. Until you got spooked and ran away.'

'I got—' She cut herself off with a shake of her head. 'What exactly do you think spooked me?'

'Who the hell knows?' Sawyer asked, the anger he'd been stifling the last seven months erupting. Fortunately, no one but her was around to hear it. 'Not me, that's for sure. You told me we made a mistake. I had to accept it.'

'But you did accept it,' she said, her jaw locked, her words steady. 'You didn't ask me why I thought it was a mistake. You said "are you sure" and "I don't agree" and that was it.'

'Because you said you were sure and that my disagreement didn't matter.'

'And you respected me *so much* that you let me go.'

She gave a frustrated—or was it helpless?—sigh. He bit back his own frustration. What was she saying? That it was his fault? He hadn't been the one to walk out. Except in the silence that followed, his heart told him it didn't matter.

'What do I need to say for you to come home?' he asked quietly.

Her eyes gleamed. 'You don't want me back, Sawyer. I'm not worth the effort.'

'You are.'

'No.' She cupped his cheek. He was embarrassed at how much the contact meant to him. How it soothed that ache in his chest. 'But you love me so much you don't see it.'

'Help me understand,' he said, his voice broken. 'Please, just help me understand.'

Her hand dropped. She wiped a tear from her face.

'Look, Sawyer, maybe I shouldn't have come. Our wounds were healing. I just opened them up again.'

'They weren't healing,' he spat out. 'They'll never heal.'

She let out an uneven breath. 'It's probably better if we don't see one another again.'

'We have an agreement,' he growled. 'Or are you going to break that promise, too?'

She pursed her lips. 'Fine. I'll come to your family events per our *agreement*. Because I promised, and I've…' She bit her lip. 'I've broken enough promises to you.' When she met his gaze now, she looked steady. 'But that's it. We need to move forward and… We need to move forward.'

He didn't reply. Moments later, she was gone.

Chapter Eighteen

One Day, Now

'Oh,' she said when she saw it. Sawyer made a similarly dismayed sound from beside her. They stared for a moment, then Zoey took out her phone and called Parker.

'A *spa*?' she asked the moment she heard his voice.

'Hold on.' There was some noise on the other end, followed by silence. Finally, Parker spoke. 'How's it going?'

'Wonderful, thanks. How are things there?'

'Good. The picnic seems to be a success and people are starting to pile in for the concert.'

'Great.' She waited a beat. 'So, um… Were you just not going to tell me the "meal" you arranged for Sophia was at a fancy hotel? Or that I was going to be led to the hotel's spa immediately after to enjoy a few treatments?'

'Oh.'

'*Oh?*'

'I…forgot. About some of it.'

'You forgot? I'm supposed to believe you forgot?'

'Yes.' There was a brief pause. 'Please.'

She managed to stop her laugh in time.

'You know you paid for these things, right?'

'I definitely know I paid for them,' he replied dryly. 'At least my future sister-in-law is able to enjoy them.'

Now she did laugh. 'You're full of it.'

'I know. According to your sister, it's one of my most annoying characteristics.' He chuckled. It cut off abruptly. 'You've got to help me, Zoey. I'm freaking out.'

She blinked. 'Like, right now? You sound fine.'

'Yeah, but not to your sister. She's onto me.' Now that he'd said it, she could almost hear him sweating. 'She's asking me questions I don't know how to answer.'

'Like what?'

'Why I'm going missing so often.'

'Why *are* you going missing so often?'

'First, it was the carriage stuff. Then I had to make sure the fireworks would go off as planned. After that, I went to the band to tell them about my plans—'

'The band?'

'Yeah. I'm going to call Soph up after the band plays.' He was smiling, she was sure of it. He was smiling at this dumbass plan of his. 'We're handing over the cheque to the charity. I'll do it then.'

'In, um…in front of the crowd?'

'Yeah. When the fireworks go off. It'll be great.'

'Will it though?' she asked, her voice thin.

Sawyer lifted his brows. She shook her head.

'What do you mean?'

'I mean…it's Sophia. Would she, um… Would she want her proposal to be that public?'

She closed her eyes as she waited for the answer. Winced when the seconds ticked by.

He swore.

'There you go.'

'How did I get it so wrong?' he asked, panic weighing down each word.

'You didn't get it entirely wrong,' she said soothingly. 'The fireworks thing is good.'

'*Zoey.*'

'Parker, it's fine. You need to take a deep breath. Now,' she barked, when she could hear his panicked inhales. 'Again. There you go.' She gave him a moment, then continued. 'Okay. Here's what you're going to do. After this call, you'll speak with the band and tell them you'll no longer need their assistance. You'll arrange for the cheque to be handed over without you. Before the fireworks go off, you'll find a private place in a nice spot in the garden. You'll tell her you love her or whatever, go on one knee, and propose to her.'

'Yeah,' he said after a moment. 'Yeah, I can do that.'

'Yes you can.' She waited a beat. 'And you'll stop acting suspiciously in front of Sophia now because everything is sorted out and you can be at ease with your plan.'

His exhale was loud. 'I owe you.'

'With the meal and the spa stuff, let's call it even,' she said dryly. 'Actually—Sawyer and I might order something for your account to tip the scales. Don't be surprised when it's charged to your credit card.'

She ended the phone call while he was still replying. Turned to find Sawyer with a small smile. She shrugged.

'I was being too nice. He can't expect that kind of treatment from our family.'

'Well,' he murmured, that stupid smile widening. 'You showed him.'

'One can hope.'

But she smiled, too. For much too long they stood smiling at one another. Like idiots.

'It was nice what you did for him,' he said eventually.

'I have no idea what you're talking about.'

'You coached him through his proposal. Which he was freaked out about, if your responses were any indication.'

'You must have misheard.'

'Take the compliment, Zo.'

She narrowed her eyes. 'Keep going and I'll tell the masseuse you have a tight spot in the nook between your neck and your shoulder.'

His eyes widened. 'I'm ticklish there.'

'I remember.'

He stared a moment longer, chuckled. 'You're the worst at taking compliments.'

'You weren't complimenting me.'

'You're a good sister. And sister-in-law. You care about your family.'

'I told you I've changed.'

'You've always cared about them.' His eyes were serious. 'You don't remember how much of your feelings you hid when your father was sick so they wouldn't worry about you?'

She opened her mouth, but it felt as if a tennis ball had been shoved inside her throat, blocking whatever she wanted to say.

'Am I wrong?' he asked quietly. 'Did you do what

you just did for a reason other than the fact that you care about them?'

She swallowed. Not so she could answer his question or comment on his observation. She wanted to speak. To say anything that would derail this perplexing conversation.

'The first time I met Parker, Sophia was basically naked in her bedroom with him.' It was the first thing that came to mind. 'He was cool as a frozen cucumber.'

'Cucumber,' Sawyer said with a frown. Derailment successful, she thought. 'It's "as cool as a cucumber."'

'You're focusing on *that* detail of what I said?'

'You know I hate it when people mess up metaphors.'

'He was as cool as a frozen cucumber,' she said deliberately. 'It's a simile. Besides, what about cucumbers make them naturally cool? Cooler than any other fruit or vegetable, I mean. There's nothing special about cucumbers. Unless you put them in the fridge or freezer, in which case they'd be cool. Hence cool as a frozen cucumber.' She rolled her eyes at his grin. 'Don't smile at me like I'm a small child you have to indulge.'

'I'm not,' he said. But the fool was still smiling. 'Your brain is still so special, Zo.'

'Is that a compliment?'

'Always.'

Her heart filled. For a moment, things almost felt like they used to. Until she remembered she couldn't change that she'd destroyed their relationship. Friendship and marriage.

'Is that why you like him? Because he's cool?' Sawyer asked into the silence. 'Parker?'

'Yeah.' She cleared her throat when the word came

out hoarse. 'He doesn't take my nonsense either, which is generally a sign of good character. And he really loves Soph.' She lifted a shoulder. 'He's a great guy.'

Sawyer was watching her carefully.

'He seems like a good guy,' he said after a while. 'Lisa had high praise for him and the article he wrote about her. Plus, he planned a charity event to aid dementia research. Guy's basically a saint.'

'I wouldn't go that far.' Not out loud, at least. 'Parker's mother has dementia. Which Lisa must have told you?' She got confirmation by means of a nod. 'I don't think he liked how helpless he felt when she was diagnosed. This was a way to process his feelings. Do something good.'

'He's also paying for us to relax at a spa.'

'There's that, too.'

'Excuse me?' a woman said, appearing out of nowhere. Both Sawyer and Zoey turned. 'Would you like to change into your robes now? We'll walk you through what we have planned once you're done.'

They followed her to the changing rooms. Before they went in, Zoey said, 'I think I figured out the cucumber thing.'

'Yeah?'

'There's a high likelihood someone with a penis made up that comparison. That's why the cucumber, out of all the fruits and vegetables, was deemed cool. Because of its phallic similarities.'

Sawyer laughed, the sound echoing against the tiles of the small space.

'By that logic, bananas would be cool, too.'

'Cucumbers are bigger,' Zoey said breezily. 'Aspirational, unlike the more realistic—' she wrinkled her nose '—for some—banana.'

She could still hear his laughter as she walked into the changing room. This time, it echoed in her chest, a ball of light that only he could get bouncing in her chest. A ball that hadn't bounced in two years.

'If you'll take off your robes, we'll be back in a few minutes.'

The masseuses left an awkward silence behind in the small room. Which was a feat, considering the room had been designed to facilitate calmness. The lights were dimmed, the smell of essential oils permeating the air. Peaceful music sounded through unseen speakers. Still, he felt awkward.

'I guess, um…'

Zoey's voice trailed off. He didn't dwell on her uncertainty. Cleared his throat instead.

'I'll turn around. You can take your robe off and cover yourself. When you're done, I'll do the same.'

'Yeah. Okay.'

He turned around, though it wouldn't help to keep his imagination from running wild. He'd known that even when he suggested it. He couldn't suddenly forget the hours they'd spent together wearing nothing. Having her nearly naked nearby certainly wouldn't help. His memories of her body haunted him almost as often as they teased him. He rarely knew which was better: knowing that he'd had and lost her; or remembering the time they'd shared and knowing it wouldn't have happened if he hadn't taken a chance.

Not that it mattered. His brain was already shuffling through the filing cabinet of his memories of her. It settled on the night of their one-month anniversary. It wasn't that different to their other nights, but it still stood out. Perhaps because of the awe he'd felt looking at Zoey. Knowing it, an unwanted desire triumphantly held up the memory of Zoey naked.

Her skin was magnificent. Smooth and brown, it was an endless desert he wanted to explore despite knowing it would have him dying of thirst. That didn't change his mind about it. It did make him think about tasting her lips, seeing if they could quench his thirst. She liked it when he lightly brushed them. She would moan, before nipping at him, opening her mouth to invite him in.

He was a dying man by then, but he didn't care. He'd run his hands along the curves of her, the dunes of the desert, gripping flesh as though it were really sand. But it didn't slip through his fingers; no, he was rewarded with the softness beneath her skin. She had a lot of that softness around her belly, her hips. Parts of her he'd been determined to explore after admiring them from a distance for so long.

Were they still there? She looked leaner, but Zoey had one of those bodies clothing didn't do justice to. Some outfits obscured the curves of her body entirely. Others exploited them. Those were the ones he preferred. She'd laughed at him when he'd told her that.

'Of course you prefer it,' she'd said. 'It leaves nothing to the imagination.'

'Good thing, too.' He nuzzled her neck. 'My imagination could never have conjured up this.'

'Hmm.' The throaty moan had gone right to his groin. 'I like that you're the only one who knows what the reality is.'

He'd kissed her, possessively, although he wouldn't have admitted it out loud. He didn't own her, had no desire to, but that admission had sent a powerful thrill through him. She hadn't complained, he thought, remembering what that moment had led to.

'Sawyer?' Her voice snapped him out of his lust-fuelled daydreams. 'I'm done.'

He grunted.

He wasn't proud of the blunt response, but he couldn't help it. His body had reacted to the memories. Knowing she was *right there* did nothing to tame it. He took off his robe, sliding under the towel on the massage bed. Lying on his stomach wasn't particularly comfortable in his current state, but that was for the best. He needed the reminder of where he was. The masseuse shouldn't see him like this. Certainly not with his wife metres away.

Ex-wife, his brain reminded him. He mentally rolled his eyes at its helpfulness *now*, after it had handed him the memories. But it was right. In all the ways that counted, Zoey was his ex-wife.

It was a conclusion that didn't help him—except it floated around his mind throughout the massage. The good news was that he was no longer thinking about Zoey's body. The bad news was that his heart was providing reasons why *exes* wasn't a good title for them.

They still had chemistry. The kiss in the carriage proved it.

He still liked her on a fairly basic level. She had a great sense of humour. His lips curved even now in memory of the cucumber. She was compassionate. Reluctantly, sometimes, as was the case with her brother-in-law, but reluctance didn't stop her. She was smart. Passionate. The way her face lit up when she talked about her job had been a delight. Loyal. She was keeping to their marriage vows despite their estrangement. So was he, but she didn't know that. Couldn't use it as motive. And damn if her buying things they didn't have during their marriage didn't kick him in the heart.

Did he describe all that as 'fairly basic'?

He hadn't even got to how she saw right through him. Right to the hurt he'd been hiding. He *was* worried that Lisa's existence meant he couldn't trust his knowledge of his family. Or that he couldn't trust his family at all. And he was angry about that. In no small part because of how hard he'd worked his entire life to make sure his actions made his family proud.

Maybe that was why he hadn't told them about his marriage until it was too late. They'd be disappointed in him. Or disapprove of him. He couldn't stand even the idea of it.

But what did they do? They kept his sister a secret. Despite the fact that he didn't think he had any siblings. Despite the fact that after his parents' death, he felt alone. How much would having a sister have changed the psychology of his childhood? Would he have been bullied as much? Would he have felt so alone? Would that conversation he overheard between his aunt and uncle weeks after they'd taken him in affected him so much?

Every time I look at him, I see her face.

He'd desperately wished he'd looked like his father then. He didn't want to give his aunt and uncle any reason not to keep him. He was a scared kid who'd lost his parents; he was desperately seeking some stability. When his aunt and uncle hadn't let his similarity to his mother keep them from adopting him, he was so relieved. So relieved he…he tried to make sure he never disappointed them.

Despite the massage, his entire body tensed.

What the hell was he supposed to do with that realisation?

Chapter Nineteen

One Day, Four Years, Two Months Ago

Zoey shouldn't have responded to Sawyer's invites. Sure, she agreed to attend family events as his fake girlfriend, but that helped *no one*. She knew that. Yet she still found herself buying a new dress; wearing it on the date that had appeared on her calendar three months before; getting her hair and make-up done.

'Where are you going?' Sophia asked as she got out her car.

Zoey swore under her breath. She'd been caught. She thought she'd be able to sneak out since Soph was getting groceries. Her mother had accepted her flimsy 'out with friends' excuse, but Sophia wouldn't let her get away that easily. Sophia knew Zoey didn't have friends. Friendship implied some kind of symbiotic relationship. But Zoey was a parasite. There was no mutual benefitting in a relationship with her.

'Out.'

'Really?' Sophia's eyes were sharp. They always were. It was highly annoying. 'Anywhere particular?' Her tone was mildly interested.

'An event.'

'Hmm.'

'A sixtieth birthday party.'

'Friend of yours?'

'Ha ha.'

'Right. Forgot you don't have friends.'

Zoey exhaled at Sophia's spot-on knowledge.

'No, wait,' Sophia interrupted. 'You do have friends. Well, you had a friend.'

'Oh, no,' Zoey said, shaking her head and opening the door of her beat-up second-hand car. It was the best she could afford. She'd bought it to prove to herself she wasn't a complete burden on those around her. 'We're not doing this.'

Moving quicker than Zoey had ever seen Sophia move, Sophia ran to Zoey's car and kept her from closing the door after she got in.

'Zo, you haven't spoken about Sawyer in years. Literal years. Ever since you got back from—'

'Soph, please. You're going to make me late.'

'Are you seeing him?'

Zoey stared ahead of her. Pure stubbornness, but it was the only way she was going to get out of a conversation she really didn't want to be having.

'Zoey.'

Sophia's voice changed into something more serious. More concerned. It was the same voice she used when she was having the 'actions have consequences' talk. When Zoey had come home after a three-month disappearance and had to explain that the university didn't want her back. That conversation had been awful. Zoey had no desire to repeat it now, especially after a year of trying to prove she could do better.

'Fine.' Sophia exhaled. 'You don't have to tell me. But be safe, okay? Call me if you need anything.'

Zoey softened. 'I am really going to a sixtieth birthday party.' She waited a beat, considering. 'Sawyer's aunt.'

'Oh.'

'You know you want to say more than "oh."'

'Yeah, but the moment I do you'll stop giving me information.'

'Good point. Moot though, since I won't be giving you more information anyway.' Zoey closed the door to Sophia's laugh, but she opened her window. 'I'll be back around eight.'

'You sure?'

'I'll let you know if it changes.'

But it wouldn't, and Sophia's question had stirred unhappiness inside her. She drove the rest of the way simmering in that unhappiness. It was likely an excuse to ignore her nerves. She kept in touch with Sawyer's aunt every now and then. Aunt Pat was an easy woman, and she'd always been kind to Zoey. Even when she didn't approve of Zoey and Sawyer pretending to be together.

When Zoey had seen the invitation to Aunt Pat's birthday, she knew she couldn't refuse it. They would have to pretend to be together again. *She* would have to pretend like that didn't kill her.

The thought made her nauseous. Then hyperventilate. She had to take the deep breaths her grief counsellor had taught her to do to calm herself. It wasn't lost on her that facing her husband, her ex-best friend, was evoking the same physical feelings losing her father had. But it *was* the end of her marriage that had pushed her to get help for her grief, after all. She'd tried to ignore it, done everything including marrying her best friend to avoid it. But that had destroyed her friendship with Sawyer and left her feeling even emptier. Things only got worse from there. Darkness had become darker until she knew she had to do something about it.

She exhaled shakily as she pulled into the driveway of Aunt Pat's house. She found an empty space at the back of a row of cars, which meant she'd have to pull out should any of them want to leave. Which was fine, since she was only coming to show her face. As soon as she did, she was *gone*.

The brick house was tall and stately. The front had vines crawling over it, and along with the white rims of the windows and the white door, added to the older feel of the house. It had a large garden, the greenest grass she'd ever seen, and trees that seemed appropriate. She had never learnt the names of trees because 'appropriate' was a good enough description for brown poles that exploded in a shock of green at their tops.

It was the kind of house that was on television. Sawyer's uncle was a lawyer, Aunt Pat a lecturer, and apparently that meant they could afford a large house in one of the most expensive suburbs in Cape Town. Zoey looked at the other houses in the area. There was a double-storey across the way that was enclosed with glass, though she couldn't see inside it. Another double-storey stood beside it, but this one was closed up like a vault. Most of the houses were similar in size—and in the fact that they all screamed of money.

A twinge went down her spine. Discomfort, she thought, walking to the front door. She'd felt it every time she visited Sawyer. She didn't like feeling like she was unwelcome, and money always made her feel that way. She was getting used to it in her job, since working with people who were more senior and thus had a lot of money was forcing her to. But the job also made her see that often, people with money thought themselves better based on the simple fact that they had it. They rarely treated those they viewed as underlings with respect, and would make demands so ridiculous Zoey often had to defer to her boss because she didn't know how to handle it.

It was nice to finally put her finger on what about Sawyer's neighbourhood made her so uncomfortable.

'Zoey?'

The door opened before she could think about it anymore. It was Carly, Sawyer's baby cousin, Aunt Pat's 'bonus' child. She'd been named after Grandma Carla.

'Hey, Carly,' Zoey forced herself to say.

'We didn't know you were coming.'

Ah, from the mouths of babes. Sure, this babe was fourteen, but she'd spoken truth and there was no way Zoey was going to—

'Haha,' Carly said, pointing at her in laughter. 'You should see your face.'

'So you've become a little brat since I've last been to visit, huh?' Zoey said, relief mingling with amusement. 'Do you know what I do to brats?'

She pulled Carly into a chokehold, pretending to mess up the girl's hair but really only pulling on her ponytail. She was rewarded with a gleeful laugh, a poke in the stomach, and suddenly Zoey realised how much she missed the entire family, not only Sawyer.

But mostly Sawyer.

'Are you done accosting my cousin?'

As if she conjured him from her thoughts—which she already knew was impossible, or he'd have been her sex slave already—Sawyer stood in the front room. He was wearing trousers and a shirt. It made her knees weak. It made her want to jump into his arms and mess up his hair. It made her want…it made her want *him*.

'Er, yeah,' Zoey said, letting Carly go free. 'We were talking.'

'That's talking?' Carly asked, smoothing her hair indignantly although her lips were still curved. 'I think you need to re-evaluate that definition.'

'The mouth on this kid,' Zoey told Sawyer. She didn't look at him to see if he agreed. 'Maybe I need to re-evaluate how to talk to you.'

She pretended to lurch at Carly. With a squeal, the girl jumped back.

'Don't you dare!' Carly said in a way that made Zoey think she was supposed to dare.

'Not now, Carly,' Sawyer interrupted. 'Your mom's looking for you. Something about a dance?'

'I told her I didn't want to do it!' Carly grumbled, her attitude changing into sullen teenager seamlessly. 'See you later, Zo.'

'See you,' Zoey said, amused by the…what could only be called stomping Carly was doing. Until she re-alised she was now alone with Sawyer.

'Hey,' she said. 'Am I late?'

'You're on time.'

That was all he said. He leaned his back against the wall. Folded his arms. Stared at her. She lifted her hand, rubbed her chin as if she were scratching an itch. Really, she was making sure no drool had slipped from her lips.

Great. On top of everything else she was feeling that day, she'd have to add horny.

'Carly's got a new personality.'

'It's been a year since you saw her.'

'I know,' she said as coolly as he'd said his words. 'I only got this one invitation to a family event though.'

'That's the only reason you'd want to see me?'

'It's what we agreed to, isn't it?' she said, dodging his question. When his face hardened, she sighed. 'Look, maybe it's a bad idea I decided to come. I'm going to—'

'You can't,' he interrupted. 'I took a gamble and told people you were coming. They want to see you.'

Panic fluttered in her belly. 'Make something up.'

'I've been making stuff up for a year,' he said, pushing off the wall. 'You're here now. Carly saw you. You have no way of getting out of this.'

She sighed again, this time in defeat.

'What did you tell them?' she asked, walking beside him through the front room into a large dining area. Food was set up on tables, as were drinks, but the guests were outside.

'That you were visiting Angie in Korea.'

'The entire year?'

He slanted her a look. 'Go with it.'

'You need to get a handle on your anger,' Zoey told him quietly. She handed him a glass of champagne, clinked it with her own glass and smiled. As though they were happy and free and not unhappily married.

'Why?' he asked sullenly. 'Is it hurting your feelings?'

She angled her back to the party, her eyes flashing.

'Hey, man, you're the one who invited me. You told me to go with it. I'm telling you that going with it isn't exactly easy when you're scowling at everyone.'

She was right, though a petulant part of him didn't want her to be. Or didn't care that she was. He was still trying to figure it out.

At some point in the last year, the hope and longing he had for her turned into something darker. It was tinged with the pain of abandonment and disappointment. Of regret and guilt. He didn't know what to do with it, so he clumped it all together, tossed it to the side and pretended it didn't exist. When he felt the ball of it roll closer, he buried himself deep into his work.

Fortunately, his company saw his availability as an asset. Apparently, a man with no family and no social life was the ideal candidate to do the dirty work on new deals. He'd been put on three new accounts in the last year, and with each, had proven he was a decent bet. He was having a meeting with his manager next week. Sawyer had heard whispers of a promotion.

His anger might have been useful with his job, but it wasn't at his aunt's birthday. He released a breath.

'Fine.'

She rolled her eyes. 'Gee, thanks.'

There was hurt beneath the acerbic tone. Both shame and satisfaction cartwheeled in his chest. He didn't like either.

'Zoey, sweetheart. With everything that's been happening, I haven't been able to talk with you.'

Zoey's smile was already in place when she turned

to welcome Aunt Pat. Sawyer was relieved. His aunt had been giving him a hard time about working too hard. Something about work/life balance and how Zoey being out of the country didn't mean he needed to stop living.

What about her being out of my life?

He wanted to ask the question more times than he could count. Instead he promised to do better and as soon as his aunt left his flat, went back to work. Zoey being here now should buy him some more time.

'Don't worry,' Zoey said pleasantly. 'It wouldn't be fair to monopolise the attention of the guest of honour anyway.'

'Oh, please.'

Aunt Pat waved a hand, but she beamed. She loved having the people she cared about around her. It was rare that it happened. Sure, they celebrated her on Mother's Day and her birthday. But those celebrations didn't include the other people she cared about. Friends, colleagues. Zoey, too. It was why he couldn't avoid inviting her. She was part of the inner circle. So he sacrificed his own feelings for the sake of his aunt's. Just as she'd done for him so many years ago.

'Tell me, how was Korea?' his aunt asked suddenly. 'It's been hell without you. Sawyer's been going out of his mind.' Aunt Pat winked at him.

'Has he?' Zoey said mildly. 'That's nice to know.'

He snorted, but ducked his head as if embarrassed, before his aunt could see the snort had been scorn.

'It was lovely. It's an entirely different world.' She spoke about some of the things she'd done, which was interesting to Sawyer, too, considering she'd never been there. Or had she? 'And of course, it was lovely to see Angie again.'

'I can imagine.' Aunt Pat squeezed Zoey's arm. 'I thought it was a bit excessive for you to be away for a year, but after what you girls went through with your father… Well,' Aunt Pat said with another squeeze. 'Let's just say you seem better. It's done you a world of good.'

'Pat,' his uncle called from the other side of the garden. 'It's time to cut the cake.'

'Just like a wedding,' his aunt said gleefully. 'Don't leave before you say goodbye, dear. Oh, and thank you for those pictures. They were lovely.'

She left them both staring after her.

'Did you actually go to Korea this year?' he asked quietly.

'No.'

'You knew a lot about it for someone who hasn't.'

'I repeated what Angie told me.'

'An expert liar then.'

'Don't do that,' she said mutedly. Lacking the fire she'd aimed at him earlier. 'I did it because you asked me to. And because we both know it would devastate her to know the truth.'

'At least someone would know the truth,' he said under his breath. Shook his head. 'No, you're right. I'm sorry. There's some…residual resentment.'

'Some?' she asked, her mouth quirking up.

Reluctantly, his mouth did the same. 'More or less.'

'I think we both know it's more.'

He chuckled. He couldn't help it, though he knew it probably wasn't the reaction he should have gone with.

'What pictures?' he asked.

'Oh.' He faced her in time to see her cheeks turn red. 'They were nothing.'

'I thought you said you weren't a liar.'

'It was for a good cause,' she defended herself, but her colour darkened.

'Come on. Now you have to tell me.'

'They were nothing.'

'Zo.'

'No, really, they were—' She broke off. Exhaled sharply. 'Fine. They were pictures of Korea.'

'Pictures… Wait—you sent her pictures of Korea?'

'The ones Angie sent me, yeah.'

'How did she know you were— How did you know—' He shook his head. 'Explain.'

She bit her lip. 'I've been keeping in touch.'

'With my aunt?'

'Yeah.'

He would let his mind process that later.

'So she asked you about Korea.'

'Yeah.'

'And you didn't think it was weird?'

'I figured you told her that's why I wasn't around.' She shrugged when he looked at her.

'You know me well' was all he said.

'It wasn't hard to figure out.'

'You knew she thought you were there?'

'Yep.'

'And you didn't think to tell me?'

'You already told me to pretend.'

'Fair point.' He paused. 'Can I see the pictures?'

'No.'

'No?'

'No,' she confirmed. 'They're…private.'

'How can pictures someone else sent you, that you then sent to my aunt, be private?'

'They just are,' she muttered. 'You're like a dog with a piece of meat.'

'A bone.'

'Bones have meat on them.'

He caught the laugh before it could come this time. 'Just show me the pictures.'

'I will not.'

'Zoey—'

'Because,' she continued, her face blood red now, 'they're photoshopped.'

'You photoshopped pictures Angie sent you? Why?'

She mumbled something.

'I didn't hear that.'

'I photoshopped myself into them,' she said, the words bursting from her.

It took him a second before laughter burst from him.

Chapter Twenty

One Day, Now

'When they said mud treatment, I didn't think this.'

'No,' Zoey murmured. 'Neither did I.'

They both stared at the small glass box. Inside were two large bowls of what she assumed were mud. Steam swirled through vents. There was a different set of holes above them they were told was a shower. Neither of them had their swimsuits. Fortunately, the box was private, so no one would see them in their underwear.

Except, of course, the other. Which was probably as problematic as the public seeing them.

'You should go,' Sawyer told her. 'Parker wanted you to experience this. I'll wait in the change rooms.'

'Don't be an idiot,' she said sternly. 'We're adults. We can see one another in our underwear. It's basically a cotton bathing suit.'

Determined to prove herself right, she stripped off her robe and opened the glass door. The heat hit her immediately, and she paused to retie her twists at the top of her head. They'd get heavy with the heat and moisture, but she tried to be thankful for it. It would provide her with a free deep conditioning. The weight was a 'suffer for beauty' thing.

She'd hated it when her mother told her that when she was a kid; she hated it now in the lie she told herself.

She shook her head, moved forward, and went to the mud bowls. The door closed behind her. She lifted both bowls, turning to offer him one. But her arm paused as she reached out, her mind stunned at what she saw in front of her.

Muscle. A bunch of muscle. Hard, sculpted muscle. Muscle that made her want to bend down and examine its lines closely. With her tongue.

She swallowed. Jutted out the bowl forcefully.

'Use this one.'

'No,' he said calmly, examining what was in his hands and what was in hers. 'I think we first do that one—' he pointed to the bowl in her hand '—and then this one.'

'You're an expert on mud treatments?'

'No.' His lips twitched. 'That one's just the exfoliator and this one is smoother.'

She looked down and saw he was right. Damn it.

'Okay, we'll do it in that order then.'

Silently, she lathered her skin with mud, hoping to the heavens she wouldn't have to watch him do the same. Her skin was prickly, and it had nothing to do with the mud. It was because her husband had somehow turned into a muscular god from another dimension and hadn't warned her of his powers. She was so aware of him, of every movement of his body. It didn't at all help that she turned away from him so that she wouldn't have to see him put mud on himself. She could picture him doing it; she could feel him doing it. It had the same effect on her body as watching him would have.

A lie, probably, but she couldn't imagine feeling lustier than she already did.

She took a seat as far away from him as possible, leaned her head back against the wall.

'Come on, it hasn't been that bad.'

His voice, low and gravelly, bridged the distance between them. It crawled up her legs, lingered between her thighs. She shifted.

'What hasn't been?'

'This reunion.'

He was watching her intently. It shouldn't have been erotic, especially with that arrogant curve at his mouth.

It was.

'It hasn't been what I expected,' she answered truthfully.

'You didn't imagine us talking, lathered in mud?'

'Surprisingly, no,' she said with a curve of her own lips. 'We were much cleaner.'

'Doesn't sound like us.'

His eyes flashed. With danger. With heat. The steam swirling around them no longer seemed to come from the vents, but from the locking of their eyes.

She dipped her head. 'Are you flirting with me, husband?'

Again, his eyes flashed. She couldn't tell with what this time; it was gone too fast. She only knew what it left behind: a warning.

What are you doing, Zoey? it asked. She leaned forward, daring herself to answer.

'Do you want me to flirt with you?'

She thought about it. 'Logically? No.'

'Illogically then.'

She smiled. 'Yes.'

He got up, moved to sit beside her, but he didn't touch her.

She angled her head. 'Tease.'

He chuckled. And though there was distance between them, she felt the vibration dance over the space and settle on her skin. It made her feel buzzed, like she'd drank just enough to enjoy being intoxicated, but not regret it.

She knew she would regret it though. She was achy with need, but there was more to it than simple desire. It was layered with emotion, the simplest of which she couldn't even peel back to look under. She was too afraid to, the fact of it something that had taunted her long before she'd seen him again that day.

She missed him. Not only as a friend, too, but as a lover. As her husband.

Damn it, she cursed herself, wondering why she'd acknowledged it.

'What are you thinking?' he asked. When she looked at him, he was staring at her again. This time, it lacked the intensity of desire. That intensity was replaced by emotion.

It reminded her of the man who'd loved her and had somehow got her to fall in love with him without her even realising it. He never shied away from his feelings. He never shied away from making her see it. After she left, that changed.

It was one of the things she missed the most. He was so careful around her. Save for that first reunion after she left, at his cousin's wedding. But she couldn't blame him. How could she be hurt with him shutting her out when she'd done the same to him?

'Too much,' she murmured a reply. 'I'm thinking about too much.'

'So tell me one thing.'

She turned her body toward him. 'You really want to know?'

Unblinking eyes stared back at her. 'Yes.'

'Okay.' But still, she hesitated. Then decided that if they were going to divorce, she'd be going through hell soon anyway. She might as well welcome the burn. 'I miss you.' His expression tightened. 'You asked.'

'What could you possibly gain by telling me that?' His voice was gruff.

'What could you possibly gain by asking me *that*?'

He exhaled. Stood. Paced the small distance between the glass walls.

'You asked me for a divorce. Now you're saying you miss me. What does that mean?'

'Does it have to mean something?'

But he was right. Welcoming the burn only led to injury.

Oh, this was a mess. One she created. She thought she was cleaning up by asking him for a divorce. Hoped that they could finally put their relationship behind them and move forward. It hung over her. Their marriage… It was one of the biggest illustrations of her recklessness. She'd taken the relationship she cherished most in the world and turned it into… into…*this*.

'Yeah, it has to mean something,' he said angrily. 'It does mean something, except I'm scrambling to figure out what. I have no idea what's going on in your head. I haven't since the moment you walked out on me the first time.'

'Sawyer—'

'Tell me,' he interrupted. 'Did I do something wrong? Did you realise one day that I wasn't enough for you? Or were you being selfish? Were you walking out on me because you were thinking of you?'

Surprise took hold of her body. While it did, she sat, staring at him. Idly, she noted his posture. His entire body was tensed. The muscles on either side of his jaw were pulsing, as though he were clenching and unclenching them. His eyebrows were basically a unibrow, he was frowning so hard. And his hands were curled into fists.

The anger wasn't something that had appeared out of the blue. If his questions, which went back further than when they'd last seen one another, hadn't given it away, everything about the way he looked now would.

'You've been keeping that in for a long time, haven't you?' She didn't wait for a reply, afraid of what he would say in this state. 'You're right. You deserve answers.'

He blinked, his frown smoothing out, his fingers unfurling.

'I am?'

She almost smiled. Managed to catch it in time. 'Yes, you're right. It's been too long that you've gone without them.' She hesitated. Inhaled. Blew out the steam that had come with the air. 'And if this is going to end, we should start being honest with one another.'

He snorted. '"*We*."'

'Yes, we,' she said seriously. Noted his expression. Tilted her head. 'Maybe we need to start being honest with ourselves, too.'

'I'm not interested in you turning this around on me again.'

'I have no intention of turning anything around on anyone,' she replied with a slight shake of her head. 'I'm going to tell you what happened. Then you can—' She stopped herself. 'I'll tell you and maybe you'll figure out the rest yourself.'

She put her hands between her thighs. It was unfortunate, considering what they were talking about and its accompanying tension, that he noticed it pushed her breasts together. Of course, that made him think about how he'd been wrong earlier; she hadn't grown leaner. She just wore clothes that covered the best parts of her, as he predicted. Did that make him right? He didn't know. Couldn't figure it out either with her breasts staring him in the eye.

Focus, Wilson.

Obeying the mental voice, he sat down on the bench, thinking—barely—about how ridiculous it was that he was covered in mud to have a conversation he'd been wanting to have for six years.

'This had nothing do with whether or not you were enough for me.' She turned toward him. 'Do you really think you weren't enough?'

'You left.'

'Not because you did something wrong.'

'You were married to *me*, Zoey. You left *me*. How can that have nothing to do with me?'

'Okay,' she said after a moment. 'That's what happened according to the logic you're using. According to me and my logic, it was more because I was selfish.'

He could hear her breathing, loud and unsteady.

'I spent a good portion of my life being selfish. I married you because I was selfish. I didn't want to face the grief of my father's death. Not my own, not my family's. It was going to change my life, and not positively, and that scared me.' She brought her legs up. Rested her chin on them. 'But then your grandmother said that thing about you having feelings for me, and for the first time since my father was diagnosed, I wasn't scared. I mean, I was scared, but not a dread kind of fear. A… I don't know, a good kind. Like, "crap, this is going to change things, but in a good way."' She turned her head to look at him, now resting her cheek on her knees. 'I leaned into that when I shouldn't have. It was irresponsible.'

'You leaned into it when you shouldn't have,' he repeated. 'You're saying that it was a mistake.'

'Maybe,' she said. 'It's complicated. I… I hate what it did to us. I went into it for the wrong reasons.' She gave him a look similar to the one she'd given him earlier. When she implied he'd gone into this for reasons other than loving her. He was too angry to address it.

She sighed. 'That doesn't mean I wish it didn't happen, or that I regret it.'

'But you do, Zo,' he lashed out. 'How can you tell me marrying me was irresponsible and in the same breath tell me you don't regret it?'

'Because it taught me that my actions have consequences,' she snapped back, lifting her head. 'Real consequences for people I love.' Her chest expanded, contracted. 'I realised that during our marriage. I knew it on a basic level when I took that pregnancy test and remembered—'

'What?'

Despite the steam in the room, colour drained from her face.

'Zoey,' he said through his teeth. 'Were you pregnant? Did you not tell me we were going to have a baby? Do we have a child?' He moved forward. 'Did you have a miscarriage?'

'Stop,' she said, voice hoarse. 'It was a pregnancy scare. I wasn't pregnant. Not then, not ever.'

The ball of feelings that had been bouncing in his chest slowly dissolved. He didn't like that she hadn't told him. But something like this, for someone like Zoey… It made sense that she didn't.

'You took a pregnancy test and remembered what?' he forced himself to ask.

She blinked. 'Oh… I…' She stammered some more, and he realised she hadn't expected him to ask her to continue. Maybe she hadn't expected to continue herself. But she did. 'I took a pregnancy test. Three, actually. With each one, I realised why I couldn't be a parent. Why you deserved more than to parent with me, too.' She lowered her legs to the ground. 'I was too selfish.' Gave him a half-smile as if she expected him to agree. 'I forced everyone around me to take responsibility for my actions. Or to save me from the consequences of them.' She paused. 'I did it a long time after I left you, too. In smaller, less tangible ways. Like I was an addict, looking for excuses not to be responsible.'

She shook her head with a bark of laughter.

'All my faults became abundantly clear with each of those tests. How I was avoiding my feelings about my father's death. How I was avoiding my family. How could I be a parent when I couldn't take responsibility for anything? Even my own feelings?' There was the barest hint of a pause, before she whispered, 'If we had a kid, I knew I would mess them up. You'd blame yourself at first, like you're doing about the end of our marriage now. But then you'd blame me.'

He swallowed at the emotion in her voice, on her face. In her body. He couldn't stand it. It was strange because his need to comfort was driven by love, by loyalty, despite the estrangement that rivalled the length of the friendship that had caused that love, that loyalty. He also didn't know how she knew him so well. Oh, he could tell her he wouldn't have worried if they had a kid and the kid wasn't a good person. But he would have known it was a lie. Apparently, so would she. And his gut told him she was right about where he'd put the blame. Wasn't he doing that now?

Somewhere in it though, he was proud of her. Proud of the work she'd been doing on herself. He didn't think she was judging herself fairly, but since he accused her of being selfish earlier, he could see where she was coming from. Strangely, his anger helped him see the same characteristics that made him love Zoey—her spontaneity, her devil-may-care attitude—could be dangerous in certain situations.

But he'd contributed to *this* situation. Relationships were two-way streets; she couldn't take all the blame. She didn't though, he realised. The entire day, she'd been implying there was more to his motives to marry her. Maybe now was the time to think about it.

When she suggested they marry, he'd been elated. She wanted to marry him! She wanted *him*. He ignored her grief and how it might have been influencing her decision because she wanted him. He ignored his own hesitance, his own instincts because she wanted him, too. He knew who she was when he married her. He knew what she was going through. And if he was being honest, when she left, he knew there was more to it than her not wanting to be with him.

Yeah, he'd married her selfishly, too.

'I wish you'd spoken to me about it.' His voice was a plea for what could have been.

'And then what?' she asked with a hiccup. 'You would have brushed it off, told me I'd be a great parent. You would have put me back on my pedestal.'

He frowned. 'I never lied to you.'

'No,' she agreed. 'But you have, or had, a distorted view of me. I couldn't do anything wrong. Even when I did, you fixed it without even knowing.' He didn't reply. She lifted her brows. 'You don't believe me?'

'I don't agree with you.'

'Hmm.' There was a long silence. 'Do you know why Dan told everyone at school I slept with him?' She didn't wait for an answer. 'Because I told them he had a small penis. He couldn't make a date one day for a completely legitimate reason, and I responded by telling everyone he had a small penis. Which, of course, made the lie that I'd slept with him easier to believe.'

She stood, pressed the button to put on the shower, but she didn't look away from him, even when the water began to wash away the mud.

'I deserved that rumour. I was being petulant and childish. But you came in and saved the day, and no one dared make fun of me. Maybe I knew that you would come in and save me.' She lifted a shoulder. 'Because you always did; and I never learnt.'

'Until we got married.'

She angled her head in acceptance. 'You would have realised it someday,' she added. 'I would keep doing irresponsible things, and one day, you would have realised you were tired of taking care of it for me. You'd see that you deserved more. That you deserved someone who gave as much as you did, and didn't only take. You'd take me off that pedestal so damn fast, we'd both forget I was ever on it. That would have been worse than this,' she said softly. 'It would have been worse.'

Chapter Twenty-One

One Day, Four Years, Two Months Ago

'I refuse,' Zoey said.

'When did you become such a wuss?'

'Carly,' Sawyer and Zoey said at the same time.

He could hear the surprise in Zoey's voice. When he looked at her, she was biting her lip. It was the usual sign she was trying to hide her amusement. He could relate. Though he meant to admonish Carly, he was amused, too.

'What?' Carly asked.

'That's not the way we speak to guests.'

He squeezed his cousin's shoulder. She was in that awkward stage where her attitude sometimes got away from her. He didn't mind it. Put her in her place when he had to. But he always wanted her to know it was coming from love.

'Is Zoey a guest now?' Carly asked sweetly. 'I thought you two were dating.'

'Anyone who isn't part of the family is a guest.'

'I could have sworn she was part of the family a couple of years ago,' Carly muttered.

'You're right,' Zoey said suddenly. 'I should do this. I can't be a wuss.'

She winked when he looked over. The flutter echoed in his chest. It wasn't what he expected would happen when he invited her. He should have though. He had no control over his emotions around her. Including anger, apparently. But beneath whatever he felt initially was the pull. The attraction. The way he couldn't help but notice how cute she looked in her dress. Or how much he wanted to untie the hair that was gathered at the base of her neck.

For the sake of his sanity, he tried to cling to the anger.

'Are you sure?' he asked. 'You're playing with Phil. You know what he's like.'

She waved a hand. 'Please. Handling Phil will be a piece of cake.'

'Roux,' Phil barked, as if on cue. 'You in or what?'

Panic danced in her eyes, but she frowned. 'Of course. What do you think I am? A wuss?'

She winked at Carly now. Sawyer reminded himself of the anger. Ignored the amusement. Tried to. But not being amused by Zoey was the ultimate test of his self-control. Like when she told him she photoshopped herself into the pictures she sent his aunt. How could he not find that funny?

Besides, amusement was easier than the other emotions. The softness that had swept through him upon hearing she was keeping in touch with his family. The wave of appreciation that she'd gone along with his lies.

Carly was right; Zoey was part of the family. Whether he liked it or not, his family saw her that way. He only had to look at Grandma Carla beaming as Zoey took her place on the lawn to know it. His aunt had been thrilled to see her, too. No matter what was going on between the two of them, his family loved her. The fact that she was here, along with everything else that he'd seen that day, told her she didn't want to hurt them any more than he did.

He could deal with his anger; fight his amusement; ignore his feelings about her for a day. It was worth it.

Someone called for the balloons to be handed out and his attention went back to the game. It was a family tradition, playing at least one game at a birthday party. It had started out tame. The game matched the theme of the party. People didn't compete for the glory. They did it for fun.

But this was his family. Competitiveness was part of their DNA. Glory was the only reason to play. If the game was ridiculous, it didn't matter. In fact, the more ridiculous, the better. Which explained why their current game was 'Protect Your Balloon.' It was pretty straightforward—everyone got a balloon to protect. Except they also had to try and pop someone else's balloon. Last person standing was the winner.

He looked at Zoey. Poor, kind Zoey. It was the first time she was taking part in the game at a party. She'd refused until today. Something about their family being 'too much.' It was true. Sadly, they didn't care.

She was going to get slaughtered.

'Ready,' his aunt called. 'Set.'

'Go' was indicated by the blow of a whistle. Carly had got it for her mother as a gift. It was bedazzled and his aunt had shrieked when she opened it. The fact that she was excited by a sparkling whistle spoke volumes about her own competitiveness.

Sawyer tried to stay unbiased since he'd been se-
lected as referee, but his eyes went straight to Zoey. She
immediately put her balloon under her dress, offering
him a tantalising glimpse of her thighs. Then, she took
her earring out and ran straight for Phil.

His cousin wasn't expecting it. Mostly because
Phil's attention was on attacking. It was brilliant of
Zoey, really. Phil's strategy was *always* to attack. Anyone who'd paid attention then would know his defen-
sive strategies wouldn't be developed. Since Zoey had
spent literal years watching them play, she used the
knowledge to her advantage. With one quick twist,
Zoey popped her earring into Phil's balloon, before
putting it back into her ear.

'What the—' Phil's curse was cut off by a glare from
his mother. 'Time out!' he shouted instead. 'Did you
see that, Sawyer? Zoey used a weapon.'

'A weapon?' Zoey said innocently. 'What are you
talking about, Phil?'

The innocence she projected was helped by the fact
that she was stroking the balloon at her stomach, draw-
ing tiny circles into it as if she were pregnant. It sent
a wave of longing through him. Not to be a father; he
wasn't ready for that. But to have a family. To be a unit
with Zoey again. Perhaps that's why he said, 'I didn't
see anything.'

Phil exploded.

'There's no way Sawyer's unbiased when it comes
to Zoey. *No way.*'

Sawyer put up his hands in surrender. 'I'm not the
only judge here. Carly?'

'I didn't see anything.'

'*Bullshit!*'

'*Philip,*' Aunt Pat shouted from where she stood. 'Don't you dare speak to your sister that way! And if you can't play nicely, you won't play at all.'

'But—'

'My birthday, my rules.'

Phil slunk off, muttering under his breath. Zoey winked at Carly. When her eyes met his, she was more hesitant, but she smiled. He smiled back, suddenly tired of resisting. He missed her. Her naughtiness and her spark. Her kindness. He missed her as much as a friend as his wife. He wanted her back, even if it meant pushing his anger aside.

'Is the time-out done?' one of his cousins asked. In answer, another blow came from the whistle. The time-out was indeed done.

Zoey's strategy was much less nefarious now that she'd taken out her main competition. She dodged a lot, but mostly, she waited for the others to take her opponents out. Which worked for all of five minutes. Then someone bumped into her hard and her balloon popped. Sawyer called another time-out to make sure she was okay.

'Favouritism at its finest,' Phil called from the sidelines.

'Yeah, well, at least I stayed in the game for longer than ten seconds, Phil,' Zoey called over her shoulder, doing a small jump so the remains of the balloon could fall out from under her dress. She grinned when Phil said some not-so-nice things back to her, which earned him another rebuke from his mother.

'You know you just put a target on yourself for next time, right?' Sawyer asked when she stopped next to him.

Her lashes fluttered and he realised what he said. *Next time.* As if there would be one. But she didn't let him correct himself.

'I'll survive.'

The whistle blew again, and the game continued. Sawyer watched, but his attention was split between the game and Zoey. She was rubbing her stomach.

'You sure you're okay?'

'It stings,' she replied. 'Not badly, but enough for me to want to soothe it.'

'I'm sorry.'

'It's not your fault.'

'We taunted you into playing.'

'I agreed to play.' Suddenly, it felt like they weren't talking about the game anymore. Zoey turned and gave him a wry smile. 'You don't get to take responsibility for my actions anymore, Sawyer.'

Carly called a foul before he could reply, and his attention went back to the game. His mind lingered on what she said for the longest time after, so much so that later, when the festivities were winding down, he went to find her. She was alone at the pool. Most of his family was on the opposite side of the lawn, hovering around the heaters now that the weather had cooled.

Candles and flowers floated in the blue water, translucent thanks to the pool lights. Zoey had her legs in the water, kicking them occasionally. There was something about seeing her straighten her legs in front of her before wiggling her toes that made him smile.

'A lot of people are enjoying the heaters on the lawn.'

'Where's the fun in that?'

'I'm not sure fun is the right word,' he said, picking

up a chair and pulling it closer so he could sit next to her. 'Warm might be more accurate.'

The corners of her mouth lifted, the only indication that she was smiling.

'Maybe I'm afraid of the warm in case it melts my icy cold heart.'

'We both know that's not true.'

'You've thought it though,' she said softly. 'Rightly so. Only a cold-hearted bitch would ruin our relationship.'

'Zo…' He took a breath. 'I was angry earlier.'

'You have a right to be.'

'But I don't think you have a cold heart.'

'No?' Her voice was breathy. 'I feel cold.' She shifted back, so that her legs stretched out in front of her without touching the water. The position allowed them to look at one another. 'I feel…numb.' She hesitated. 'Then I come here and I spend a day with you and your family and I wobble.' She laughed lightly. 'I think that means I've already melted, doesn't it?'

His instincts tingled, like a superhero sensing danger. He supposed that wasn't the worst analogy. He hadn't used his power in a while, but he knew when Zoey was hurting. He couldn't tell if it was from the numbness, the coldness or because of what she felt around him.

'What's going on, Zo?'

'I'm a mess.'

He lowered to the ground, taking her hand. 'Talk to me.'

'No,' she said with a shake of her head. 'You're part of why I'm a mess. Or maybe I'm a mess because we're not friends or lovers or anything at the moment.'

She sighed. The sound was sad and mingled with the stir of the wind around them. He noticed she didn't let go of his hand.

'Fine. Give me a rundown.'

She smiled. 'Old school, huh?'

'Yeah,' he said with a faint smile. 'Old school.'

She meant it literally since the last time they'd done this was in school. Sometimes they wouldn't see one another for a while, and a lot would happen. So they developed the rundown: a quick summary about what was going on in their lives with a quick descriptor of how they felt about it.

'Okay.' It was a couple more seconds before she continued. 'It's still hard without my dad. My mom's in pain. So am I. Sophia is…well, she's doing her best to get us through it.' She rubbed her chest. 'My life isn't the same without you. It's another constant pain. There are days I wish I could talk to you, but I know I don't deserve that.'

She pulled her hand from his. He felt the absence of it as acutely as he did the absence of her in his life.

'Your turn.'

'Me?' he asked, his brain still trying to figure out what to do about her revelations.

'That's how the rundown works.'

Fair point.

'Um… I've been working really hard. Aunt Pat's worried, but it helps distract me from…from how different my life is without you.' He hesitated, but pushed on. 'I didn't realise how big a part of my life you were until you weren't there.' He swallowed the pain. 'Of course, I keep thinking about the end of things. How we got to this.'

She searched his face. Then she lowered back onto her forearms and slyly said, 'Simple, straightforward problems for the both of us, I see. Just like old times.'

The chuckle vibrated in his belly before he mirrored her position. When he got there though, the floor seemed more inviting so he lowered completely and lay on his back. Seconds later, she did the same thing.

'Things are tough at work?' she asked, breaking the silence.

'Not tough. There's a lot to do, but I'm offering.' He found a star in the sky that looked like it was twinkling directly at him. None of the others seemed as bright, so he kept looking at it. 'I might be up for a promotion.'

Her head whipped to the side. 'Yeah?' She punched his arm lightly. 'That's pretty damn impressive, Wilson. Good job.'

She bumped her shoulder with his, and the gesture warmed him. No—it was the praise. Or both. It was such a simple thing, but he loved her approval. He wondered how much of his hard work was so he could get it. In case she came back, and he could show her what he'd built for them.

But she wasn't coming back, he thought. Not for the first time. The second year of their separation had forced him to face some hard facts. Which was why he'd been so cold to her when she arrived. The hope inside him was small. It was that hope that was working for her, waiting for her to return. He needed more time to communicate the realisation that she wasn't returning to that hope. But it would happen. Eventually.

For now, he had these moments. Short and painful, but the sweetest pain. He'd never known what that meant until now. Until this. Until her.

'How about you?' he asked. 'How's work going?'

'Okay, I think?' she said. 'I'm still finding my feet. You know how the corporate world sees young women. They keep waiting for me to announce I'm leaving to start a family or something.' There was an awkward pause. 'Sorry,' she muttered.

'Don't apologise. Unless there's something you want to tell me?' he asked easily, though he wasn't sure how it came out that way when his throat was so tight.

She snorted. 'Please. We both know I'd make a terrible mother.'

'What?' He frowned. 'I don't think I agree with that.'

'You should. I made a terrible wife.'

'Not when you were trying.'

'But I stopped trying, didn't I?' she asked lightly, but he didn't for one minute believe she found the conversation easy. 'You can't do that when you're a parent. Or you shouldn't.'

'What are you saying?'

She slanted him a look. 'I just said it.'

'No, you tip-toed around it.'

'I called myself a terrible wife. How is that tip-toeing around it?'

'I'm not talking about you as a wife. I'm talking about that parent comment.' When emotion rippled across her face, he knew he was right. 'You think your parents stopped trying to raise you?'

'My father's dead, Sawyer,' she said flatly, although there was a twisted kind of amusement in her voice. 'Of course he stopped trying.'

'Maybe even before that, too, huh?'

Her lashes fluttered. 'Sure. Maybe.' The excuses

poured out. 'He was sick though. How could I expect him to be the same man he was before the tumour?'

'Easy. You were a kid. He was your dad. The tumour didn't change that.'

'Except it did, didn't it?' she said, looking up. 'This is so stupid. I'm still crying about something that happened almost two years ago.'

'Losing someone doesn't go away, Zoey.'

Her gaze sharpened on him. 'You feel like that about your parents?'

About you, too.

Instead he said, 'Yes. I miss them all the time. I have questions that can't be answered, and answers I don't have the questions to.'

'You've always been pretty zen about losing them,' she noted softly.

'I didn't know them. Aunt Pat and Uncle Ben were good to me.'

'But they're not your parents,' she chided gently. Rolled her eyes when he looked at her. 'Who are you talking to, Sawyer? I know you better than you know yourself.'

She flopped back down on her back. He looked at the sky again. He couldn't find the star he'd been looking at earlier. That was the thing about stars. From this distance, they weren't very distinctive. But human beings? His head shifted to look at Zoey before he could stop himself. The answer to that question settled itself in his mind.

Yeah, human beings were distinctive. Unique. Special. There was nothing, not work, not a person, who could replace Zoey in his life. He wasn't sure he wanted to. So he had to ask himself whether it was enough to have her in his life and no longer have romantic feelings for her.

He'd made that decision once. When he met her, he knew he loved Zoey. But he put those feelings aside because being around her was more important than being in a relationship with her. She was the first person to make him feel like he was chosen. Not thrust into a new family because his parents had died and left his aunt and uncle custody. Not included in family outings and events because he was now supposed to be a part of them. No, Zoey had picked him out of so many other people. He wasn't going to spoil that with a crush.

Of course, it wasn't a crush. He knew that now, lying next to his wife under the night sky. But he had to figure out what was better for him. And just being there, being able to lie next to her? Being able to make her laugh? That seemed better than nothing.

'You were wrong about being a bad wife.'

'Please. You know I was.'

'Why?'

'You know.' She waved a hand. 'I didn't do spouse things.'

'You listened to me when I got home at night. Supported me. Made me feel like I wasn't alone.'

Her eyes took on a sheen. Because his throat was growing thick with each word, he went for something lighter.

'You were also amazing in bed, which was at the top of my list for what I wanted in a spouse.'

'What?' she asked, but she was laughing.

'It's right here—' he patted his shirt pocket '—in this list I keep of what I want in a partner.'

'You keep a list of characteristics you want your partner to have in your front pocket?'

'Yep.'

'And sex is right at the top?' she asked. He nodded. 'Right off the bat?'

'I have my priorities straight.'

'Sure.' She straightened. 'Can I see it?'

'The list?' When she nodded, he shook his head. 'Nah. It's irrelevant.'

'Because I'm already your wife?'

'Exactly,' he said. 'Good thing I added smart to the list, too.'

Then it happened. In quick movements—so quick, he didn't even know she'd moved—she was straddling him. Pinning his hands to the ground. Placing her butt over his groin to make sure she had the best grip.

'What are you doing?' he asked. If she asked, he'd blame his breathiness on her knocking the wind out of him. Although he wasn't sure she'd believe him since his blood was pumping to the part of his body she happened to be sitting on.

'I want to see the list.'

'You know there's no list.'

'Hmm.' She wiggled down on top of him. His attempts at resisting arousal went out the window. 'Maybe I wanted to see if you still think I have what it takes to be your wife.'

'Zoey—'

'Tell me you don't want me to kiss you.' Everything about her had gone serious. No more teasing. No emotion either. Only the fire of desire. 'Tell me.' She leaned forward.

Gravity had the fullness of her breasts edging to

the front of her dress. His eyes automatically dropped. When he dragged his gaze up, the fire got hotter.

'We shouldn't do this.'

'Probably not,' she agreed. 'But we all know I'm not one to have good ideas. I have bad ideas.' She stopped centimetres from his face. 'I'm irresponsible and spontaneous. Which means if you want me to kiss you, I will.'

'I… I can't tell you that.'

There was a stunned beat, but she nodded and began to shift away. 'I understand. You are responsible. And you're right. I was being—'

She broke off before she could finish. Because he was kissing her.

Damn it. He was kissing her.

He pulled her down so hard that their lips smacked together. But neither of them complained. Instead, they both moaned, as if they were tasting the finest dish made in the finest kitchen.

He missed the taste of her. The smell. Like a garden full of flowers the morning after it rained. Fresh, new, sweet. But there was a groundedness to her. Idly, he wondered if he was thinking about her perfume or her personality. Then she inched her tongue between his lips and he wasn't thinking anymore. He was letting her tongue tease his. Allowing her to claim him and give him more memories to torment him.

If he lived long enough. He was currently so aroused he thought he might die from the intensity. She was making little movements with her hips that he didn't think was seduction. It was reaction; instinct, almost, as if she wanted him to soothe the heat he could feel against his hardness.

Silently, he thanked the universe for creating dresses that made it easier to fool around in.

She let out a breathy sigh against his lips when his hands found her hips, pulling her more firmly against his erection. The strokes of her tongue grew more intense, those movements of her hips a little more intentional.

'Zo,' he said, pulling away from her. 'If you keep doing this, I'm not going to be able to go back to the party.'

'I thought we dispelled the myth that people can see when you've been making out with someone when we were in school?'

She spoke against his throat, her tongue trailing over that line at his collarbone. It was his *spot* and she knew it. Which was why she was now sucking at it gently. She'd leave a mark, and damn if he cared.

Somehow, he managed to pull himself out of the daze.

'I didn't mean that. I meant—' he paused when she kissed her way to his ear '—that my pants would be ruined, which is not the kind of gift I want to give Aunt Pat today.'

She stopped the kissing, then pulled away. There was a twitch on either side of her mouth that told him she wanted to smile, but she was trying not to.

'Oh,' she said. 'I'm sorry.'

'No, you're not.'

'No, I'm not.' She didn't fight the grin this time. 'But I do understand why that might be awkward for you.'

'Thank you,' he said dryly.

'My suggestion,' she continued, 'is that we make excuses as to why we have to leave and meet at your place to finish this.' She blinked. Colour flooded her cheeks. 'If you want to, I mean. And if you're—' his eyes lowered to her throat as she swallowed. He raised it to her face again '—free to do so.'

'Free?' he repeated. 'You mean if I'm not seeing anyone else?'

She shrugged, but blushed harder. It was so charming that he didn't even want to tease her.

'I'm not seeing anyone. I'm married.'

Her face… He could only describe the expression as a glow. He was unreasonably proud he'd put it there.

'Good,' she said. 'Ditto.'

'Good.'

'So…'

'So, you better get off me so I can make up an excuse as to why we're leaving early.'

She caught her bottom lip between her teeth, then smiled. 'I *should* probably get off you then, huh?'

'Yes.'

His arms tightened around her waist when she tried to leave.

'One more kiss won't hurt though…'

It was in that second meeting of their lips that he realised he could never only be friends with Zoey. His body responded to her as if it had been created by her hands. For her hands. His instincts were honed to her emotions; his mind constantly tried to understand her.

He needed her in his life, as his wife, because that's what they were meant to be. He knew it as surely as he knew he was going to take her to his flat and make love to her.

The only consolation was that he'd only have to decide what to do about it after he had one more night with her. He wasn't sure if that was torture or a blessing.

Chapter Twenty-Two

One Day, Now

Things were horribly awkward since that mud treatment.

Sure, blame the treatment, an inner voice said. Zoey ignored it. Because *obviously* it wasn't the treatment, but the conversation they had in that small box. As soon as she washed the mud from her body, she left, ignoring that there was at least another thirty minutes left. She used the thirty minutes to compose herself instead. She couldn't leave feeling as shaky as she did. As raw.

She admitted her deepest flaws to the man who had somehow always seen the best in her. She needed him to see that she could never live up to who he thought she was. That it would have hurt them both eventually.

She shook her head, trying to dry her hair. Since she didn't want to do anything more vigorous than gently squeeze the water from it for fear of fuzz, she left it to air dry. Two women entered the cloakroom, and she took it as a sign that privacy was no longer an option. With one more look in the mirror—who was that woman with the wide eyes staring back at her? The shakiness she saw there surely couldn't belong to *her*—she joined Sawyer in the waiting room.

Only to find him denying someone access to his feet.

'No,' he said, for what was obviously not the first time. 'I'm not interested in a pedicure. Thank you, but no, thank you.'

'Sir,' the woman said with a quizzical look. 'You realise you've paid for this? You've chosen the treatments with this package. I don't understand—'

'I'm not trying to be rude, ma'am, but no one is touching my feet.'

'Is there a problem?' Zoey asked, stepping in before the woman could ask another question that would anger her usually laid-back husband.

'You're having the pedicure as well?' the woman asked, visibly relieved. 'I was just telling your—?'

She gave him a sly look. 'Husband.'

'Your husband that we'll be doing the treatments here while we offer some beverages.'

'Excellent. That sounds great to me.' She gave Sawyer an innocent look. 'Doesn't it, honey?'

'No,' he said flatly. 'You know how I feel—' He lowered his voice and turned his back to the woman. How rude. The only time she witnessed him be rude was in these circumstances. 'You know how I feel about people touching my feet,' he whispered fiercely.

His feet. He was only rude when someone wanted to touch his feet.

'What will you give me if I get you out of this?' she replied in the same tone.

'What do you mean "what will I give you"?'

'I mean, you obviously don't know how to get out of this since you're biting the beauty therapist's head off. So you need me. In return, I have a simple request.'

'Something tells me this isn't going to be simple.'

'Oh, no, it is,' she assured him. 'A moment alone when we get back to the park.'

His expression became unreadable. 'Why?'

'You don't get to ask questions.' Because she didn't have answers. 'It's part of the deal.' She tried to obscure the hand she held out to him with her body. 'Deal?'

'Zoey—'

'Do you *want* them to touch your feet?'

He gave the most dramatic sigh she'd ever heard. 'Fine. You win. As always.'

She smiled, despite the jab. 'Wonderful.' She turned to the therapist. 'I'm sorry for my husband's behaviour. Ever since he lost a toe, he hasn't felt comfortable with letting people see his feet.'

'Oh,' the woman said, her mouth forming the same word. 'I'm sorry. We weren't informed his toe was—'

'Cut off,' Zoey completed for her. 'By the cartel who kidnapped him for information on his boss. You know what?' she said immediately when the woman began to look sceptical. 'He doesn't like talking about it. And frankly—' she lowered her voice, inserted a tremble '—neither do I.'

She made a show of grasping for Sawyer's hand. He gripped it back, but so firmly it was almost painful. She hardly deserved it. It wasn't like anyone was going to find out all his little piggies could still go to the market.

She cleared her throat. 'Would it be possible for us to switch his pedicure for a manicure? He has all his fingers, so he won't be upset about that.' She gave him a look to make sure of it.

But Sawyer seemed amiable. 'That would be appreciated.'

'Well, of course,' the woman said with a shake of her head. She was probably trying to figure out how she got herself into a situation where she was contemplating a client's missing toe. 'You can take your seats here. Our therapists will be with you in a moment. I'll send the butler through for your drink orders as well.'

They took their seats. When she disappeared around the corner, Zoey turned to Sawyer. 'What's your thing about your feet again?'

'I lost a toe to a drug cartel on behalf of my employer,' he replied dryly.

She grinned. 'Some of my best work, even you have to admit.'

'I don't know if I'm feeling that generous yet,' he said, but there were the tiniest curves at the corners of his mouth. 'But to answer your question, I don't like people being around my feet.'

'But why?' she pressed. 'I know there was a reason. You told me in our early days, when I still used to think tickling you would have an effect.'

'It did. Not on my feet though.'

'Yes, you made that abundantly clear.' She ran her tongue over her top lip. 'It had something to do with tickling though, didn't it?' Then it hit her. 'Phil used to tickle you there. You hated it.'

He sighed, defeated now that she already seemed to know his secret.

'Yeah, he used to pin me down and tickle me. Now I don't like people there because I like having some control over the area. I don't like feeling helpless or whatever.'

She wanted to reach out and grab his hand, but she didn't want to hurt his pride. She didn't know if she would, but she wasn't going to take chances with things being so weird between them.

'You know,' she said after a moment. 'Phil might be a bully.'

'Yeah, he definitely is.'

She wrinkled her nose. 'I never liked him.'

'Is that why you popped his balloon with your earring at Aunt Pat's sixtieth?'

She gave a delighted laugh. 'I always wondered if you saw that. You were very convincing when you said you hadn't. We never spoke about it afterwards.'

'We had other things to occupy ourselves with after,' he commented.

It hit its mark. Her mind immediately jumped to how she'd gone to his flat—not the one they'd once shared, since he'd moved into the city to be closer to work—and made love. She'd ripped off his clothes; buttons literally flying because she was so determined to get him naked in case he changed his mind. She'd needed him so much that night. Losing him had created a hole only he could fill. Apparently, literally, too.

It would have been more amusing to her if the night they'd shared had been quick and hot. But he'd lingered, his lips brushing over her skin like whispered promises. When he made her orgasm, there'd been tears in her eyes because she'd felt like she was being worshipped. Perhaps it was also because she knew she would have to go back to her life after, where such worship was banned and only authoritarian-like control was welcomed.

When she lifted her eyes and realised he was watching her, her face burned. She was saved from the question she was sure would come when the butler arrived to take their orders.

'Today is the second time you said you'd be a bad mother,' he said softly. Suddenly. Without warning. She was glad she didn't have her drink. She definitely would have spilled it. 'The sixtieth birthday was the first time.'

So he was thinking about that night, too. Or was she projecting?

'Well, it's true.'

'You seemed pretty great with your niece today.'

'Because she's a great kid.'

'Who said you won't have a great kid?'

She shook her head. 'She's Angie's, which means she already comes hardwired with the right equipment.'

'What are you talking about?'

'She has a good foundation. Solid parents. Great examples.' She accepted the drink from the butler, but didn't take a sip from the champagne. 'My kid would have my flimsy genetics and then me as a mother.' Now she did drink. 'I don't think that's the way for me to go.'

'Zo.' Sawyer's voice was soft. 'What the hell are you talking about?'

'I already answered that question.'

'Yeah, but this time I was asking about your answer.' He shifted, and somehow, managed to get her to look at him. 'Do you really believe that?'

'Sure,' she said, smiling although she was sure it looked as shaky as she felt. 'Look, I've accepted who I am. That means I don't get to be a mom.'

'You'd be a great mom.'

'No, I wouldn't.' She shook her head in emphasis.

'Let's change the topic. Let's go back to your missing toe.'

'Zoey,' he said, firmly now. 'You're kind and caring. You have more passion in your pinky toe than most people have in their entire body. Assuming you have a pinky toe, of course.'

It made her smile. Damn him.

'Have you made mistakes? Sure. But we all do. You can't keep punishing yourself. Learn from them.' There was a quick pause. So quick she almost didn't think it existed. 'And, from what I can tell, you have learnt from a lot of your mistakes.'

It meant more to her than she could ever say, that he saw her. Because she *was* trying. She was trying so damn hard to be a better person. Sometimes, it felt like no one saw it. She would make a mistake, fall back into the habit, and they'd see that. There goes Zoey, they'd say. Irresponsible Zoey. Better clean up her mess before she makes it worse.

It had happened in the park earlier that day. When she told her sisters about her marriage, they wanted to fix it. She didn't blame them; she blamed herself. She'd forced them to think that they had to fix things for her. But what she realised since trying to be better is that sometimes, they wanted to fix *her*.

If only it were that easy, she'd thought many times. If she could fix herself, she would have. She would have been the responsible person. The kind of person who could have kids and be a mother. She would be someone who could be a wife. Sawyer's wife. Someone who *deserved* him.

She downed her drink, blaming the prickling at her eyes on the bubbles.

'Thanks,' she said when she thought she had her voice under control. 'It's nice of you to say that.'

'I'm not only saying it, Zo. I believe it.'

'I know you do. Because you're a great guy.'

'Zoey—'

He couldn't go on because the beauty therapists arrived. Zoey immediately engaged hers in conversation, though she hated talking to people while they worked on her. It made her feel weird. She didn't want them to think that because they were working on her, they had to entertain her as well. Although this one didn't seem to mind, and chatted happily.

'I love your hair,' the woman, Zinzi, told her.

'Thanks.'

'Where did you have it done?'

'Oh, I did it.' When Zinzi stared at her blankly, Zoey took a twist and unravelled it until the root. When it was unravelled, she shook it with a smile. 'It's mine, too,' she said, because she'd had the question of the ownership of her hair many, many times before. 'I twist it most of the time.'

'Why?'

'Have you seen how much there is?' Zoey asked, unoffended. 'Plus, I like how it looks.'

'I do, too.'

But Zinzi kept studying her quizzically. Zoey let it go. She'd been twisting her hair for years despite the warning of what the style would do to her hairline. The twists were loose for the most part, and she only tied them up when she had to, so she was doing her part. And okay, yes, fine, she wore it in a wash and go at least twice a month, for two days max, otherwise her generous mass of hair got tangled, and detangling took ages.

They were finished soon after, and they went to the cloakroom to change. She shot off a message to Parker asking if the spa was it, and thankfully, got an affirmative in answer. She met Sawyer at the spa's front desk.

'Parker says we're off duty.'

'A relief,' he replied, though he looked distracted. 'I was sure we'd have to spend the night in the room he's booked.'

She laughed, ignoring the jokes her mind begged her to make. 'I called for a car to take us back.'

'Thanks.'

They waited in the front of the hotel for a couple of minutes in silence. When a black car began creeping its way down the narrow road, Sawyer spoke.

'I'm not that great.'

'What?'

'Inside. You said I was great. I'm not.'

'Okay,' she said slowly, wondering where he was going with it.

'You were right earlier when you said I was angry at my mom and grandmother. I am. I did so much so that they wouldn't be disappointed in me, and they hid that I had a sister. I feel... I feel betrayed.'

He dropped the bombshell confession before the car came because he didn't want to talk about it. He was angry, betrayed, and it all felt so raw and ugly that he couldn't entertain those feelings. Doing so required strength and energy he didn't have, at least not at the moment. Seeing Zoey, speaking with her, touching her, kissing her... All of it had ripped away his armour.

Her judging herself so harshly made him think about his own flaws. It was more than that though. It was that she seemed to see something in him, in their relationship, that he couldn't. He could sense it close to the surface. He could feel that it was entangled with how he saw her and how he saw his family. But it wasn't clear yet. What was clear was that he had his own flaws. And if she was going to judge herself according to hers, she better judge him in the same way.

That's why he told her about how he felt about his family. It was the *only* reason he told her. It had nothing to do with his compulsion to open up to her and get the poisonous emotions out of his body so he could heal.

'Don't think you're getting away from this conversation,' she muttered from beside him. 'You owe me a private moment when we get to Kirstenbosch. Guess what I'll be using it for?'

He didn't reply, but he appreciated the heads-up. Not that he hadn't expected her reaction. She was like a dog with a bone when she wanted to be. He'd handed her this bone, too, so he couldn't be upset. By the time they reached Kirstenbosch, he still didn't know what he'd say. Everything he came up with made him sound petulant. Or vulnerable. He couldn't figure out which was worse.

At some point during their drive, the sky had gone from light blue to something darker. Not night yet though. It was an in-between time of day where magic seemed possible. Sawyer had no idea why he thought so. No, he did—because of Zoey. She was magical. Being around her made him think anything was possible. Maybe that was why she'd always helped him heal. From the loneliness of growing up without parents. From worrying he'd be a burden to his aunt and uncle. Her choosing him as a friend had made him feel less alone. And if she'd chosen him, surely he couldn't be a burden?

She gave him courage to face hurt. To trust. But when she'd walked out on him, that magic had disappeared. He'd begun to question whether he'd really healed. Regressed to being someone who let his emotions fester and poison him. That's why he refused to discuss his aunt and grandmother's decision to keep Lisa's existence a secret. He refused to even think about it—and the fact that his mother wasn't the person he thought she was. None of them were. That refusal to think had been the same way he'd approached the end of his marriage.

There were a lot of similarities between what he was doing with his family, and what he'd done with Zoey. It was probably why he thought they were linked. He tip-toed around anything that made him feel vulnerable. With his family, he tried to be the perfect adopted son, nephew, cousin. With Zoey, he tried to be the perfect friend, lover, husband. He did everything he was supposed to. Then, when things didn't go the way he wanted them to, he blamed himself.

His day with Zoey was making him realise none of these emotions, responses, beliefs were healthy. Nor was his anger at realising it.

They entered the garden without speaking, the pulsing of the music from the concert the only sound. When she began walking in the opposite direction, he followed without question, though he did say, 'You're going the wrong way.'

'No, I'm not.'

Seconds later, they were standing outside a food stall. There was a short line. Sawyer attributed it to the fact that it was the time of night where alcohol was more important than food. When they got to the front, Zoey grinned.

'Ricardo.'

'You,' the sour-faced man behind the till said. 'What do you want?'

'I'm bringing my friend for the healing bacon-wrapped cheese stick.'

The softening of the man's expression was so subtle Sawyer would have missed it if he wasn't watching the man closely.

'Two, please.'

'You need healing, too?' the man asked.

'Not this time,' she said, her smile widening. 'This time it's just for pleasure. Also, I'll pay you.'

His reply was a mutter in a different language, though the heat in his tone was mixed with affection. It puzzled Sawyer—he couldn't quite figure out their relationship—but he enjoyed the back-and-forth. It sounded easy, familiar. Soon he was making up situations where Zoey would have an easy, familiar relationship with a food provider.

Did she use him for the events she planned? Was he an acquaintance? A friend? A lover?

Wow. That escalated quickly.

'Is this the friend who hurt you?' Ricardo asked as he handed them the sticks with food on it.

Sawyer's eyebrows rose by themselves.

'Ricardo.' Zoey's voice was light, but there was a warning in it. 'I thought you'd know better than that.'

'Maybe this is payback,' he said slyly.

There was a beat of stunned silence, then Zoey laughed. One of her belly laughs that had everyone in the vicinity looking at her in genuine amusement.

'You're petty.'

'Smart.'

'Petty,' Zoey said again. 'Luckily I like it. And I like you.'

Ricardo smiled. It did wonders for turning the dragon into someone who looked almost human.

'My offer still stands.'

'Thanks,' Zoey said sincerely. Her tone turned cheeky. 'So does your invoice.'

His laughter followed them as they walked away. Despite himself, he asked, 'How do you know that guy?'

'Oh, he and Sophia got into it this morning. Almost. I ran interference.'

'You met that guy this morning?'

'Yeah.' She looked at him. 'Why?'

'You guys were talking like you've known each other forever.'

'Oh.' She waved a hand. 'He's a grump. After living with Soph for years, then meeting Parker, I know how to deal with grumps.'

He shook his head, though his heart told him he should have known. Zoey didn't need to know someone a long time to make an impression. He'd fallen for her the day he'd met her, hadn't he?

'He seemed to know personal things about you.'

'I have no boundaries.'

He stared at her. She laughed. Somehow it turned into a sigh.

'I was upset earlier. I…bumped into him. Since then, he's been more amiable than usual.'

'What upset you?'

Her eyes crinkled, but she wasn't laughing. 'I asked you for a divorce. It upset me.'

'Well,' he said, ignoring the ridiculous hope in his chest. 'I intend on taking you to the cleaners, so you had a right to be.'

She gave a polite little snort. 'I haven't accumulated much wealth in the last six years, but you're welcome to try.' She paused. 'Though you have, haven't you?'

'I do okay.'

Now she did smile. 'I don't intend on taking *you* to the cleaners, Sawyer. You don't have to be vague.'

He smiled back. 'It has nothing to do with that.'

'Let me guess,' she said after studying him for a moment. 'You're being humble. It's not as impressive as you think.'

'I'm not being humble.'

'Just not used to sharing personal information with me anymore.'

He took a deep breath, and followed her to a bench when she walked away without waiting for an answer.

'That's not fair,' he said when he was ready. 'I've shared more personal things with you today than I have with anyone else in the last six years.'

She made a non-committal noise.

'Do you want to know how much I earn?' Frustration gave his question an edge.

'No.' She sighed. 'I'm sorry. That comment was uncalled for.'

'Where did it come from?'

'Annoyance.' She gave him a half-smile. 'I don't like

being outside your life. I know I don't deserve anything else,' she added quickly, 'but not knowing…'

'This isn't about my job,' he said, understanding.

'No.'

'You're annoyed you don't know what I'm feeling.'

'Even after all this time, you know me so well.'

He finished his cheese-bacon stick instead of replying, taking in their surroundings as he did. Tall trees hovered over them, dark now that night was falling. They looked as though they were reaching for the stars that were beginning to twinkle. The music was still audible, though the tempo had changed. Gone was the pulsing in rapid beats, replaced by languid melodies.

'I know you, too, you know,' she said into silence. 'You think having a normal reaction to a stressful family situation makes you a bad person.'

'Oh.' When the surprise passed, he shook his head. 'You're sneaky.'

'I know.'

He gave a half-hearted laugh, but didn't say anything else. He was still trying to figure out whether she was right.

'You're loyal, Sawyer,' she continued despite his lack of reply. 'You always have been. But sometimes…' She inhaled deeply. 'Sometimes that loyalty becomes an excuse for you not to feel your feelings.'

'No,' he said immediately. Automatically. But damn if it didn't ring true.

'Your expression is giving away that you know I'm right.'

'Okay,' he conceded. 'Maybe you *are* right.'

'Maybe.' Her voice was so dry he almost choked on

it. 'You said something about betrayal earlier. Where do you think that emotion comes from?'

'This is getting annoying.'

'Me seeing right through you?' He grunted. She grinned. 'I'm not trying to annoy you. At this moment, anyway.' The grin grew, before slowly fading. 'I only mean to say that your other feelings are as important as your loyalty.'

'You think my anger is as important as being loyal?' His heart was pounding. It somehow felt lethargic. 'Being angry with my family for not telling me the truth is the same as being grateful to them for taking me in? Being pissed off that everything I know about them is a lie is the same as wanting to make them proud?'

She immediately reached for his hand. He moved it away before she could take it. He didn't need her comfort.

No—it was worse. He *did* need it.

'How are those things equally important, Zoey?'

'Because you feel them.'

'That's too simple.'

'It doesn't have to be complicated.' Her voice was gentle. 'All of your emotions have validity simply because you feel them. Does that mean you have to be ruled by them? No. Should they make a difference to how you approach your family and your life? Maybe.' She shrugged when he looked over. 'You've been pushing down how you feel about the Lisa situation because you think you shouldn't be feeling it. How would things change if you didn't think that?'

He took a long time to answer her.

'My relationship with my aunt would be different.'

'How?'

'I'd ask her how she could have kept this from me. She knew how much losing my parents broke me.' He frowned as another thought occurred to him. 'I don't think I've ever told her that, actually.'

'Why not?'

'I was… I was afraid she'd think I was being ungrateful.'

'For grieving for your parents?'

'For making their lives harder by grieving for my parents.' He couldn't believe he only realised it now. 'I told you they struggled after my parents died. Aunt Pat said I reminded her of my mother. She was in pain.'

'That might not have had anything to do with you.'

'I thought it did. I thought… I wanted to make her life easier by being easy. I didn't want to say or do anything that would make her regret it.'

'You thought you were being loyal.'

'I used it as an excuse to ignore my grief,' he said, acknowledging her earlier comment. 'It made me feel alone and unwanted. A responsibility rather than a choice.'

'Except they did choose you,' Zoey said. 'They didn't have to. You have other family members. Your grandmother could have taken you in. But they *did*, and it had nothing to do with whether or not you were a good kid. I mean, they're Phil's parents and they still love him.' She rolled her eyes. 'I think you had some leeway.'

He shook his head. The realisation made his feelings harder to articulate verbally.

'Your grief could have changed things with your aunt. Your anger now could change things with her. But she loves you, and you love her, which means you'll get through it.'

'Like we did?' he asked absently. Wished he hadn't almost immediately. 'I'm sorry.'

'Don't be.' But her expression closed up. 'I encouraged you to feel what you feel.'

'But you were talking about my family,' he said with a small smile. 'So we'll keep talking about that to avoid talking about us.' He continued without waiting for a reply. 'I am angry that they didn't tell me. I'm also angry because I got it wrong. I thought they were people who deserved my loyalty. But *they* aren't loyal. Not to me, not to Lisa. And it isn't only loyal, it's cruel.'

'Because they did what they thought best at the time?'

'You don't know that.'

'Neither do you,' she shot back. 'You're letting your anger give you answers to questions you haven't asked.'

'What happened to feeling what I feel?'

'I also said don't let your emotions rule you.'

'You don't get to decide that.'

'But you do.' She paused. 'You better make a smart decision. Because letting the wrong emotion lead can take you down a bad path.'

'Like marriage?'

She exhaled. 'Okay, let's do this. Let's talk about it since you can't let it go.'

'You asking for a divorce feels like a betrayal, too,' he ground out. Apparently, it was too close to the surface to pretend he didn't know what she was talking about. 'I'm angry that after everything we've been through together you don't think we deserved more.'

'You mean after everything *you've* done for me,

don't you?' Zoey's voice was so polite it didn't sound like her. 'You're doing the same thing you did with your aunt with me.' She stood. Faced him. 'You did everything right with me and this is how I pay you back. With no loyalty. Am I right? No, don't answer that. I know I am.'

She crossed her arms. It was halfway between sass and shielding herself. He felt a twinge that she thought she had to. But it was only a twinge. He agreed with her, after all.

'I've grown, Sawyer. I'm better now. And yet I don't think I'll ever be good enough for you,' she said. 'You're uncompromising with your expectations. Sometimes you expect too much. And you don't even know that you do.' Her arms dropped. 'I'm not the person you made me out to be. I don't think I could ever be. And that was part of the problem.' She met his eyes. 'I have flaws. I make mistakes. Breaking your heart was one of those mistakes. I'm trying to own up to it, but you still see it as me not living up to a standard you set.'

Her voice got softer, though it was no less passionate. 'Asking you for a divorce isn't about betrayal. It's about making up for how I broke my best friend's heart. It's about making things right instead of avoiding the pain of the situation like I did before.'

He opened his mouth to reply, but words weren't coming. They got stuck on their way from his brain to his mouth.

'I'm exactly like your aunt and your mother and grandmother. A human being who might not always do the right thing. But I learnt. So did they, based on the way they treated you. They could have given you up for adoption like they had with Lisa,' she clarified. 'Maybe that experience with her made them realise they didn't like what they did before. But you don't see that because you're stuck clinging to this black-and-white idea of loyalty and betrayal and…and *family*.'

'You're an expert now, are you?' he asked bitterly, and hated himself for it.

'Maybe,' she replied, crossing her arms again. 'Or maybe all my flaws and mistakes make me more compassionate for other people's.'

Chapter Twenty-Three

One Day, Three Years Ago

'You're still getting that girl to pretend to be your girlfriend,' Grandma Carla said, shaking her head. 'After all this time. I let it slide because she made you happy. But you're not happy anymore.'

Sawyer gaped at his grandmother. They were sitting alone in the corner of the hall. Zoey had disappeared to get them something to drink, and Grandma Carla had started talking almost as soon as she left.

His first instinct was to come up with an excuse. He overruled it almost immediately. His grandmother was sharp, though she'd grown frailer this year than any other before. Her eyes were warm and patient, amused even, but it was the sharpness that told him not to lie.

'How long have you known?'

'All the time.' She leaned back, surveying the room with those sharp eyes. 'I thought it was funny. Especially when you were trying so hard.'

'Not hard enough, apparently.'

'No—*too* hard. You didn't have to pretend, Sawyer. You were both in love already. You just needed encouragement to be together.' She sighed wistfully.

'I thought I succeeded that night of Jill's graduation. I was sure I did. Poor Zoey looked like she swallowed a frog when I told her to do you right.'

His lips curved. 'You did succeed.'

'I did?'

'Yeah.'

He almost continued, told her the truth, but stopped himself in time. If he told her about the marriage, it would no doubt disappoint her. He hadn't invited his family; he hadn't told anyone about it. Most significantly, their marriage had failed. Which begged the question of why he was still pretending Zoey was his girlfriend. And why *she* was still pretending to be his girlfriend.

They had seen one another three times in three years. He only invited her to the big events, which thankfully, seemed to be tapering off as his family grew older. He explained her absence with lies at smaller family gatherings. Zoey was in Korea for a year. There was an important work project she had to focus on. Her family needed her because of what they'd been through. He wasn't proud of that one, but people shied away from others' grief. He'd learnt that after his own parents died. He never thought he'd use that knowledge, but life could surprise in that way.

Despite the minimal number of times he and Zoey had seen one another, they somehow managed to make their relationship more complicated every time. With emotion; with sex. He couldn't tell his grandmother all that. He couldn't bear to have her see him as the mess he was. But he was tired. Tired of keeping the secret. Tired of pretending to be the good grandchild. After minutes of deliberation, the fatigue won.

'We're married.'

Her gasp was more a wheeze than an intake of air. When it was followed by a bout of coughing, he took her hand and rubbed it slowly.

'I'm sorry. I shouldn't have sprung that on you.'

'Well, dear,' Grandma Carla said, patting his hand with her free one. 'I can't imagine how else you could have told me but to spring it on me.' She frowned, the thoughts basically jumping out her head, so intense was her concentration. 'I was only hoping for you two to be together. I didn't intend for you to marry. At least not…' She trailed off. 'I'm sorry, my darling.'

'For what?'

'If you're married, but you're both unhappy, it must not be going well.'

Astute observation. Unexpected, though not altogether. His grandmother always saw through him. When he was being made fun of because he didn't have parents, he hadn't told anyone. He didn't want to cause a scene, or make them worry about him. But Grandma Carla walked into his bedroom one night and asked him about it. With the few pieces of information he gave her, she figured out the rest. She told him family was family, no matter what it looked like. It had comforted him more than he could say.

'I guess you could say that,' Sawyer allowed. 'Not what you wanted to hear, right?'

She looked thoughtful. 'It's my first great-grandchild's first birthday. I have enough to celebrate. Though I did hope you'd have better news for me.'

'Me, too.'

She patted his hand again. 'Time is precious, my

boy. Go for the things you want in your life.' There was a short pause. 'Leave behind the things you don't want.'

'Are you saying I should divorce Zoey?'

'I'm saying you better figure out what you want with that girl and do it. You both deserve better. Now,' she said, 'she's coming. I'm going to give her a hard time. Ask her when she intends to make an honourable man out of you. Just to see her blush.' She sighed happily, as though even the thought brought her joy. 'She does have such a beautiful face, doesn't she? I'll support whatever you want, Sawyer, but I do hope you want her.'

Chapter Twenty-Four

One Day, Now

Zoey's heart was crushed. Partly because it hurt her to see Sawyer like this; partly because him lashing out felt like physical strikes to her body. But this experience made her see two things. One, she wasn't stuck. She had been moving forward, even if her progress had been slow and tedious. The fact that she could ask Sawyer for a divorce, knowing it was the best thing for them proved it. Two, was harder. It forced her to face that, despite that forward movement, she was lingering in the fear that she wasn't good enough for him. That she would never be.

His response made her think that fear had validity. She'd been caught by it. That he thought she'd betrayed him, and that he couldn't see how much she was trying to do right by him. At the same time, it freed her. It told her that she might not be stuck, but Sawyer was. In the past, in his emotions. In the false idea that the people in his life owed him something because he'd given them something of himself. Those expectations would always break down his relationships. Because they had nothing to do with the people he was in relationships with; only himself. All of it came from the hurt and fear he experienced as a child. She knew it. But he didn't, and until he did, they weren't right for one another.

She still wanted them to be.

Oh, she'd spent the day thinking about how much she missed him. How much she wanted him in her life. But she'd been so determined that the divorce was right, she hadn't allowed herself to think of the alternative. Now, after their day together, she remembered how amazing the alternative could be. He was caring. He made her laugh. He teased her body and her mind. He knew her better than anyone else. She hadn't found anyone in the last six years she connected with as much.

Sawyer felt like home even though Zoey had forged a strong one with her sisters in the years since her father's death.

But her father's death had been a catalyst, as was their marriage. They showed her that being taught one thing shouldn't dictate her perspective on that thing for the rest of her life. People took care of her for as long as she could remember, but that brought pain into their lives and hers. So she changed, but she still had a long way to go. Her argument with Sophia the day Cal had been born proved it. She'd thought of Sophia one way, and it had hurt her sister. She had no interest in continuing with that, so she adjusted. Adjusting and changing was always going to be part of her life. But she couldn't be with someone who made her feel like that didn't matter.

'I'm sorry,' he said into the silence. 'I reacted poorly.'

Her reply was to watch him. A strategy that would

keep him from hearing the pain in her voice since her heart was breaking.

'I think… I might have…' He exhaled. 'I think I have some things to work through.'

'Yes.'

That's all he'd get from her.

'You deserve compassion. So does my family.' His fingers clenched and unclenched. 'It's harder with them. They never…' He exhaled. 'They didn't ever make me feel wanted like you did. I know they wanted me,' he added quickly. 'I can see that. But feelings aren't nearly as cut and dried as logic.'

'No,' she agreed.

She only had to look at the fact that logic told her they needed to divorce. Her heart, on the other hand, told her she was still madly in love with him. She literally bit her tongue to keep the sob from coming out.

'I don't deserve your kindness,' he said quietly. 'Or your understanding.'

She closed her eyes. When she was steadier, she sat down beside him and said, 'I don't understand you.'

He chuckled, but looked down at his hands. 'That's fair.'

'You expect too much, Sawyer,' she whispered. 'People can't love in the same way you do. You're a good man, so giving and generous and sacrificing. It's not so easy for the rest of us.' She wiped her cheek, though there was no wetness there. Which was…surprising. 'I can only give you my best. Except…maybe you're not ready to give me yours.'

'Why not?'

It was barely above a whisper.

'You deserve to have time to figure out what you're

feeling. To work through it. I don't think you can do that still being married to me.' He started to protest, but she cut him off. 'We both need to be in the right space for a relationship to work. I don't know if you are. I don't even know if *I* am, honestly.'

'You wouldn't be able to see it if you were,' he said quietly. 'You've changed and grown, but you still put yourself down. Doubt yourself. You've never seen yourself clearly, Zo. Even now, after all the work you've put in.'

'I… That's…'

'I'm sorry I made you feel—' He broke off. 'I don't know how to describe how I made you feel. Or maybe I just don't like it.' He went silent for a beat. 'I guess I'm trying to say that how I made you feel may have come from how you see yourself, too. I'm not shifting the blame,' he added quickly.

She took a moment to process. 'I…see that.' She cleared her throat. 'Maybe you have a point.'

'Your mistakes don't mean you don't deserve happiness,' he pointed out gently.

'But what if my next mistake hurts you again?' She forced it through her lips. 'You have standards, Sawyer. How I see myself doesn't change that. So what if I don't live up to those standards? Will I be betraying you again? Could we ever be happy with that hanging over our heads?'

He didn't answer, which was an answer in itself. As the silence extended, hopelessness danced in it.

She and Sawyer were both stuck now, it seemed. In this reality where they wanted to make things work, but couldn't. She didn't know if she deserved him, it was true. But she also didn't know if he was ready for her. Since he didn't know it either, there was no answer. Only the hopelessness. The realisation that no matter how much they loved one another, love wasn't enough.

'Well,' he said after a long time. 'I guess this is it.'

He sounded as empty as she felt.

'Yes,' she said. She thought, *No. Please.*

'We can't see one another anymore.'

'Okay.' *Please don't say that.*

'It's too hard.'

'I know.' *But it's worth it!*

Isn't it?

He released a breath, his eyes unbearably sad. 'For what it's worth, you've surpassed every standard I've had for you.'

'Even when I left?'

'Yeah, maybe.' He offered her a small smile when she looked over sharply. 'You realised things weren't healthy and did something about it. I refused to see it, and myself, and stewed in it for the last six years. That's pretty extraordinary. Of you.'

'Please,' she scoffed, though her heart was pumping. 'You're putting me on that pedestal again.'

'It's your own fault. In the seven years we were friends, you helped me build it. You proved you were worthy of being there.' He took her hand. She let him. 'I didn't understand why you left before today. I get it now. And you're still worthy of happiness, Zo.' His voice softened. 'If you don't believe anything else, believe that. And that I'm so damn proud of you.'

She swallowed. It didn't help. Her voice still came out like she was a little girl. 'P-proud of me?'

'More than I can possibly say.'

There were definitely tears now. She didn't bother

blinking them away. They left her eyes in quick succession, but as quickly, Sawyer wiped at them. She gripped his wrist, squeezing her thank-you. His lips curved and their gazes caught. It had her heart scrambling, trying to get out of her chest to him.

To where it belonged.

'Oh,' she said softly.

She was never going to get over him. Not as a friend, but as a lover. As a partner. As a spouse. She loved him. Always had, and she always would.

But that didn't change a thing.

He leaned forward as she thought it, and selfishly, she accepted. One last kiss. A goodbye. Their lips touched and she closed her eyes, letting herself have it. His mouth moved tenderly against hers, as if they were lovers who couldn't be with one another and only had this one moment left. *Because* they were lovers who couldn't be with one another and only had this one moment left.

They were both saying goodbye. She wondered if he knew it.

Her mouth welcomed his tongue without coercion. Tasting the sweetness of him she moaned, threading her fingers through the thick black strands of his hair. His hands danced over her skin, then gripped her waist more firmly, pulling her toward him though she couldn't move any closer. He solved that problem by lifting her over his lap. She responded by dropping her hands to around his neck, and pressing herself more firmly against him.

It deepened the kiss, and her body, already alert from his expert kissing, sighed. Demanded more. Her aching breasts wanted his hands to touch, his mouth to tease. The throbbing between her legs wanted him to fill her, to ease away that tightness and release her from her thoughts and her conscience.

Sawyer stood then, scooping her in his arms. She wrapped her legs around his waist as he walked forward and pressed her against a tree. 'Privacy,' he paused long enough to say against her mouth, then continued. Although now, his hands were a lot more searching.

He pulled her top up, groaning when it allowed him to touch her skin. She was so damn hot that she wanted to pull the top off altogether, but something in her head warned her against it. Probably the part of her that didn't want to get arrested. She shoved his t-shirt up, too, her hands immediately skimming the muscles she'd admired in the sauna. They rippled beneath her fingers; mirroring it, satisfaction rippled inside her. Her thumbs grazed his nipples and he swore against her mouth. Then he wrenched his mouth away to trail kisses down her neck.

She angled her head and arched her back at the same time, both movements completely outside of her control. The kissing stopped almost as quickly. She opened her mouth to protest, but when she saw him staring at her, his eyes hooded with desire, emotion brimming just behind it, she stilled.

'What?' she asked shakily.

'We shouldn't do this like this.'

'No, we should,' she said, pressing a kiss to his chest. 'There won't be another opportunity for us to—'

She broke off when his face hardened. When he stepped back, allowing her to lower to the ground, she realised it was too late. There wouldn't be another opportunity for anything other than a verbal goodbye.

'You still want to go through with it then?'

What gave you the impression that I didn't? she wanted to ask. But he was straightening his clothes, and she was straightening hers, and she had her answer.

'I'm sorry,' she said, hands dropping to her sides. 'You're right. We shouldn't have done that.'

He gave her a curt nod.

'Have a lawyer draw up the papers.' His tone was as curt as the nod. 'You keep what's yours. You can take whatever's mine. Send them to me and I'll sign.'

'Sawyer—'

'It'll be over soon.'

When he turned his back to her, she realised she'd been dismissed.

Chapter Twenty-Five

One Day, Two Years Ago

He was clenching his fists. As they sat in the front pew of the church, Sawyer was clenching his hands in his lap. It meant she couldn't thread her fingers through his. Couldn't squeeze them when he came back from carrying the casket that held his grandmother's body. Couldn't comfort herself as much as she needed to comfort him.

She hadn't been invited to this family event. There was no reason for her to pretend to be Sawyer's girl-friend now that Grandma Carla was…

She couldn't even say it. Back to where she started, she thought idly. She hadn't been able to say that her father had died either. Not until after two years of grief counselling. It had just come out then. Once, at a work function when her colleague had inquired about why she still lived with her mother.

'My dad died a couple years back. She's a bit lost without him.'

That had been her answer. She only realised it when she got home. She wondered if it would take Sawyer as long, too.

What could she do to make it better? She felt help-less. More helpless than when her own father had died. Maybe because then, things between her and Sawyer had been good and she could turn to him for com-fort. Things were different now. Despite the moments they'd spent together over the years—the days, really, whenever an invitation to an event would pop up in her inbox—they weren't in a good place. She couldn't be there for him when he needed her.

But she'd come today, even though he hadn't asked her to. Even though he hadn't told her Grandma Carla had died. When Carly sent her a message to tell her the news, Zoey knew she had to come. She didn't once hesitate when she arrived. She immediately went to sit with his family. Didn't glance away when he saw her and his face tightened. He'd come to sit next to her, hadn't it? It was enough.

She told herself that at the end of the service, when he left the church behind the casket, not checking to see if she followed. She *was* following, but she stood aside. She already offered condolences to the people she cared about when she arrived. The rest would be pretentious. So she was okay with standing aside, greeting those who greeted her.

It was a long time later that he came toward her. He walked without purpose, which was new for him. She hated it. Hated that hunch of his shoulders. Her heart ached to soothe him. To help him. To take care of him like he'd taken care of her.

This was hard, she thought suddenly. And realised it was too much like her father's death. His funeral. Her breathing sped up.

'I didn't tell you about this,' he said when he stopped in front of her.

'I know.' Inhale, exhale, she instructed herself. 'I came anyway.'

His jaw set. She took a step forward. She would offer him a hug. Just one hug. The hurt in his eyes stopped her.

'You shouldn't have.' His voice was hard. So unlike her Sawyer.

Her heart pounded against her chest.

'I'm sorry.'

'You should go.'

She swallowed. Nodded. Because frankly, she was on the verge of a breakdown. She could sense the grief around her, a menacing spirit waiting for her to be weak so it could possess her body. She supposed it could sense how much Sawyer's words, his demeanour, his sadness broke her. But it had another thing coming. She wouldn't fall apart in public.

'I will.' Her lashes fluttered. 'I'm sorry about your grandmother. I know how much she…' She couldn't finish the sentence without choking up. She cleared her throat. 'I know.'

Something softened in his eyes, but he responded with a firm nod.

'Thank you.'

They stood in silence. Cars began to pull out of the car park. Behind Sawyer, Carly waved at her. She didn't wave back, but gave a small nod. They'd agreed not to do anything that would make Sawyer suspect Carly had told Zoey about Grandma Carla.

'I should go,' Zoey said, dragging her eyes from Carly. Sawyer was looking at her. Staring in that intense way he had, though it wasn't warm as it had been before.

'Okay.'

She took two steps back, still facing him. She realised it, turned. Another two steps later, he called out, 'Zoey.'

She turned back so quickly she was almost embarrassed. But she couldn't be embarrassed with this much hope, this much *maybe he wants me to stay* pulsing through her body.

'We shouldn't see one another anymore.'

Her lips parted. Breath rushed through. Her brain coached her lips to speak, and slowly, she obeyed.

'Do you mean—' She cleared her throat when the question came out hoarse. 'Do you mean we should—'

'I mean there'll be no more invitations,' he interrupted.

He doesn't want a divorce.

She nearly collapsed from relief.

'You don't want me to pretend to be your girlfriend anymore.'

'There's no reason to.'

She wondered how many times her heart could break in a day.

'Okay. If…if that's what you want.'

She'd give him one more opportunity to change his mind.

'It is.'

Somehow, she hadn't expected it.

'Okay.'

She sucked in her bottom lip. Her insides were quivering from strain but she straightened her spine and walked toward him. She kissed his cheek. Couldn't help but do it. He stiffened. It felt like someone had crushed the pieces of her broken heart with a careless trample, but she didn't let him see it.

'Goodbye, Sawyer,' she murmured.

A nod was her only reply. She turned to walk to her car, didn't look back. She drove to the steep hill that had been christened Lovers Lane because of its popularity as a make-out spot, in no small part because of the privacy it offered. There were other cars there, obscured by the large trees and shorter bushes. She had no desire to check what they were doing. She only wanted privacy. As soon as she parked, she let herself fall to pieces.

Chapter Twenty-Six

One Day, Now

'You're breaking up with me, right?' Sophia asked as soon as Parker stopped between some trees. 'You should have done it before this event. Then I wouldn't have wasted my time stressing over—' She broke off with a sigh. 'That's a lie. I probably still would have stressed. But from a distance, which is worse because I wouldn't be able to help.'

'Are you done?' Parker asked, his infuriatingly handsome face tight. When she nodded, he continued. 'Why the hell would you think I'm breaking up with you?'

'You've been acting weird,' she pointed out. She refused to be comforted by his disbelief.

'How?'

'You've been… I don't know, distant.' She shrugged, pretending like it was no big deal. But it was. A very big deal, actually. 'Not like yourself.'

'Yeah, well, I've been distracted.'

'By someone else?' Sophia demanded, only half-joking. She was fairly certain Parker was smart enough to know not to cheat on her. 'I'll kill them.'

He chuckled. 'Not by someone else, no. Thank goodness, too, or you'd be in jail. Hmm.' He tilted his head. 'I wonder if they do conjugal visits?'

'You think I'd want to sleep with you in a jail?' she asked, amused despite herself. 'Wait—you think I'd sleep with you if you were cheating on me, thus forcing me to kill someone, and that's the reason I'm in jail?'

'Glad to see you have your priorities straight.'

'Jails are unhygienic.' She sniffed. 'I don't want to catch anything.'

'You're worried about *that* and you're in jail? Again, good to know what your priorities are.'

She smiled. She loved doing this with him. The back-and-forth had always been one of the most enjoyable and frustrating parts of their relationship. It hadn't happened in so long—it was part of why she was worried. So maybe that was why now, it felt like a trick. Like this glimpse of how things hadn't been for over a month was some kind of illusion. Soon, Parker was going to tell her he changed his mind and didn't want to be with her.

It had gone away, that fear, over the months they'd been together. Over eighteen months, she thought. Their relationship had started because of one amazing day together. They'd basically gone through the motions of an entire relationship in those hours. The rest of their days together had been less dramatic. But it had solidified their relationship, and she'd fallen deeper in love with him. It terrified her almost as much as it amazed her. Parker did nothing to deserve that fear though. He'd proven day after day that he was there and he wanted her, just the way she was.

So she managed to stomp down the fear. For a while,

she'd even believed it didn't exist. Then he started acting weird and it had come back. A small voice in her
head in the middle of the night asking her if she was
sure he still wanted her. Maybe she'd done something
wrong. Maybe he changed his mind.

Maybe, maybe, maybe.

She hated that she reverted to those worries. That
she was giving them any time at all. So she pretended
they weren't there until he did something strange again.
Or until the next night came and the whispers returned.

It was freaking her the hell out.

'What's been distracting you?' she asked softly, hoping it would give her some answers.

'This.'

And he got down on a knee.

On one *freaking* knee.

'I can't imagine my life without you,' Parker said
in a low voice. She understood why he led them so far
away from the concert now. She complained, but now
she was glad. She could only just hear him. 'Since I've
met you, I've been happier than I ever thought I deserved to be. If you say yes, I'd like to spend our entire lives making you happier than I probably deserve
to make you.'

She wasn't ashamed by the tears that heated in her
eyes. She wasn't even annoyed by it. The only thing
she felt was gratitude. And love. A deep, illogical love
for this man.

Her man.

'So—' she sniffed '—to clarify, you're not breaking up with me?'

'Obviously not.'

'Are you getting *annoyed*?'

'Are you going to make me stay on my knee this entire time?'

'I mean, I haven't even seen the ring.'

'Oh.'

He went into his back pocket, patted it, then tried his other one. It took a few more seconds of frantic patting before he found it in the small pocket at the front of his jeans.

He was so adorable.

'Do you like it?'

She stared at the diamond on its gold band. Bigger than she might have expected; more beautiful than she ever expected. It was plain and perfect. Pretty much how she'd describe herself, frankly.

'I love it.'

'Does this mean you're saying yes?'

'If you *need* me to answer…'

'Sophia,' he growled.

She laughed. 'Of course it's a yes. Do you honestly think I'd waste over eighteen months with you if I didn't intend on—'

He cut her off with a kiss. A hungry kiss that was equal parts passion and tenderness. Her body immediately went on alert, as it always did when he touched her.

'Hmm,' she said when he pulled back. 'Maybe I would agree to conjugal visits. I have needs, after all.'

He chuckled, nipping at her throat. 'What you need is me.'

'Okay.' She dragged out the vowel. 'You haven't put the ring on my finger though, so what proof do I have?'

'Oh, yeah.'

He slid the ring onto her finger.

She took a few moments to admire it. While she did, she heard fireworks go off. Her head shot up, and she watched in wonder as colour spread over the night sky.

'Did you do this?' she asked, still looking at the spectacle.

'Yeah. I mean, I told them it was for the event, so they'd pay for it, but it was all for you.'

She chuckled, wrapped her arms around him and rested her cheek on his chest.

'You're stuck with me forever now.'

She felt the rumble of his laugh.

'I suppose so.' He kissed her head. 'Although I'm sure there's a return period. One hundred days, and if I'm not satisfied with the product, I get to return it. Or exchange it. I'm not fussy.'

'Exchange.' She snorted. 'Such a brazen joke to make when I just told you I'd cut off your arm if you cheated on me.'

'I thought you said you would kill the person I'm cheating with. When did it become chopping off an arm?'

'At some point during this conversation I decided torture would be more satisfying.'

'You decided that while I was proposing to you?'

'Yeah. I'm in love with you and I agreed to spend my life with you. The only appropriate response to you leaving me or cheating on me is the utmost pain.'

'I love your sadistic brain.'

'If it makes you feel better, I wouldn't derive any pleasure from it.'

He laughed, holding her tight. 'It does.'

She sighed happily. 'This was a nice surprise. Much better than how I thought it would be.'

'You expected me to propose?'

'I expected you to break up with me. So obviously, this is better.'

'Oh. I thought you meant you thought I'd propose in some pathetic way.'

'Well,' she said, thinking it over, 'there is a part of me that worried—not that hard or frequently, I might add—you'd do something public. Or over-the-top romantic.'

His body tightened beneath her hold. She shifted back, looked up at him.

'I didn't mean to offend you.'

'I'm not over the top.'

'No, of course not,' she said. 'But some guys completely forget who they're proposing to and get caught up in the actual proposal. One of my colleagues at work got proposed to with a flash mob.' She shuddered. 'To each their own, I guess,' she said as an afterthought, 'but that is not my own.'

'Good thing I did it privately where no one could see us then.'

'Thoughtful and romantic.' She pressed a chaste kiss to his lips. 'It was perfect. Because it was about us. Thank you.'

'Of course.'

'I'm so glad you know me so well.'

He smiled. But—was that *mischief* dancing in his eyes? Relief?

'Like the back of my hand, my love.'

Sawyer wondered if Zoey had finally figured it out: it wasn't that she wasn't good enough for him; it was that *he* wasn't good enough for her.

How could a man who made her feel insecure about herself be good enough? How could a man who didn't know how much baggage he carried be worthy? Worse was that he couldn't get himself out of his emotions. He was still angry at his family. He still felt betrayed by them. And by Zoey, though he understood her motives and feelings now more than ever.

He thought, when they started kissing, things could be different. Even though seconds before, he realised he had to accept the reality that their relationship was over. But he always hoped with Zoey. He thought she might see that they were good together, that they could figure things out together as they had today. But she couldn't trust that she wouldn't hurt him. And he couldn't trust that he wouldn't see it as a betrayal if she did.

Betrayal. It was such a strange word. An even stranger concept. It entailed offering someone trust and having them break it. With his family, it had also come from being indebted. Being afraid. The night he'd heard his aunt complain about how he was a reminder of what she'd lost changed him. Perhaps the grief of losing his parents had, too. He couldn't trust. He had to prove himself. Betrayal had come because despite that, they hadn't even thought him worthy of the truth.

The same thing had happened with Zoey. She had been going through so much during their marriage and she hadn't trusted him to help. Even though he'd shown her time and time again that he wanted to help. Why hadn't she told him the truth then? Was it really because he'd made her doubt she was enough for him?

Everything inside him stilled. When his brain started working again, he remembered what she told him. He had standards. Expectations. He couldn't deny it when the way he felt about his relationships clearly proved it. She was struggling to see herself clearly; of course that would make his standards seem impossible to meet. It would affect someone who was grieving, who was already feeling insecure and vulnerable, even more.

He hadn't intended on making her feel that way. But what did it matter when she did? Either way, his reaction then—*now*—told her she couldn't feel safe with him. His actions had spoken louder than his words. Than the reassurances that she was more than enough and deserved the world. His actions told her that when she made a mistake, he would feel betrayed. If she was honest with him, he would punish her for it by responding that way. All because he was clinging to an idea of what he thought he deserved.

It must have put pressure on her. More so because she assumed he saw a better version of her and was holding her to that standard. No wonder she was doubtful of his proclamations that she was good enough.

The truth was that the reality of Zoey in the past and in the present *was* good enough. She *did* deserve the world. Her actions proved it. She was trying. To own up to her mistakes; to be a better person. And in return, he projected years' worth of his own crap onto her. Even when she was trying to clean up a mess they'd both made.

Maybe divorce was for the best.

'Hey.'

He looked up sharply when he heard the voice, his muscles tensing. But it was only Lisa, peering down at him with concern on her face.

'Hey.' He cleared his throat. 'What are you doing here?'

'Zoey told me you were here. May I?' she asked before she continued. He answered by gesturing to the bench. She sat. 'She said you might need some support.'

'Still looking out for me.'

He didn't mean for her to hear it, but she said, 'Seems like it.'

There was a long pause where they both stared out ahead of them. It was punctuated by a punch. A literal punch to his shoulder.

'What the hell was that for?' he asked, rubbing the skin.

'That's for making me worry about where you were today.' Lisa scowled. 'I had to hear it from Parker, who went missing for an hour before that. So, for, like, an hour, I was hoping you were okay.'

He closed his eyes briefly. 'I'm so sorry. I wasn't thinking.'

'No, you weren't. Damn it.' She sighed. 'Honestly, I'm not sure whether this panic is from me as a mother, or me as a sister.'

'As a mother? Why would you be mothering me?'

'It happens when you have a child.' She rolled her eyes. 'Suddenly, your concern for everyone you care about is heightened. I don't recommend it.'

He laughed, some of the tension inside him releasing. 'I appreciate your motherly/sisterly concern.'

'Is this sisterly concern? You're my first sibling, so I'm not sure.'

'I think so?' he replied with a small smile. 'Although I've never felt the way I feel about you with Phil.'

She laughed. She'd met Phil a few times. Apparently, it was sufficient enough for her to understand the reference.

'I'm glad I found you,' she said, taking his hand. When she threaded her fingers through his, she said, 'Is it weird that I'm sitting with my brother on a bench holding his hand?'

'Nah,' he said. 'I think we're entitled to hold hands. We didn't get to do it when we were kids and we had to cross the street and stuff.'

She laughed again. They sat contently for a few minutes, before she said, 'I really like Zoey, you know. You sure you guys can't figure things out?'

He squeezed her hand before letting go and threading his own hands together. 'No. She's made it clear she doesn't want to be—' he hesitated '—friends anymore.'

'Hmm.' Another few seconds of silence. 'You know you already told me there was more than friendship between you?'

'Oh. Yes.'

'So you and Zoey were together?'

He sighed. 'Yes. We were best friends for seven years, then we—' He broke off. Realised he was done with lying about it. 'We were best friends, but I was always in love with her.'

'Aw.'

'I believe this is proof of you fully transitioning into the annoying big sister.'

'I'm sorry,' she said, but she was grinning. 'Okay, tell me the rest.'

'When she found out I was in love with her, she realised she might have feelings for me, too.'

Lisa sucked in her breath. He couldn't even get mad

at her for being dramatic because he was pretty sure she *was* that intrigued by the story.

'What happened?'

'We got married.'

'*What?*'

'A quickie wedding, two weeks after we proclaimed our love for one another.'

'That is…quick.'

If he were in the mood, he would have smiled at the restraint.

'Yeah. We were young and in love. Foolish.'

'Been there.'

'It lasted three months.'

'You got it annulled,' she said disappointedly.

'No. She left. Didn't tell me why until today.'

'Why did she leave?' She put a hand out before he could say anything. 'No, don't tell me. Whatever it was, it's private.'

'And complicated. Not the kind of story you can tell your sister in the middle of the night.'

She nodded. 'I'm sorry. The divorce must have been more painful if you didn't know why it was happening.'

'I didn't say divorce. But the break-up was painful for those reasons, you're right.'

'Wait a minute.' She was frowning. 'You didn't get an annulment and you're not divorced—but you're broken up? What does that mean?'

'We're still—'

'You're still married!' she exclaimed before he could finish. 'You're still married?' she said again. 'Sawyer, that's wonderful!'

'She asked me for a divorce today.'

If she were a balloon, she would have deflated. No—popped.

'Shit. I'm sorry.'

Now he did smile. 'It's okay.'

'What I was going to say before you told me about the divorce thing—which is really inconvenient considering what I wanted to tell you—is that if you're still married, you still have a chance.'

'No, we don't.'

'Of course you do,' she said with a hand wave. 'Neither of you asked for a divorce in how many years?'

'Six.'

'*Six?*' She gave a quick shake of her head. 'No, I will not get distracted. My point is that if neither of you asked for a divorce, there must be something inside you both that wants to work things out. It's been six years. You found a member of your family you never knew about during that time, for heaven's sake. You can win your wife back.' She frowned. 'If you want to.'

'I don't think that's going to happen.'

'Why not?'

'I'm an idiot.'

'Oh, honey,' she said soothingly. 'Don't worry about that. She would have known that when she married you.'

The topic of their conversation should have meant he wasn't in the mood to laugh, but he couldn't help it. 'Thank you.' Just like that, the amusement went away. 'It's fine, Lisa. We…we weren't meant to be.'

She studied him. 'Is it? You look like you've lost your best friend. And your wife.'

He gave her a dark look.

'You're done then?' He released a harsh breath. Be-

fore he could speak, she continued. 'I'm not talking
your relationship. I'm asking if you're done fighting
for her. See,' she said after a minute, 'it's that silence
that makes me think you're not.'

She took his hand again. They sat like that for a
while. He didn't say anything because he could sense
she was working on a Big Speech. The music was still
pumping loudly in the distance. Idly, he wondered what
time it was. He hadn't been checking his watch when
he was with Zoey. Probably because he felt so lucky
to spend time with her.

Panic fluttered at the thought, but not for the reasons
he thought. It wasn't because he would miss her; it was
because he might have lost her. For real this time. He
thought he'd been protecting himself by telling her they
couldn't see one another again, but now he wouldn't
even have that. He had nothing. Because he was an
idiot. Stubborn, and stuck in his ways.

'I almost gave up,' Lisa said. His attention instantly
focused on his sister. 'When I started looking for you.
It was so big, you know.' Her mouth tilted up at the
side. 'So very big. I didn't know what I would find. I
didn't know if I really wanted to find it.' She bit her lip.
'My parents warned me that it might not go the way
I wanted it to. There was a part of me that acknowledged that as truth, but another part…it thought they
were being protective. Maybe even a little selfish. If I
didn't find my birth parents, I would only have them.'

'What do you think they meant now?'

'A little of all three,' she answered after a moment.

'And you? Which do you think is the right one?'

'A little of all three.' Her lips curved. 'But mostly
because it didn't go the way I wanted it to. My biolog-

ical mother's gone. The people she cared about most knew about me and didn't try to find me. My biological father...' She didn't finish the sentence. He squeezed her hand. 'But then,' she continued, squeezing back, 'I found you. Getting to know you has been one of the best things in my life.'

The smile on his lips was genuine, his entire body filled with emotion.

'Same here. It's kind of nice and weird that we have things in common.'

'Same hair.'

'Same competitiveness.'

She laughed. 'Exactly.' She let go of his hand and shifted to face him. 'I'm not telling you this to make you feel good about yourself. Or bad,' she said with another laugh. Probably at the frown her words had immediately inspired. 'I'm telling you this because if I gave up, I would have lost something more special than I could have ever imagined. I don't think you want to lose that with Zoey.' She waited a beat. 'I don't think you want to lose Zoey.'

He didn't. But if he wanted to be with her, he had some growing up to do. Part of what Lisa had said had shown him that, too. She had so much more to be upset about than he did. They hadn't given him away without any answers. He'd got to know his aunt and his grandmother, and knew they cared about him. He got to know his mother through them, too, and had always known how much she loved him.

One day, he would tell Lisa about their mother. About how she must have done what she did because she had a reason. His mother had too much love for her family not to. The reason he hadn't already done so was because he was selfish. He made his sister's existence about him. Doubted everything he knew to be true about the family who had loved and raised him because of it. Because of some misguided feeling of betrayal.

He'd done the same thing with Zoey.

It was time for some serious self-reflection. Because when he went back for Zoey—he saw now that there was no other choice—he wanted to offer her something better than what he had before. He wanted to support her as she grew, and he wanted to grow with her.

He also just wanted to make her happy. To see her smile every day. To hear her laugh or tease or make fun of him. He wanted them to have a family for no other reason than the fact that they loved one another. There would be no more ulterior motives. He only wanted her and the future he knew they could have together.

Now he had to make her see she wanted it, too. And he would.

Zoey had never pegged her family for the squealing kind. Or maybe she just couldn't remember the times they wanted to squeal. Her father's sickness had changed them. His death had turned some of those changes into permanence. She put squealing firmly into that category.

Although she did think her father would have been amused by it.

'Tell me again.'

'Angie,' Zoey groaned. 'They didn't go to Paris and get engaged in front of that fancy tall building.' She ignored the smirks aimed at her. 'They got engaged right here among some trees. There's not much more to tell. No offence,' she told Parker and Sophia.

'Offence taken,' Sophia said with a frown. 'You're being very rude.'

'Do you want me to apologise for being honest, Ms Straightforward?'

'She kind of has a point,' Parker said.

'Hey.' Sophia poked him in the stomach. 'This—' she wiggled the fingers of her hand that giant rock was on '—means you have to be on my side always and forever.'

'Of course,' Parker said, eyes light with amusement. And contentment. And pleasure. A man who knew exactly what he wanted and had got it. 'You're being rude, Zo.'

But he winked at her. She must have been going soft because she smiled at him.

She knew he was grateful for what she'd done that day. But she couldn't bring herself to be gracious about it yet. Sure, she brushed it off when he'd drawn her to the side to thank her after Sophia had announced their engagement. Honestly, her displeasure had nothing to do with him and everything to do with Sawyer. She spent a day with him and it had done nothing but remind her of why she'd fallen in love with him. Why she was still in love with him. Why she couldn't be with him.

Maybe that was why she couldn't deal with Angie's squealing.

'Maybe we should go get some coffee to celebrate?' Angie suggested.

'We have champagne—' Sophia broke off when Angie nudged her. They exchanged a look. Sophia said, 'Yes, coffee sounds like an appropriate way to celebrate my engagement.'

'Great,' Angie said brightly, though Zoey caught the pinch her oldest sister gave Sophia. 'Zoey, can you help us carry?'

'Why?' Zoey asked with a frown. 'There are five of us. I don't want coffee, so four cups. You two have two hands, and two times two is—'

'Five,' Sophia interrupted with a roll of her eyes. 'We'll need five coffees when Byron gets back from the bathroom.'

'Seven if you count Lisa and Sawyer coming back,' Ezra added.

Even hearing his name was a punch to her heart. She needed to get out of there. But she couldn't exactly leave when her sister had just got engaged. Her family seemed delighted, and they were happy, and she was a miserable old grump who was spoiling everyone's mood.

Great. She was turning into Sophia.

'Fine, I'll go,' Zoey said, grumbling. It was probably her best option. At least this way she could avoid Sawyer, even if it was only temporarily.

They walked for about five minutes before her sisters dragged her into a small alcove surrounded by trees and started making demands.

'What's going on with you, Zo?' Angie said, her eyes concerned but her voice sharp. It was the kind of thing Zoey had seen her do with Cal.

'What are you talking about?' Zoey asked, feigning disinterest.

She stared at her nails, wondering if picking that piece of dirt she saw in her middle finger's nail would be misconstrued. She was sorely tempted not to care. But she did. So she resisted.

'This,' Angie replied. 'Exactly this. This…this attitude is not like you. You weren't even happy for Sophia.'

'Of course I was,' Zoey said, folding her arms. 'I hugged her and everything.'

'Yes, but you'd be the one squealing, not me.' Angie rubbed at her throat. 'I've been trying to get you to say something about it for ages and you've ignored me.'

'You were doing that on purpose?' Sophia asked, turning to Angie. 'Thank goodness. I thought I was going to have to talk to Ezra about getting you to a doctor.'

'Why Ezra?' Angie asked. 'You could have told me.'

'It would have annoyed you more if I'd gone over your head.'

'I'm the head of our household so technically you'd be going under my head.'

'How did you manage to make that weird?' Sophia shook her head. 'Anyway, Zo, Ange is asking about why you're acting like such a brat.'

'I'm sorry,' Zoey said sincerely. She didn't like being miserable, let alone spoiling Sophia's big moment. 'I didn't mean to be. I just—'

To her horror, her eyes began to burn. She looked up, because she heard somewhere that it would force the tears back into her eyes. It didn't sound legit, but she wasn't looking for logic. She was desperate. Desperation sometimes meant listening to rubbish.

When she thought she had that under control, her lips started trembling. She pressed them tightly together. She could do nothing about the thickening throat though. Or the broken heart that was making her body react in these weird ways. It was so *frustrating*.

She thought she was imagining the sound when she first heard it. She recognised it immediately, her brain filling in the beats even though it was coming from outside her. Slowly, her head lowered and she opened her eyes.

Her sisters were making the sound in union, the *bum-bum, bum-bum, bum-bum-bum-bum*, while marching in a circle. Angie was taking the lead. Naturally. She was the only one of the two who'd done this before. Sophia was following along, but under protest, Zoey imagined. Only she didn't have to imagine. Sophia's slow moves and menacing frown told her she wasn't happy.

Why would she be? The marching included pretending to be various kinds of animals. They waved their hands from side to side, then lifted their legs. Zoey kept her eyes on Sophia because she was the most entertaining to watch. It was like her sister was playing a complicated round of Simon Says, only there weren't verbal commands, and she had to watch Angie's body for her cue. She absolutely hated it, but she was doing it because Zoey was down. Soph was doing the Terrible Dance for *her*.

How many times had Zoey and Angie done it for Sophia? Whenever Sophia was in a mood about something and nothing else cheered her up, Zoey and Angie would do the Terrible Dance. There was no fixed choreography—although no one would know that now, considering how closely Sophia was following Angie—their only instructions to make the dance as ridiculous as possible. It never failed to make Sophia smile.

It only succeeded in making Zoey cry.

'Zo,' Angie said, as soon as she noticed. 'Zo, Zo, Zo, I'm sorry.' She put an arm around Zoey's shoulders and guided her to a nearby bench. 'I'm sorry you had to see Sophia dance like that. It truly was terrible.'

'Hey,' Sophia protested without heat. She sat on Zoey's other side, so that Zoey was sandwiched between her older sisters. 'Was it really that bad?'

'Yes,' Zoey hiccupped. 'But it's…supposed to be… so…it's…fine.' She patted Sophia's knee. 'Thank you.'

'Zoey,' Angie said, her tone more insistent now. 'What's wrong?'

Zoey didn't have the energy to lie anymore.

'I…still…love…Sawyer.'

The admission broke her heart again, which brought a fresh batch of tears. She was just so sad at what she'd lost. Not only Sawyer, but her father. Maybe if he hadn't died, she wouldn't have lost another man she loved.

And there she was, not taking responsibility for her actions all over again. Blaming her *dead father* for choices *she'd* made. She was a mess. She didn't deserve Sawyer's admiration. She didn't deserve his…his love.

It made her cry harder, and she gripped Angie's top and cried into her sister's chest. Angie put her arms around her, made soothing sounds as she rubbed Zoey's back. Angie wasn't that much older than Zoey, but she'd done this kind of thing often. When they were all in school together and Zoey had got hurt, she'd go to Angie. Angie would never turn her away. Even when her hair stuck out in tufts because she'd taken off all the ties her mother had given her that morning. Even when her face was covered in a mixture of dirt and tears. Angie would hold her, rub her back, and try to make it better.

She couldn't make it better now. No, nothing could

make it better. Zoey had to live with the consequences of making poor decisions before she knew any better.

And still, even in that, she didn't regret marrying Sawyer.

After a long while, she drew back from Angie. She couldn't bring herself to look her sister in the eye, so she stared at her palms in her lap. Seconds later a tissue was thrust into her hands.

'Where did you get that from?' Sophia asked Angie softly.

'From my pocket. Is that really important?'

'Well, she's clearly not in the state to talk right now. Excuse me for trying to figure out whether you're some kind of magician, pulling tissues from your sleeve.'

'Sophia,' Angie hissed, her voice still low.

Of course, Zoey could hear them perfectly.

'Why are you rubbing your breasts?' Sophia replied in the same tone. 'It's weird. Stop.'

'My milk still responds to tears.'

'Are those spots—'

'Yes,' Angie cut her off. 'I didn't put in nipple pads because I pumped— Does it matter?'

'Were you rubbing your boobs because they were producing milk?'

'Yes, the milk thing. They're also kind of achy.' Zoey tilted her head in time to see Angie look at the round spots in front of her top. 'I guess this is one kind of welcome to the family for Parker, isn't it?'

'If you think you're going back—'

Sophia broke off. It took Zoey a moment to realise she was the reason why. A giggle had escaped from her lips. She wasn't sure if it was because of Sophia's inability to be serious when Angie asked her to be, or because Angie was practically fondling herself in front of them. It was likely both, coupled with how indignant Sophia seemed about Angie facing her fiancé with a shirt that had big round wet spots at her nipples.

Welcome to the family indeed.

Her thoughts coaxed another giggle from her lips, and before long, she was full-on laughing. She wiped the tears from her face with the tissue, which wasn't in the best condition, she could admit, but since Angie wasn't offering her another one, it was all she had. When she finally stopped laughing, her sisters were staring at her with twin expressions of amusement and concern.

'Are you done?' Sophia asked. 'We need to know if we should call your counsellor.'

'Sophia!'

'What?' she asked Angie. 'I'm being serious. I'm sure her counsellor would take a call from Zo if she's having some kind of attack.'

'Oh, you're being serious.'

'Of course I am.' Sophia didn't seem bothered that Angie thought she was joking. 'If Zoey needs someone to talk to, there's nothing wrong with that.'

'I don't need to talk to my counsellor,' Zoey said, a strange calm coming over her. Likely due to exhaustion from experiencing such an extreme range of emotions.

'You have one?' Angie asked.

'Yeah. I started seeing one after Dad died. Well, no. I started seeing one after I realised Sawyer and I wouldn't work out and left.'

'Wait—*you* left him?'

'Yeah.'

'But you said you still love him?'

'I do.'

'I don't understand,' Sophia said. She looked at Angie. 'Do you?'

Instead of replying, Angie asked Zoey, 'Why did you leave him?'

'Back then? I thought that one day he'd figure out I wasn't enough for him. And I didn't want him to take responsibility for me like you guys had to.' She didn't care that she was spilling secrets she'd kept close to her heart for years. What was the point now anyway? 'I realised that if he did, I'd let him. Because that's who I was. Am.' She let out a huff of air. 'I don't even know anymore.'

There was a stunned pause.

'Maybe,' Angie said slowly, 'you did that before Dad died. And who could blame you? You were doing what you were taught. We all were.'

Sophia confirmed with a nod.

'But that wasn't who I came back to,' Angie continued. 'When I got back here you were a responsible person. I gave Soph the credit for pushing you out of the darkness I left behind when I went to Korea after Dad died, but she told me it was you.' There was a beat. 'When you came back after those three months you went missing, you were different.'

Zoey blushed. 'That was after I left Sawyer.'

'You mean the three months was after you left Sawyer?'

'No,' she answered Angie. 'I was, um, living with Sawyer for those three months. When I got back, things were different because I realised I didn't want him to take care of me. I wanted to be different. Better. Not a burden.'

'We're family,' Sophia interrupted whatever Angie was about to say. 'Family does what needs to be done.' She said it with a half-smile. 'You were never a burden, Zo. Did I wish you could be more independent? Sure. But I realised your dependence was as much my fault as it was yours. So I changed that. You changed letting us take care of you. Long before I even gave you credit for it, I think.'

'So,' Zoey said, letting it linger until she processed the words. 'You don't think I'm dragging you down anymore?'

'We never thought that,' Angie said. 'Do you think we thought that?'

'Obviously, if she's asking us,' Sophia answered. 'The more important question is why you don't realise we had as much to do with our family dynamics as you did?' When Zoey didn't answer, Sophia pushed some more. 'Zo, you're taking all of this on yourself. Why?'

'Because it *is* me.'

'We were there, too.'

'But what does it say about me that I was fine with you guys taking care of me?' she asked with a rasp. 'I was living my life while you guys took care of Dad and Mom and me. I tried to make things easier by being happy all the time, but—'

'You tried to make things easier?' Angie asked. 'Wait—you weren't genuinely happy?'

'Dad was dying,' Zoey replied. 'Of course I wasn't happy. But you had a lot on your plate. I didn't want to add worrying about me to that.'

'Sounds to me like you were taking care of us, too,' Sophia commented. 'Which begs the question—why are you punishing yourself for something you didn't even do?'

'Please. You still had to look after me. I didn't do anything worthy of your care.'

'You were you!' Angie said at the same time Sophia said, 'What?'

'Plus,' Zoey said, getting into it, 'I made terrible decisions. I married Sawyer. I stopped going to university. I let you—' she gestured to Sophia '—clean up that mess.'

'You stopped going to university?' Angie asked.

'Not the time,' Sophia told her.

Angie nodded. 'Yeah, you're right. Look, Zo, if we all punished ourselves for hurting the people we love, I'd have to do so for going to Korea after Dad died. But it was an important part of working through my grief and becoming the person I am today. Based on everything you've told us, marrying Sawyer was part of that for you, too.'

She blew out a breath. 'Yeah, it was. But I don't like that I hurt him in the process. Or that I might have hurt you two.'

'Does it look like you've done irreparable damage?' Sophia asked. 'Angie's happy. So am I. We all had to go through what we did to be where we are. It's a part of growing up.'

Something shifted. It took time to realise what it was. She'd been cleaning the clutter in her head, her life, for six years. Working on herself. Trying to be better. But for all of that work, she refused to clear one thing: the guilt. She blamed herself for her past. Punished herself. For all her talk of moving forward, Zoey saw that she was still stuck, at least in this one place. The rest of her had improved and moved; the guilt had spurred that on. Except the guilt itself had never changed.

If she wanted to make herself whole again, she would need to let go of it. She owed herself that much. She might even deserve it. It would mean she could be fully present in her family. She could interact with her sisters without anything tainting it. She could hope for her future again, not be resigned to unhappiness. Not only because letting go of that guilt would mean she no longer had to begrudge herself happiness, but because she understood now. It wasn't easy to let go. It took time and experience to get unstuck.

She'd been unfair to Sawyer for judging him when he'd had neither. But she saw him clearly now. His confusion, his hurt. His feelings for her that had always been there—and, if she let herself believe it, were still there, despite the mess they'd made. She saw herself clearly enough now, too, to know her feelings were demanding she give him another chance. She give *them* another chance. To grow together; to become better together. It would be worth it, her feelings said.

She… She believed them.

'Zo,' Angie said softly. 'You deserve to be happy as much as we do. I think that might mean being with Sawyer.'

'I think so, too.'

There was a stretch of silence.

'It seems like a good time to mention this,' Sophia said, 'but apparently being reckless and irresponsible brought you something you might not have got if you weren't that way. Sawyer, I mean.'

Zoey rolled her eyes, but smiled. 'I got it.'

'You had to marry him to be the adorably responsible dweeb you are now.'

Since she thought it herself, she didn't reply. She did belatedly punch Sophia for calling her a dweeb.

'I said adorable, too,' Sophia muttered. 'It's worth remembering next time you're being hard on yourself.'

'That you think I'm adorable?'

'That everything you experience is part of making you who you are,' Sophia said dryly. Then her expression changed. 'This is weird, right? Talking about this stuff, all three of us.'

'You mean bonding?' Angie asked.

'Yeah.' Sophia shuddered. 'It's like we're a family or something.'

'Imagine that.' Angie shook her head, before resting her gaze on Zoey. 'I think you need to find Sawyer.'

'So we can give him a hard time,' Sophia added, standing. 'None of this supportive BS for him. He needs to prove himself worthy first.'

'After all the work our Zo's done?' Angie squeezed Zoey's shoulder before standing up, too. 'It would be wrong not to at least *check* he deserves her.'

She smiled at her sisters as a part of herself healed. The guilt had finally been cleared because they helped her. She had a family. They loved her exactly as she was.

Maybe she still had a marriage, too.

With the thought, hope stirred the pieces of Zoey's broken heart as if it were a gentle wind. When they lay together in a pile, Zoey realised she couldn't fix it by herself.

She needed to find Sawyer.

Part Three

'We're choosing each other.'

Chapter Twenty-Seven

One Day, Now

'Sawyer, I need to—'

'Zoey, can we—'

They stopped at the same time. Stared at one another. Sawyer did his best to ignore the people around them who were staring, too. Their family cared about them, but they really needed to mind their business.

Then again, they were having this awkward moment in a crowd of hundreds of people, not just their family. But as soon as he'd seen Zoey walking back with coffee—apparently, it was celebratory, although he didn't understand why they were celebrating with coffee when champagne cooled in a bucket nearby— he knew he had to speak with her. If he didn't do it immediately, he'd lose his nerve.

Apparently, she felt the same. She handed him a coffee and said the words he'd spoken over. Now they were both staring at one another.

He was the first to recover.

'Could we go somewhere private and talk?'

'I'd like that very much.'

'So polite,' Sophia murmured. Sawyer caught Angie

nudging her in the ribs before he gestured for Zoey to walk ahead.

When she stopped, he was out of breath. She'd walked the incline of the garden like someone possessed, then climbed the stairs to the highest point of the area with ease. When she turned to him though, the moonlight helped him see the pink of her cheeks, the rapid rise and fall of her chest.

'Sorry,' she said between breaths. 'I wanted to get away from the music.'

He only then realised he couldn't hear that faint throb anymore. He didn't notice how much it bothered him until it wasn't there and the silence felt like a gift. Lowering to one of the steps, he waved a hand. He wasn't sure what he meant by the gesture, but moments later she lowered next to him. Far enough away that he couldn't reach out and touch her. Pity, although it was probably for the best.

'It's beautiful, isn't it?' he asked when silence filled that space between them.

She nodded, then blurted out, 'I love you.'

The coffee he still held in his hand slipped. He gripped it just in time, though a good portion of it slid through the drinking hole. He paid no attention to that, or the searing on his hand.

'Excuse me?'

'You heard me.'

'I heard you say you love me,' he repeated. 'Is that right?'

'Yes.'

He took a long time to respond. When he did, it was as logical as he could expect. 'Why?'

Her lips twitched. 'You want to know why I love you?'

'No. Yes.' He tried again. 'I want to know why you're telling me this.'

'Because I don't want a divorce.'

The sound he made came from the vicinity of his throat. He believed some would describe it as 'strangled.' It fit, he realised after a moment. He did feel like something was strangling him. Hope, perhaps.

'Are you going to say something?' she asked, that wonderfully familiar expression of amusement on her face.

He shook his head. She laughed. The sound rolled over him, caressed him. Encouraged him to say, 'I don't want a divorce either.'

Her laughter faded, but she shifted closer to him.

'I'm sorry you got hurt when I left,' she whispered. 'I had to, to grow. To be who I am now.' She released a shaky breath. 'It doesn't make what I did right. I should have spoken with you. I was afraid I would become someone I didn't like—who you wouldn't like— if I let you take care of me. I was afraid one day you'd hate me.'

'That wouldn't have happened. I understand why you'd feel that way though. I'm sorry for contributing to it.' He exhaled. 'I'm sorry for the pressure I put you under.'

'Oh, you didn't—'

'Zoey,' he interrupted. 'You were right. I had standards. I didn't think about them, and I never intended on making you feel like you had to live up to them. But you did feel that way, and I'm sorry. I'm… I'm sorry.'

He wasn't sure what more he could say on the topic, so he decided on a second apology. She nodded slowly. It wasn't an answer—but what answer could she give to an apology? Apologies didn't require a response. People thought they did because they were giving it to someone and they expected something in return. He didn't.

He felt immeasurably proud that he didn't. Not the biggest evidence of growth, but he'd learnt something today. He'd strive to learn more, to be better, in the future.

'So,' he said into the silence. 'Do you like yourself now?'

'Hey, now,' she said with a smile. 'That's a heavy question.'

'You led me to it.'

Her cheeks lifted. 'I suppose I did.' She inhaled deeply; exhaled sharply. 'I think I do. I like that I want to be better. I like that I've changed, and that I'm still changing.' She hesitated. 'I don't like that I was punishing myself for being a human being. I... I don't like that I was judging you for being one, too.'

'I deserved it though.' His fingers itched to brush her face, her hand. Her skin. 'I wasn't perfect through everything that happened.' He gave himself a moment to figure out his words. 'I love, but somehow, I turned that love into something... I don't know. I suppose selfish is the best way of describing it.'

'You were never selfish.'

'Those expectations the people who loved me couldn't live up to? That was being selfish. I was expecting people to respond to things in the way I would, rather than the way they needed to. Then I reacted to *that*, and made people I cared about feel like I didn't care about them. Or like I wouldn't, someday, if they did something to hurt me.' He took a sip of the coffee to give himself something to do. After, he forced himself to continue. 'There's also how I let something my aunt said in grief dictate my entire life. How I made your grief about us, Lisa's adoption about me.'

'You also tried your best to be the kind of son, nephew, brother and husband you could be proud of. That matters.'

'But it's made me unhappy. Not the trying. I wanted to try. It means something to me to try,' he said, realising the truth of it. 'My mistake was letting those attempts be tainted by my emotions when they were constantly changing. Or by other people's intentions, which I had no way of knowing.' He set the coffee down.

'You can know your own emotions though. So what do they say?' Her voice was so soft and understanding.

'I don't like that my family kept Lisa's existence a secret. I feel guilty that they decided to keep me, but not her.' It was painful picking through it, but he knew he had to. Even his marriage, which was so precious to him. 'I hate that I made you feel the way you did in our marriage. And I… I probably shouldn't have married you.'

'Sawyer—'

'You asked,' he cut her off. 'And I have to say it.'

She nodded, eyes tight.

'I was in love with you. I let that cloud my instincts even when I told myself it didn't. To me, that means I wasn't ready to get married either. I needed to realise this stuff about emotion and intention before I could be ready. I needed to go through our marriage, finding out about Lisa and today to see that though.' He exhaled. His chest felt lighter. 'You didn't betray me,

Zo. You gave me the best thing that could have ever happened to me.'

'Sex?'

He laughed. 'Sure, although I didn't mean that specifically. I meant marrying me when I wasn't ready.'

'If that's the case,' she said, shifting closer again, 'I should thank you for marrying me when I wasn't ready, too.'

'I was only in it for the sex.'

Her laugh was husky. 'You spent a lot of our three months together proving that.'

'That was just making up for our wedding night.'

'There was nothing to make up for.'

'I don't deserve you,' he said with a smile, though it was more thoughtless than anything else. When he did think about it, he continued. 'I know how it feels to be insecure in a relationship, Zo. I don't think I've ever believed I deserve you. Now, I think it more than ever. But if we want this to work—and I'd like for it to work—then we have to set that aside. We have to trust one another. In the present, too. No anticipating things that might happen in the future.'

She reached for his hand, which was a little awkward with the distance between them. They moved at the same time. They sat, legs pressed together, hands tangled.

'You're right.'

'Thank you.'

She smiled. Squeezed his hand. He understood she was trying to soften her next words when she said, 'I don't think you've processed or worked through everything we've spoken about today. Mostly because I know I haven't.'

'I've started to.' His heart thumped painfully as he considered the rest of his answer. 'But I understand if you don't want to be together while we figure it out.'

The next seconds were the longest of his life.

'You know, when you asked not to see me anymore at your grandmother's funeral, I spent weeks crying. I was heartbroken. But I was also so relieved.' She absently rubbed her knee with her free hand. 'It was better than a divorce, I told myself. We were still linked. We still had a chance.' She looked at him. 'Divorce was never an option I *wanted*. I thought it was necessary.'

He reminded himself to breathe.

'I was focused on fixing my past mistakes. I thought that meant no ties to one another anymore. We wouldn't have that link and we'd finally move on.' She ran a hand over his hair. 'I don't think fixing my mistakes means divorce anymore. I think it finally means listening to what I want.'

'What's that?' he whispered.

'To stay linked with you. To move on from what happened *with* you.' The sides of her mouth tilted up. 'Neither of us is perfect. Both of us are responsible for what happened in the past. But we can be responsible for what happens in the future, too. We'll never be perfect, but we can try to be better. That's enough for me.'

'It's always been enough for me.'

She smiled, then sucked a lip between her teeth. 'You can't take care of me.'

'Yes, I can,' he replied gently. 'You need to trust who you've become, Zo. You won't let me take care of you because you can't, or won't, take care of yourself. That's no longer who you are. But you will let me take care of you because you understand taking care of you is part of how I love you. Protecting you, helping you, supporting you… They're how I'll be a husband to you.'

She blinked rapidly. He immediately understood she was overwhelmed. He rubbed her hand.

'Fine, but then we work through things together,' she said thickly. 'That's how I'll be your wife. I'll encourage you to feel what you feel and not judge yourself for it. You need to be patient with yourself. And with me.'

'Of course.' He slid an arm around her shoulders and kissed her head. 'I choose you. How can I be anything other than patient?'

'We're choosing each other.' Her expression softened. 'I like this.' She traced his face.

'My beard?'

She pulled his ear in rebuke. 'Talking with you. Figuring things out.'

'Good.' He nudged his coffee away with his foot then turned to face her. 'We'll be doing it for the rest of our lives.'

Then he kissed her.

He kissed his wife.

Epilogue

One Day, Four Years Later

'Why did we decide to have another one?' Angie whispered to Ezra, caressing her stomach as if she were assuring the baby inside she didn't mean the words. 'It took me an hour to get Cal into that dress. An hour, Ez! It takes less time for me to put my shoes on, and I can't see my feet.'

Ezra rubbed her shoulders. Wisely, he thought, he didn't reply.

Angie's stress levels had been through the roof since they discovered they were expecting again. It wasn't so much a decision as a late night, *oh the kid's asleep and we haven't done this in forever* consequence. Angie had gone off the pill after having Cal and they'd decided condoms would be a good idea. Fools, the both of them. How could they be a good idea when neither of them remembered to use one?

He probably would have said something about how their upcoming arrival wasn't a choice if he had replied. He also would have reminded her how excited they were to have another baby, despite the surprise. Cal was almost six years old, naughty as hell, and she needed to learn some responsibility. A younger sibling would work nicely. They would also round out the family quite nicely.

He stroked Angie's arms with firm pressure. She groaned, which got her a dirty look from some of the other patrons in the glass-enclosed building Zoey and Sawyer were renewing their vows in.

'It's not a church. Relax.'

Angie didn't say it loud enough for those people to hear it, but Ezra knew the sentiment made her feel better. Hiding his grin, he pressed a kiss into her hair.

'We just got unlucky with Cal.' He mentally told his daughter he didn't mean that. 'This next one will be an angel. No energy, good, obedient.'

'Do you think so?' Angie asked with such a happy sigh, Ezra couldn't help the smile that curved his lips.

'Absolutely.'

The organ began to play, and they all stood. First through the doors was Cal. She looked adorable in her white dress. Angelic as she threw the flower petals down the aisle.

'Oh,' Angie said. Ezra handed her his handkerchief. He packed it in knowing she'd need it. He hadn't expected himself to need it, too. 'That's why we're having another one.'

He watched his child who was growing up way too fast finish her trip down the aisle. He held Angie tight against him, a hand possessive on her stomach.

Yeah, this was why. It was his why for everything he did.

'Personally, I don't see why they'd waste the money having another wedding,' Sophia whispered to Parker.

They were at the end of the row, next to Angie and Ezra, their mother sitting on Angie's other side. Thank goodness. If Charlene had heard that comment over the organ music, Sophia would never hear the end of it. Or rather, she'd never see the end of the disapproving looks.

'Not everyone's like you, babe,' Parker whispered back.

'Smart?'

'Cheap.'

She poked him in the ribs, which forced him to turn his laugh into a cough. Ah, there was the disapproving look from Charlene. Good to know things hadn't changed too much since she'd moved out.

Not that that was a measure of comparison anymore. She'd moved out five years ago. She'd been married for four of those years since she and Parker had tied the knot a short while after he proposed. Only their family members were there. Mostly because she and Parker didn't have any friends.

But that was okay. They had one another.

And, of course, their family.

The corniness of it nearly made her groan. She wouldn't, of course, because the organ had already tested the baby in her arms and she'd just got Ariah to quieten. In time to see her parents share another wedding day.

'Honestly,' she whispered to the baby, who she was quite fond of, to be honest. 'Your parents are so extra.'

Ariah looked back at her with Zoey's exact eyes, and Sophia's insides puddled. It was like having her baby sister without any of the sass. A dream. In all honesty, she loved being an aunt more than she could have anticipated. It was a responsibility she took seriously. And never once did she feel like she was missing out on anything because the kids weren't hers. Because they were her family, and that was enough. Family was always enough.

Speaking of…

'Your mom was okay this morning, right?' She turned to Parker. Ignored the evil eye she was getting from Sawyer's family. 'With the rush and looking after this one, I didn't even think to ask.'

'Yeah, she was okay.' He sighed. It was a deep sigh that told her Penny Jones wasn't okay. But her son was being eternally optimistic. 'She didn't know who I was, but she knew Dad. That's enough.'

She studied him, then handed him the baby. 'Here, hold her.'

'Wh—' He was already holding the baby. 'Why?' he asked again, automatically bobbing.

'So I can do this.'

She stood on her toes and kissed him. A soft, reassuring press of her lips. He was smiling when she lowered to her feet.

'What was that for?'

'For being you. And for being so strong. I know this is hard.'

'You could have done that *and* tell me that with Ariah in your arms.'

'Yeah, but your appeal goes up when you're holding her. I need to use every opportunity to do that since we've been together so long and you've let yourself go.'

His still-defined biceps flexed in response, though it was probably because he was holding a baby. Probably.

'You're one to talk.'

'Please,' she snorted, taking the baby from him again. 'I have a mirror. I know what I'm about.'

He smiled and a hand rested on her waist as she turned back to the front of the room. 'Yeah, so do I: me.'

She let him have that egotistical jab. Just this once.

'You look beautiful,' Sawyer said, not for the first time.

'I look like I gave birth a few months ago and had to have my dress tailored a million times because my weight's fluctuated so much.' That was the first time Zoey had given that particular answer. Normally, she just went for 'thank you.'

'Like I said, beautiful.'

He kissed her. It was soft and tender and went right to that achy place between her legs. It had been such a long time since she felt anything like that. No one had warned her about what having a baby would do to her libido. Not even Angie, the traitor. No, Angie had spent all her time telling Zoey how much she wanted Cal and the new baby to have a cousin. Now Zoey wondered if her lack of a warning was strategic.

'Get a room,' Sophia called sharply.

Zoey laughed as she pulled away from Sawyer. She stuck her tongue out as Parker and Sophia danced by, and they both did it back. Her family was so immature. She loved them so much.

Most of all, she loved her husband. This wonderful man who had such patience with her. Who loved her as she was and supported her growth. Who put family first and let himself grow. When he'd proposed to her—his first time, since she'd suggested they marry the last time—she was six months pregnant, doing the dishes. He was on his knee, waiting for her when she turned. She'd dropped a glass in surprise.

She'd said yes though. Fallen into his arms and welcomed the love he lavished on her. Enjoyed his pleasure as she did the same.

Almost six months later, they were dancing together at their wedding. Lights and flowers and trees decorated the small venue. Later they would return to the house they'd built. They'd feed their daughter and make love. It would be perfect.

'I hope you're prepared for tonight,' she said when they were far enough away from prying ears.

'What do you mean?'

'It's our wedding night.' She dropped her voice. 'You'll be deflowering me. Have you prepared?'

He nearly tripped, nearly brought her down with him. It would have been worth it for the look on his face alone. She laughed, and waved away the concern of the people around her.

'One too many drinks,' she said, although she hadn't seen Sawyer take one drink that night.

'You did that on purpose.'

'Yes, it's called teasing.'

He growled at her. She laughed.

'Come on. It's been such a long time since I've felt this light. Let me have it.'

Rolling his eyes, he acquiesced. 'You're happy?'

'The happiest.' She snuggled closer to him, resting her head on his chest. 'It's perfect.'

'It does look good.'

'I wasn't talking about this. I was talking about our life together.' She looked up at him. 'You've given me so much to be happy about.'

'And you deserve every last bit of it.'

'So do you.'

She was smiling when he kissed her again. Her heart burst with contentment. And love.

With Sawyer, it was always love.

* * * * *

Reviews are an invaluable tool when it comes to spreading the word about great reads.
Please consider leaving an honest review for this or any of Carina Press's other titles that you've read on your favorite retailer or review site.

To find out about other books by Therese Beharrie or to be alerted to new releases and other updates, sign up for her newsletter at theresebeharrie.com/newsletter.

Acknowledgments

I want to start by thanking my editor, John Jacobson, for the support they've offered me not only for this book, but this entire series. They've truly been the biggest cheerleader of my vision for each book. When I pitched *One Last Chance*, especially, I told them the format wouldn't be linear or typical (I think I was hoping they'd talk me out of it!). John enthusiastically encouraged me to do exactly what I wanted and helped me turn this book into what it is. The effort John has put into me and *One Last Chance*—and the entire One Day to Forever series—means they'll always have my gratitude.

Thank you to the entire Carina Press team for the support they've given this series. I'm proud to be part of a publisher walking the talk when it comes to diversity. To Olivia Dade, for her constant, unwavering, *wonderful* support, and Talia Hibbert, who beta read scenes I was uncertain about and helped me make them better while cheering me on. You have no idea how much your friendships have come to mean to me. To Bianca and Lunelle, I appreciate you more than I can say, and to my family, whose complexity has helped me write the Roux family with nuance and love.

And to Grant, my best friend and the best person in my life. I work as hard as I do for myself, because you helped me realise I deserve to, and for you, because you deserve for me to give my best. Every word of support lingers in my brain as I write. I write heroines who are unapologetically themselves deserving love because you love me exactly as I am. You're the reason I believe in happily ever after.

Readers, thank you for supporting my characters, my stories and me. I wouldn't be here, writing who I do, without you. I can't articulate how much you all mean to me, but please know that it's a lot. My desire to write different kinds of characters who deserve love is so you believe you do, too. Because you do—and that includes from yourself. Please believe it.

About the Author

Being an author has always been Therese's dream. But it was only when the corporate world loomed during her final year at university that she realised how soon she wanted that dream to become a reality. So she got serious about her writing, and now writes books she wants to see in the world featuring people who look like her for a living. When she's not writing, she's spending time with her husband and dogs in Cape Town, South Africa. You can find her on Twitter at www.Twitter.com/ThereseBeharrie and Facebook at www.Facebook.com/theresebeharrie, or catch up with her on her newsletter at theresebeharrie.com/newsletter/ or her website, theresebeharrie.com, where she keeps a writing blog.

Chapter One

She won't care if I'm not here.

The words were on the tip of Sophia Roux's tongue. She glanced over at her mother, who was sitting at her side. Charlene Roux worried her thumbnail, staring off into the distance. Sophia's sister, Zoey, was on Sophia's other side. Zoey alternated between pacing the small space of the hospital waiting room and annoying Sophia. The latter was currently happening. It was part of why Sophia was plotting her escape.

'Babies don't care who's there when they're born,' Sophia whispered to Zoey. She ignored that Zoey was tapping her thigh with a finger. 'Besides, the baby hasn't even arrived yet. Let me get back to my life.'

Slyly, she looked over at her mother. Charlene wasn't paying any attention. Sophia wouldn't be punished for trying to escape.

'Angie would stay if it were your baby,' Zoey replied, all logic despite the thigh-tapping, which was gradually increasing in speed. 'She'd probably be in the room with you.'

'Hell, no,' Sophia said with a shudder. 'One, I'd have to want a baby for that to happen. Two, even if I did,

I can't imagine wanting to see people after I pushed a baby out my vagina.'

'Sophia!'

Oh, damn. Her mother had heard *that*.

Zoey snickered. The three people who were sitting in the row in front of them looked scandalised. Sophia wondered if her mother's reaction was because Charlene was offended, or because those people had heard her.

She hadn't meant to raise her voice, but surely she hadn't said something scandalous? They were in a hospital, for heaven's sake. She could have sworn she'd used the scientific term for where babies generally came out of in church.

Because it wasn't like God had created vaginas or anything.

'I'm sorry,' Sophia said. She was speaking to her mother, but she eyed the people still looking at her. 'I meant after I negotiated the terms of my baby's release with the stork who only delivers to hospital rooms where my partner and I are present.'

'Sophia,' her mother said again, her tone disapproving, if reserved. 'Can't you try to support your sister instead of...' Charlene lifted her hand, dropped it.

Sophia purposefully unclenched her jaw.

'I'm here, aren't I? Supporting Angie.' *Even though Angie didn't support us when we needed her. But let's forget about that, shall we?* She pulled herself back to the present. 'All I'm saying is that Angie's baby will have done the equivalent of an intergalactic move. Would you want to entertain guests after that?'

Zoey laughed. Her mother did not.

Not that it surprised her. Charlene had always disapproved of Sophia's sense of humour—amongst other things. Though the sense of humour issue was likely because Sophia hadn't inherited it from her father or mother. She wished she could say it was a combination of their genes, but that wouldn't be true either.

Her mother had no sense of humour.

Miraculously, Sophia didn't snort out loud at her little joke. Instead, she simply sat, her conversation with Zoey ended by the Vagina Saga. Time ticked by slowly. As it did, Sophia felt her soul die.

She'd already been there for ninety minutes. Angie had been in labour for longer, but Ezra, Angie's husband, had told them it was pointless coming to the hospital since it was still early. The only reason the two of them had gone to the hospital was because Angie had tested positive for some bacteria and needed to be put on antibiotics so it wouldn't be passed to her baby.

This did nothing to change Sophia's mind about not wanting a child.

In any case, Charlene had decided not to take Ezra's advice. She'd wanted to come to the hospital immediately. She'd demanded Sophia and Zoey go, too. Sophia had wanted to say something about it, but then she'd seen Charlene's expression. Her mother was terrified.

To be fair, terror *was* the state Charlene lived in since her husband's death. Sophia sympathised. It was scary to build an entire life around someone, then have to live it when they were no longer there. But she wouldn't coddle her mother. She wasn't Angie, who soaked up everyone's emotions as if she were a wet sponge, cleaning up their messes in the process. Nor was she Zoey, who would do whatever she wanted to regardless of the people around her. Yes, Sophia felt for her mother; she also needed Charlene to get her act together.

But after five years of dealing with her mother's terror, Sophia knew when to pick her battles. This was not one of them. Today's terror came from a mother's fear for her child. So Sophia bit her tongue, woke Zoey up, and now they were in the waiting room…

Waiting.

She'd sent Ezra a message as soon as they got there, but there'd been no reply. He'd either turned off his phone or put it on silent. Or he simply wasn't interested in checking it.

When Angie had introduced him almost two years ago, Sophia had realised he was different to the men she knew. He watched Angie with an intensity that made her think he was trying to anticipate Angie's next move. He paid attention to Angie even when she wasn't paying attention to him. Sophia could only imagine what would happen when Angie actually needed his support.

But it had been ninety minutes. Almost two hours now, she saw, checking the clock on the blue wall of the waiting room. The bubble of anxiety around her mother was growing larger and larger. Charlene needed an update, and Sophia needed to get out of there before she got trapped in the bubble. Not because she would feel the anxiety, but because she nearly always popped the bubble. Her mother didn't need that today.

She stood.

'Where are you going?' Zoey asked. Charlene's gaze rose with her. It was curiously blank.

'I thought I'd try to find some news,' Sophia told Zoey.

'I'll come with you.'

'No,' she said immediately. Zoey's eyes widened. 'Sorry, Zo, it'll be easier if I do this myself.'

'Okay.'

Zoey's voice was breathy. It was the tone she used when she was hurt but didn't want to show it. Sophia softened.

'Can I bring back something for you?' she asked, wanting to make it better. 'Chips? Chocolate?' When Zoey didn't look up, Sophia lowered her voice. 'Both?'

There was a long pause before Zoey looked at her. 'Lightly salted chips. Fruit and nut chocolate. And something to drink.'

'Of course,' Sophia said with a smile. She turned to her mother. 'And you, Mom?'

'A water, please.'

Sophia nodded, her smile disappearing as she walked away from her family. She felt hollow and full at the same time. The hollowness was because these events made her remember her father. Nothing much had fazed him. Generally, that attitude had spilled over to her mother. Charlene wouldn't be the mess she currently was if Daniel Roux had been there.

Sophia didn't engage with that hollowness. It was simply there. An observation. A consequence of death.

The fullness was more dangerous anyway. Emotions that swelled into the hollowness. Resentment, betrayal. A cesspool of negativity that Sophia fed each time something like this happened.

When she felt out of her depths with taking care of her mother. Or when Zoey needed someone who could nudge her in the right direction. Whenever she thought that Angie would be better equipped to deal with the remaining members of her family. When they thought so, too.

But after their father's death, Angie had run. All Zoey and their mother had left was Sophia. They'd often made it clear they didn't think it was enough. When Angie had finally come back, Sophia could see why. Angie was exactly who they needed her to be, even if she had come back a little changed.

Sophia hadn't changed though. And the differences between her and her older sister were sharp and aggravating. It didn't matter that Sophia had picked up the slack when Angie couldn't. It only mattered that she was there when *Angie* needed her. Because families were there for one another.

Except their family had conditions.

If only Sophia adhered to those conditions, too.

'What are you alluding to, Dr Craven?'

'We suspect your mother has dementia,' Dr Craven said, obliging Parker Jones's request and cutting the bull. Parker wasn't sure if that was a good thing now that he'd heard the words come out of his mother's doctor's mouth. 'There's no one test I can administer to give you certainty, but the testing we have done up to this point has made me fairly confident. The behaviours you've described over the past few years are also good indicators.'

An unreasonable wave of guilt washed over him. They were making this diagnosis based on information he'd provided. Behaviours he'd questioned his mother on and she'd brushed off. Now those behaviours were part of how they knew she was sick.

He felt sick.

'The good news is that it's in the early stages. Your mother still has good years ahead of her. It will require some adjustment, but there's no reason why things can't be normal for the foreseeable future.'

How is that good news? he wanted to ask. He didn't. Instead he looked through the small window in the door of the room where his mother lay. She was alone. His father had stepped in and paid so she could have privacy.

Parker blew out a breath. 'Can I see her?'

'She's sleeping.' There was the briefest of pauses. 'I'm more than happy to answer your questions, Mr Jones.'

'That won't be necessary,' he replied woodenly. He held out a hand. 'I appreciate you caring for my mother.'

When Dr Craven had shaken his hand, Parker walked away, leaving the confused doctor behind. Parker knew what the man was thinking. Someone who'd just been told his mother might have dementia shouldn't walk away. He should have questions. He should ask those questions so he knew what to do next.

Parker was well aware of what he should have done. It was why he'd walked away.

Not his best moment, he could admit. But there was too much going on in his head for him to think logically. He hadn't been able to since he'd got the call from his neighbour telling him his mother had been hit by a car. Fortunately, the car hadn't been going fast, and Penny Jones's injuries were minimal—a broken arm, a cracked rib, some bruising. The real problem was the police report an officer had conveyed to him shortly after the incident.

A car hadn't bumped into Penny; she'd walked in front of it.

He gritted his teeth, quickened his steps down the white hallway of the hospital. Though he wasn't in any of the wards, the smell of sterility that attempted to mask illness churned his stomach. The walls were tall, the windows high, not allowing him a necessary glimpse of the outside world. He needed to prove to himself that he wasn't trapped. Not by the terrible building he was in, or by his mother's possible illness.

Or perhaps he needed to be around people, he thought, his legs still moving despite the fact that he didn't know where he was going. If he made his way down to the cafeteria, he'd be exposed to the busyness that was always there, regardless of the time. Busyness meant noise, which meant people, and energy. Surely that would distract him. Pull him out of his own head.

Instead, he lost his breath.

He didn't know what had happened until it was too late. He was already falling, propelled by a force that couldn't only have been a person since his breath was knocked out so completely. He was on the floor when he realised it wasn't someone with machinery or the like. It *was* only a person. She looked tiny, sprawled on the floor across from him, though her expression made him think she had little to no awareness of this fact.

He got to his feet, held out a hand to help her to hers. But she was already up, gathering the snacks he only now realised had scattered at their collision. He lowered, reaching for a water bottle, but she snatched it away from him before he could get a grip on it. When she was standing again, she glowered at him. He frowned. Neither of them said anything for a moment.

'You're not going to apologise?' she asked in a prim voice.

'Are you?'

'Why would I apologise?'

'You walked into me.'

'*You* walked into me.'

'Really?' he asked lightly, though annoyance had stretched its wicked arms and gripped his tongue. 'How do you know that?'

'You weren't paying attention.'

'The fact that you can say that tells me you *were* paying attention, which means you knowingly walked into me. Your fault.'

Her mouth opened, as if she wanted to say something, but no words came out. It drew his attention to her lips. Plump, with an intricate network of creases imprinted into their fullness that he'd never seen before. They were neither pink nor red, those lips, but fell somewhere in between, or formed a fascinating combination of the two.

'Hey,' she said sharply. 'My eyes are up here.'

He lifted his gaze. 'I was trying to figure out what you'd say next. Nothing good, I imagined.'

Colour spread on her cheeks, making him notice the dark spots on the brown skin for the first time.

'This is what I get for speaking to a man I don't know,' she muttered, rolling her eyes. 'Listen,' she continued more loudly, 'I don't care that you're a jackass who knocks people over with their tank-like body and then refuses to apologise. I—'

'Why not?' he asked.

'Why not what?'

'Why don't you care?'

'I can handle it.'

He smirked. The colour on her skin grew deeper.

'Continue,' he said, folding his arms. Her eyes dipped to his biceps. Then she met his eyes and he swore the look she gave him could set the world on fire.

'I don't need your permission to continue.'

He waved a hand.

'Out of curiosity—are you just an annoying person?' she asked. 'Or are you saving this side of your personality for me?'

He only smiled, because that seemed to annoy her more than anything and for some perverse reason, he enjoyed seeing the way her colour changed when she was annoyed.

'Of all the days I could meet an inconsiderate—'

'Unfair,' he interrupted. 'I'm not inconsiderate.'

'Considerate people apologise.'

'We've already established that you were the one responsible for this. Usually the person responsible for the action apologises to the victim.'

Her entire face tightened. 'Victim?' She barked out a laugh. 'Get out of my way. I have enough of those in my life.'

The abrupt change in her demeanour had him giving her space before his brain could catch up with what had happened. When it did, the anger that had taken a backseat to his amusement flared.

'Now you're being rude, too. *You're* the annoying person in this equation.'

She whirled around. 'Hey, buddy, you don't get to call me rude when you're being rude yourself. When you're purposefully going out of your way to get a reaction from me.'

Now he opened his mouth. Shut it. Because she was right, and he would not tell her that. He wouldn't lie either.

He clenched his jaw, hating that she'd put him in a predicament where he couldn't have the upper hand. Her eyes dipped to his mouth, and she smirked.

'It isn't so fun when you're on the other side, is it?' She walked away.

Don't miss
One Day to Fall *by Therese Beharrie*
Available now wherever
Carina Press ebooks are sold.

www.CarinaPress.com.